To Karen

DUE DILIGENCE

D. J. Harrison

Published in Great Britain by Open Circle Publishing in 2012

ISBN 978-1-909607-00-2

Open Circle Publishing
49-51 St Thomas's Road
Chorley
Lancashire
PR7 1JE
www.opencirclebooks.com

For Anne Marie

1

'Jenny Parker, Signor Casagrande will see you now.'

I extract myself from the soft chair, dragging my heavy laptop case over my shoulder, and follow the receptionist. She walks across the immaculate white stone floor that gives a feeling of opulence to this steel and glass office building. Her body is beautifully proportioned, smooth under her simple dress; I shudder at how my short legs and large bottom must suffer in comparison. She must be in her mid-thirties, a similar age to me, but the ravages of age, childbirth and constant worry seem to have passed her by. She is the graceful embodiment of all I imagine myself to be on a good day. Today is not a good day.

Paul hovers at my side but she turns to dismiss him. 'Mr O'Rourke will be down shortly for you, Mr Unsworth.'

I'm heartened by Paul's obvious discomfort, he considers himself to be of more than equal status and the snub will dent his masculine pride quite nicely. Although it's not unusual for Landers Hoffman to send two accountants on a due diligence assignment, I could manage much better by myself. I'm anxious to get home to my child as quickly as possible; male colleagues, in contrast, welcome the free hotel room and the opportunity it gives them to try their luck with the nearest female, usually me.

The receptionist leads me up a chrome and steel staircase and deposits me in an office lined with display cabinets containing model racing cars. On the corner of the large desk is a cube of glass encasing a yellow racing helmet with a green stripe.

A thin-featured man enters wearing a perfect grey suit and immaculate shirt and tie. His sharp eyes appraise me and I meet them for a brief moment. What I sense behind them is a strange mixture of excitement and fear, with fear the predominant component. Why?

'Giuseppe Casagrande.' He gives a short, stiff bow then offers his hand.

'Jenny Parker, Landers Hoffman Accountants, Manchester office.' As I look across at him, our eyes meet again and he unashamedly holds my gaze. His dark brown eyes penetrate deeply and make me feel exposed and unprotected. Breaking away from his stare, I look instead at his clothes which appear to have been poured over him while molten. There is no part of them that is not a perfect fit. The white shirt cuffs protrude a satisfying amount from his jacket sleeves. His shirt collar is neither slack nor tight. His tie is perfectly knotted, cascading a delicate blue tracery which perfectly complements the suit, which looks handmade, beautifully tailored and fitted with precision. Nobody in my experience dresses like this. It's a tradition from another age, another world.

His eyes are still on me; not on my body, not weighing me up, not imagining me naked, not feeding lascivious thoughts, but gazing into my soul. As our eyes meet I experience a shudder of fear similar to the one I detected in him when he first entered the room and to my dismay I feel scared and vulnerable.

The silence has gone on long enough and, dry-mouthed, I begin. 'My colleague and I are here to conduct a due diligence audit on behalf of World Ordnance Systems. We would be very grateful for your assistance in helping us get the job done as soon as possible. It's all fairly routine; I'm sure you'll all be familiar with due diligence procedures.'

'But we've already had a visit,' Casagrande says. 'Your Mr Youngs came. He conducted a full investigation and pronounced himself totally satisfied.'

My heart jumps at the mention of Martin's name. 'So I understand. However Mr Youngs is currently unavailable because of family commitments and we've been sent to expedite matters in his absence.'

Yesterday, Paul bundled me unceremoniously into a tiny meeting room as soon as I arrived at the office. Breathlessly and in a strangely loud half-whisper, he told me about Martin's unfinished business here and why we hadn't seen him recently.

'Between you and me, Jenny,' he said, 'his wife has been in to see Eric. She expected him home two days ago and he hasn't been in touch. She doesn't know where he is and apparently she told Eric that she'd thought for some time that he had a…well…that he was having an affair, you know.'

I was shaken by these revelations. My face burns again as I remember Paul's words and I'm still reeling at the implications. Nobody knows about Martin and me, nobody, absolutely no-one at all. The idea that flashed across my mind, that there could be another mistress, is absurd. Martin's wife can only be referring to me. I'm shocked that she should know, but not surprised. Martin and I have been seeing each other on a regular basis for almost a year now. Wives tend to notice when husbands return home to them without any vestige of sexual energy remaining. Most worrying of all, I've heard nothing from Martin myself.

Casagrande cuts through these thoughts. 'This acquisition is very important to us, it cannot be delayed by personal problems at some accountancy firm. I hope you understand, Signora Parker.' The gaze again holds mine and I nod while trying not to squirm.

My discomfiture is alleviated when the receptionist reappears and takes me along the corridor to a large room where Paul is sitting in conversation with two men.
A short portly man with bushy grey hair is the first to rise.

'Mark Sullivan.' He reaches out and grasps my hand weakly. 'This is Liam O'Rourke.' Sullivan indicates a tall man with caterpillar eyebrows and thick black hair.

Sullivan makes the mistake of setting Paul off with the inevitable polite question about our trip to see them. 'How was your journey down here?'

In response, Paul inches his way down the highways of England describing every turn and obstacle as if it were of great interest to our hosts. I sigh inwardly and settle back in the comfortable leather chair. A striking black lady with wide

3

flashing eyes and beautiful tight curls comes in and distributes hot drinks.

Paul is a boring man. He's one of Martin's managers and someone I find deeply irritating. It was Eric who insisted I came all this way with Paul to cover for Martin's unexplained absence. Eric is the managing partner, not a man to be denied if I want to keep my job, no matter what childcare problems it gives me. Now, Paul is sitting at the table peering down his long skinny nose, head shining in the fluorescent light. I notice his shirt buttons protruding beneath the black cardigan, tight across his ample belly, like pieces of coal on a snowman. There seems little harm in the man unless I count his inability to know when to stop his flow of drivel. On my own, I could have this due diligence exercise done in half a day. Paul's presence means I have to spend the night away. Little Toby will be inconsolable when he realizes his mother won't be there at bedtime. Tim will do his fatherly best but I know it won't be good enough.

I spread out the paperwork on the table and try to divert Paul off the M40 and back to the matter in hand.

'I realise that you may think some of these questions are going back over the same ground but please bear with us,' I look up and smile before getting stuck in. 'There are transactions amounting to over thirty-five million pounds which are referenced as consultancy costs. Although we have a breakdown of the payments we do need further clarification. Can you give me a description of the services provided, please?'

Sullivan is all smiles of accommodation while O'Rourke is shrouded by serious melancholy as we grind through the information. I make pages of notes, Paul witters on ingratiatingly. The body language coming from Sullivan and O'Rourke is all sham and deception, the atmosphere resentful. I have to remind myself that we are not looking for problems; we're here only to demonstrate that we do our job in a reasonably responsible manner.

Eric made it quite clear that this visit has to gather the detail to justify our positive report. Landers Hoffman's fees are conditional on the acquisition going ahead. If a few financial warts are uncovered after the event we only need to make sure they were blemishes we couldn't have been expected to see.

Paul appears oblivious to anything other than his own pompous voice. It's a situation that I've observed many times before. He asks what he imagines are important questions and expects me to write down the answers. This would be a reasonably efficient way to do business if only he listened to the answers. This failure on his part leads inevitably to him repeating the questions over and over again until I manage to stop him or night falls or the subject dozes off.

I write down Sullivan's description of the company's activities. Associated Composites design and manufacture components from exotic materials, supplying the aerospace and automotive industries. They have factories in various parts of Europe, including Monaco and Andorra, places I associate more with holidays than manufacturing, though I suppose everywhere needs some form of industry.

As I take notes, I feel a little disappointed that of all the exotic locations being reeled off, I have to end up here in Northamptonshire. The way Paul drives it would have been quicker to fly off somewhere, anywhere, rather than endure his unerring ability to find the most congested motorway and the longest delays. A false note in Sullivan's voice makes me snap out of my daydream and start paying serious attention. Things are not going well. Paul is conducting this visit in a manner that irritates the hell out of me. There is a long list of queries, things that need explanation or additional evidence, but he seems more interested in justifying his own actions and ingratiating himself with Sullivan and O'Rourke. Most annoying is the way he remains oblivious to the fact that they're constantly being evasive. I can see that they are lying, covering up, avoiding straight answers. Paul continues, smiling and accommodating, pretending to be a man of the world in the company of equals.

2

As I sit on the edge of the giant bed alone at last in the functional tidiness of my Travel Lodge room, the feeling of vague unease I had after first examining Associated Composites' accounts has grown into a realisation that there is something very wrong. Every attempt I make to get to the bottom of things is met with ill-disguised fudging and at this rate of progress I could be here for a long time. I really do need to get home tomorrow; I'm concerned about what's happening there.

Tim tells me all is well, Toby has been a good boy; he has eaten all his tea and he went to bed at the right time and is sleeping now. Even over the phone I register my husband's insincerity, he might as well be Sullivan or O'Rourke, but I have to comfort myself with belief.

I imagine a world where I no longer have to deal with Tim and for an instant I feel a lightness – which evaporates quickly as all the thoughts crowd back in about Toby needing a father and how I couldn't manage financially without Tim.

A firm rapping on my door jolts me back to the here and now. There's only one person who knows my whereabouts and that's Paul. Our arrangement is to meet for dinner at eight, it's only seven fifteen and I'm sitting in my underwear looking forward to a relaxing shower. A tide of anger tempts me to shout, 'Fuck off and leave me alone,' but instead an inane, 'Who is it?' actually emerges.

A soft voice with a disarming accent replies. 'It is I, Giuseppe Casagrande. My apologies for disturbing you, Signora Parker.'

My heart beats faster in shock, I peer through the tiny peephole and a distorted version of Casagrande is indeed on my doorstep.

'Wait, one moment.' I cast around for something to wear, quickly dress and open the door. He walks in majestically and sits down on the chair by the desk. He is alone, dressed in a dark blue suit now, looking even more expensively elegant. I realise that I felt compelled to admit him; refusing him entry was something I didn't consider. Now he is here I feel my discomfort increasing and wonder if I should have sent him away. After all, I am a vulnerable woman alone in a hotel room.

'Thank you for seeing me.' He waves to encompass the room. 'And in such unconventional surroundings. I fear you might find me not entirely professional.'
He smiles to reveal perfectly white, perfectly even teeth. I wonder whether they're his own. I also wonder what he would possibly want with me. His manner seems more assured now and less disturbing than I experienced at the office. There is a cool charm, the air of a man operating in his own element, performing work that he is good at and comfortable with. The thought that this might be rape or murder is easily dismissed. His suit is far too expensive for him to be engaging in anything messy.

'I am asking for your help, your assistance, Signora Parker. The people I represent require the takeover to proceed smoothly. It is very important to them. It is not something that they can allow to fail and it is very close, practically complete: a done deal as you say.'

I begin to mentally phrase my queries – what people? Why do they want it so much? Why me? How can I possibly be of any help? – but Casagrande's tight manner and precise economy of words convince me that this is no question and answer session. He is here to speak, I am supposed to listen and, I feel a pang of worry at this, agree to do whatever he wants. He places a thick document case on the desk. It's black leather and blends in comfortably with the general opulence of his attire.

'Here, this is for you, an indication of our serious nature and good intentions. I am sure you will find its contents convincing. All you need do is make sure that your firm delivers a positive report on Composites, something that says that a thorough check has been made and that all is as it should be. Something that will smooth the process of the transaction.'

He pushes the leather case towards me and stands up. A sudden realisation of what the case might contain grabs my stomach. Of course it could be some of the extra documentation that Paul has requested but I have my doubts. Then excitement grips me and I can hardly stop myself from zipping it open and checking out my suspicions. In the presence of Casagrande this seems inappropriate, almost insulting, and I resist. As he turns for the door I manage to voice my uncertainty.

'Wait. I don't know how I can help you. It's not up to me; it will have to be a partner that signs off the due diligence on your business. I'm only an accountant, I don't think I can help.'

There is a stern look on his face as he turns towards me.

'Signora Parker, let me explain. Where I come from there are two kinds of people. In the north, if you do not do what is asked of you then a member of your family is taken and pieces of them are sent to you until you do what you are asked. In the south, if you don't do what you are asked, then you are killed. You need to be aware that the people I represent are from the south.'

With that he opens the heavy door and leaves me standing in numb incomprehension until the fearful implications begin to sink in. I no longer have any desire to open the case. It can only bring certainty to the situation I am in. I lie down on the bed and close my eyes hoping to wake up to find the world the place it was before Casagrande showed up.

3

Paul is making a pass at me as we finish our dinner. He is full of self-importance which has been fuelled by drink and the company of people he perceives as important and influential. People who he thinks like and respect him. The same people who regard him as a nonentity and instead enlist my help to further their interests. Or perhaps Paul was included, why not? Another threatening speech wouldn't seem to be beyond Casagrande. If that were the case Paul has shown no signs over dinner, or has he? I think back and try to filter out any useful items from the torrent of conversation.

The references to work were confined to speculation about Martin, which made me freeze with indignation, and grand designs for Paul's future career which include occupation of Martin's corner office and made me want to hit him. As for Associated Composites, he expressed the view that things had gone well and that we should be away in good time tomorrow. My breath catches in my throat. As long as Paul is happy to sign off a positive report I appear to be off the hook. If not, at least according to Casagrande, I will soon be dead.

My life is in the dithering hands of this smug man who is in the process of ordering yet another bottle of wine, this one to take to the room with us.

'I thought we could have a drink in my room while we sort out the paperwork for tomorrow,' he leers.

It's gone ten and I'm absolutely tired out. If it had been up to me I would have stayed asleep after Casagrande's visit. Instead Paul banged cheerfully until I joined him, no rest, no shower, only sitting in a pub restaurant eating microwave in the bag food and feigning interest in what Paul has to say. Now he's trying to get into my knickers as if it were some benign ritual to be conducted whenever male and female colleagues were away together. It might have worked for Martin but this is very different. I need to get back to my room to check the contents of the document case and to sleep, even if it brings nightmares.

'That's very thoughtful,' I remain pleasant despite my increasing disgust, 'but I'm very tired, Paul, and I have terrible stomach ache.' I rub my belly as convincingly as I can.

'Oh dear!' He looks crestfallen, my meaning beginning to dawn. 'Was it the meal, something you ate?' He just has to check to make sure.

'No, no.' I speak softly, as if sharing a secret. 'Nothing I ate, it's just something we women get, you should be glad it doesn't happen to men.' I give a weak smile and he responds by losing all interest in paperwork.

'I'm sorry to hear that.' I bet he is. 'You get some rest, Jenny, we'll meet for breakfast and discuss things then.'

I leave him with his fresh bottle of wine and as I walk past table after table occupied by solitary business itinerants I see one or two who might find Paul's invitation more attractive than I do.

Safely back in my room, I lock the door and put on the chain. Trembling slightly, I unzip the case and take out its contents and arrange them neatly on the desk. There are no documents, only twenty pound notes, used ones. These are held in bundles by elastic bands. There are ten bundles, one hundred notes in a bundle. Twenty thousand pounds – freedom or death.

4

Tim is doing his abandoned schoolboy impression, hurt that I left him and wanting all my attention now I'm back. The house looks as if it's been ransacked by hungry burglars, the kitchen is strewn with soiled pots, spilled food, mess everywhere. I start to load the dishwasher before I realise it hasn't been emptied and now the dirty and clean sit enmeshed. Tim sits among the devastation, completely oblivious, anxious to engage in conversation for which I've no need or energy.

'What did you get up to last night?' he asks, not for the first time.
I feel irritated enough to tell him that his worst fears came true, that I got myself laid and that yes, I enjoyed it more than doing it with him. But even that wouldn't have got him off his arse and helping to clean up the mess he'd made, though it might give me a momentary stab of satisfaction.

'Nothing,' I mutter. 'I was dog tired, just as tired as I am now. Can't you clear the table for me?'

He would be very interested to hear about my visit from Casagrande and the small bonus of a case full of twenty pound notes which now lies concealed safely, I hope, under the shoe boxes at the bottom of my wardrobe.

As I work and ignore Tim's bleatings, I consider the money. I should never have taken it in the first place but I had little choice. There was Casagrande, all charm and impeccable manners, uttering the most serious threats as if it were an everyday thing for him. To refuse the case would have caused offence and signalled my rejection of his request. For all his smoothness there was an air about him that makes me sure that he would take that very personally and very seriously.

A sudden insight into his behaviour grabs hold of me. He was describing his own position as well as mine. The people he was referring to had obviously asked him to make sure the acquisition went through and the consequences of failure would apply equally to him. Casagrande might not have been making

11

threats, only passing them on. Now I realise just how high the stakes must be for a man in his position to be so in fear of his life that he resorts to bribery in a desperate attempt to save it. My blood freezes at the revelation.

Giving back the money wouldn't help either of us. If the deal goes through I don't expect to see the man ever again. If it doesn't, well – it absolutely has to. It must, and there is some comfort in knowing that Casagrande will be doing everything he can to make sure of it.

5

I close my eyes and breathe in deeply, then exhale slowly. The walls around me dissolve and I am sitting high above Manchester. To my left is the top-heavy slice of the Hilton, in front of me the glass apartments lean expectantly over the black waters of the Irwell. I relax to allow the urine to stream out, feeling the sensation as it passes through my body. Breathing softly, I allow its release until it trickles to completion and I reach down to gently dab away the drops clinging to my hairs with the wad of tissue.

As I do so a faint tingle of arousal reminds me of Martin's sensitive fingers there. This is quickly replaced by an uncomfortable stinging, courtesy of Tim's unwelcome thrusting. My eyes open to the pale grey cubicle, I smooth down my skirt and prepare to face another day at Landers Hoffman, Accountants.

As I slump back gratefully into my chair Emma arrives in a cloud of optimism. Emma always seems positive, she radiates bright energy and her conversation is sprinkled with shoes, handbags, dresses and guinea pigs.

'Jenny, they've started fighting again,' Emma announces as if this were a news bulletin I've been anxiously awaiting. 'We've had to split them up.'

Emma and I have adjacent work stations. I would like to describe them as desks but what I have in reality is half a desk. Emma sits diagonally across, occupying the other half. In this way the large square office can accommodate twenty-two hard-working souls while the two outside walls provide windowed offices for the more senior staff. Their translucent partitions at least let in some daylight, even if we do get it second-hand. Emma is still talking, still describing the idiosyncrasies of guinea pigs and I'm wishing I had her vitality and the undoubted luxury of being able to worry about minor guinea pig activities. My worries crowd in on me, stifle my breath, rob me of energy and threaten to crush my spirit.

Toby was ill again this morning; he was throwing up in the car on the way to nursery. At the time I managed to get a coveted place for him at Sunny Trees they made me sign a long form which promised, among many other things, that I would never under pain of dire consequences present them with a sick child. No coughs, runny noses, sickness, diarrhoea, rashes, temperatures, conjunctivitis: the list went on and on. All these ailments are forbidden by the nursery but seem endemic to my little Toby. There is hardly a day goes by when he doesn't exhibit at least three of the forbidden symptoms and he often manages the entire list.

Every day I turn up hoping nobody will notice his snotty nose and hand him firmly back to me, the consequences of which would indeed be dire. I have to work to pay our mortgage. Tim's wages are less than mine and believe me, mine are nothing to be proud of. There is another reason I need to work and to progress my career. I want to be able to afford to get a nice place just for Toby and me. I want to be independent. I want to have a life of my own.

Emma pushes a piece of paper across the desk. It has an intricate lattice work diagram with arrows, annotations, labels and two big-eyed animals staring out at me.

'That's the cage I'm building,' she proudly indicates. 'There's a separate downstairs and upstairs for each of them, a little stairway and a place they can sit together. The wires will stop them biting, I'm sure they'll be really happy. I've worked out the living area and they both have more space than you need for half a dozen guinea pigs.'

I return the diagram and make some positive noises. 'Brilliant, I'm amazed, what a super cage.'

I look across to the corner office and I can see that it's still empty. Martin has the best office with windows on two sides overlooking the city. I worry again at his continued absence, for selfish reasons, too; if he's not here then the slim chance of us stealing an hour together at his apartment is lost. He doesn't feature in my long term plans, nor I in his. He will never give up his Cheshire wife, Cheshire house, Cheshire kids and Cheshire lifestyle. Short-term, though, I need the things he provides, the oases of pleasure in my desert of toil and self-sacrifice: I need the way he makes me feel. It's worth all the guilt and more besides.

Emma's excitement has changed to softness, a caring concerned manner as she somehow detects my inner distress.

'Are you all right, Jenny?' she asks.

I automatically reply, 'Yes, fine,' before I can stop myself. 'Actually I'm not great,' I admit, 'I seem to have wasted my life.'

Emma wrinkles her nose as if failing to understand my contradictory answers.

'I've wasted my life,' I repeat and see her wince as she takes it in. 'Where's it gone? I'm thirty-four now, I'll be forty before I know it and soon after that I'll be old and useless. Where did my twenties go? The best years of my life vanished in a haze of pointlessness. I swear I spent ten years either drunk or getting drunk. Now look at me.' I spread my arms to encompass the black shirt, white top, black tights, black shoes, the uniform I wear every working day.

'What do I look like, Emma? Greasy hair, bad skin, big bum. Look at me, where has all my fire gone? You'll never believe it but I was once the life and soul of every party. Now I'm a boring mother, over-worked and over-stressed. The last two years have been all about Toby and never about me.'

'Rubbish.' Emma speaks with a false joviality that fails to hide her discomfort. 'You're great, you have done well, you are doing well. You've got a lovely little boy, a good job, you're ever so well thought of and most women would die for your slim figure. All the men here fancy you like mad.'

I start to smile back at her but just then Paul Unsworth calls me into a meeting room, a pokey box with one square window looking out on the slab-sided neighbour that was built in a time long past, when concrete was considered chic.

Paul appears nervous. As he speaks his eyes flicker between my chest area and a piece of wall behind my left shoulder, as if looking into my eyes might turn him into stone. He's explaining the situation in his own roundabout way and I'm thinking of Toby's sickness and worrying if he's kept down his morning milk.

'While Martin's off, there's a lot of extra work to be covered. I really can't believe he would leave us all in the lurch like this while he gets his end away.' Paul continues to dribble out words, noticing nothing beyond the unchanging pattern on the walls or the shapes beneath my blouse.

I sit quietly while he slowly reveals the point of the conversation by circling around it, heading off in several unpromising directions then settling gently on to it. While I wait, I feel a rising anxiety about Martin, about the seemingly universal acceptance that he has gone off with his mistress, about the fact that I know for sure he hasn't, about the awkward situation that means I can't tell anybody.

I am sure that neither the bumbling incoherent Paul nor anyone else possesses any inkling about my relationship with Martin. This conversation is merely a prelude to him passing over some work that he can't be bothered to do himself. Paul proves me right when he nods to a stack of fat ring-binders on his table.

'That looks like an awful lot,' I say. 'I won't be able to do anything with it for a few days, I've still got some of the Manchester United players to sort out. There's a large payment for a suite at the Hilton in one of the player's accounts but the hotel bill has the name Chen Xi and a company, Chengdu Industries. There's obviously been a mistake, I've asked the hotel for more information and I've arranged to talk to the player at Carrington tomorrow.'

'Oh. Eric likes to deal with that sort of thing himself, anything involving Man U players. Give him that file.' He looks at his watch. 'This other stuff has to have priority, Jenny.' He taps the binders. 'I'm way behind on it, what with having to do the due diligence report on Associated Composites.' He leans

16

forward and whispers loudly, 'Eric was very pleased with the job we did down there.'

I'm unimpressed but very relieved. I even meekly accept the pile of work Paul is dumping on me. It's a small price to pay for his compliance.

Martin's absence is beginning to worry me more and more. Where is he, why would he just up and leave? My heart gives a small jump and sends extra blood thudding to my head. What if he really has left his wife to be with me? Almost as soon as this thought surfaces I dismiss it. Martin has been almost too honest with me in that respect and I can't believe anything has changed. No, whatever his wife might surmise, Martin has not left her for another woman.

My heart sinks and my eyes brim with tears as the realisation washes over me that Martin might be dead.

6

As soon as I can reasonably leave my desk for the lunch break I hurry outside and walk quickly to the flat. Martin bought four of these, 'off plan' as he described it. His idea was to sell them at a profit as soon as they were ready. People were doing this all the time, he said, and there was good money to be made. It seems that this business didn't work out in the way he intended and he was left with the choice of selling at a huge loss or putting them out to rent.

The one we used was the show flat, slickly decorated and tastefully furnished in order to demonstrate what a Manchester apartment should look like. I suspect he kept this one off the market just for us, it being less than a five minute walk from the office.

As I click the key in the lock and let myself in, I suddenly feel a pang of fear and uncertainty. What if Martin is here, dead and rotting away? There's no smell of putrefaction in the air but I proceed nervously, scared of what I might find and at the same time fearful of discovery. I can think of no credible excuse for my being here and my ears strain for any sounds of occupation. There is nobody here, dead or alive. The flat is exactly as I left it ten days ago. The bed is in a state of wanton abandonment and the teacups are stained with brown rings.

Without Martin here, without my usual state of excitement and adventure, the place is seedy and depressing; a glorified hotel room for two selfish adulterers to take sexual pleasure from one another. I sit down on the side of the bed, suddenly bone-weary with the whole situation. I risk so much for so little and now I can't believe I acted so stupidly. Whatever Martin's fate, I cannot afford to be found out. Tim might be laid back and easy-going, but the discovery that his wife, the mother of his son, has been regularly screwing another man would soon change that.

18

I take a couple of Tesco bags out of a kitchen drawer. These were once used to carry in food for our illicit lunches, treats for post-coital consumption. Now I need them to secrete anything that might betray my presence. She may turn up here at any time; the cynical eyes of a suspicious wife are something I have to guard against.

Pulling out the top drawer of the bedside cabinet I pour its contents into a bag. A large plastic penis, used only once with disappointing results, flops soggily into the bag, followed by an assortment of vibrators and several pots of lubricant. I hide them by squashing in a cheap dressing gown bought at Marks & Spencer's during a cold snap. I can't think of anything else that needs to be removed but, nevertheless, methodically open each drawer and cupboard and peer in with Martin's wife's eyes. All clear, only the bed in its magnificent disarray stands testament to the activities it accommodated. There are semen stains on the sheets, if you know where to look.

I'm considering stripping the bed and taking away the soiled items when I hear the sound of a key scraping in the lock and the front door opening.

7

My heart stops, my breath catches in my throat, I am frozen with terror and indecision. In the twenty or so times I was here before, nobody ever knocked on the door let alone entered the flat. Apart from Martin, of course.

I hear footsteps, the noise of something being dragged, a clunking noise and the door swinging back violently and hitting the wall.

My panic pitches me headlong into the bathroom where I lock the door and listen to the pounding of blood in my ears. I'm trapped, there is no way out of this now without revealing my guilt and my shame. Tim will find out, Toby will be taken from me; I will be cast out of Landers Hoffman. My life is at an end.

I should never have taken the chance involved in coming here.

I look around me to discover that this is a really horrible little bathroom with no external wall to provide a window and some natural light. I never realised it before, having used it only for a quick pee and a wipe-down before scurrying back to the office. It's built like a hotel bathroom, as small as possible and just as tacky. There's a small hand basin that presses against my thigh, a mirror that reveals a gaunt woman and a bath shrouded by a curtain.

Beneath the bass drum in my ears, I hear someone banging around in the bedroom I only just escaped from. Keeping deathly still, I pray that whoever is out there will go away and leave me undetected. Leaning against the thin white door, I try to locate noises, strain to hear where they are, hope they will recede. There is a moment of silence when I lose touch with the movement coming from outside, then the door handle next to my right arm clicks as it receives a heavy twist. The whole door shakes as if a heavy sack has been thrown against it. An involuntary screech leaves my throat and echoes around the bathroom despite all my efforts to retrieve it.

A female voice responds, betraying equal alarm.

'Hello?' A thick foreign accent scrambles the remainder of the query into an indecipherable babble. I breathe again, thankful for the cool air returning to my starving lungs, grateful that there is no plummy Cheshire voice, steadied by realisation of what the commotion has been all about.

'Who is it?' I hear my voice several pitches above its normal tone. 'What do you want?' I ask the questions I am now convinced I can already answer myself.

'Sorry, thought nobody here. We cleaning.'

'Well go away and clean some other time,' I shout, releasing some of my tension in anger.

In defiant confirmation of my sudden change in status, I walk boldly over to flush the toilet, run the taps in the basin then wait for a few minutes before sliding back the bolt and walking purposefully out of my hiding place.

There is nobody left in the flat, the cleaner has disappeared as quickly as she came. And without catching sight of me. My position remains uncompromised, there is no witness to my clandestine activities.

I sit on the bed and try to quiet my trembling nerves. Of course there had to be a cleaner, Martin would hardly have done it himself and couldn't afford to let his wife even know he had this place.

My sin turns from despair to presumption.

Now that I have managed to concentrate on my breathing for a few seconds, I feel myself becoming calm, almost relaxed. The crisis is over; I have been spooked by a cleaning lady, no harm done, no need to panic. In fact, I handled it perfectly, if I ignore the emotional aspects.

I stand up and retrieve the bag of dildos. A sudden fear grips me as I realise my handbag is missing. I left it on the bedside table when I was emptying the drawers and now it's gone.

*

Back at the office, having dumped the sex toys in a public refuse bin, I search through my handbag desperately trying to discover if anything is missing. I discovered it lying beside the bed, contents spilled onto the floor. There's a distinct possibility that it had fallen that way but I'm worried that it has been rifled through. Thank God my purse appears untouched. I know exactly how little money was in it and it's all there.

Nothing appears to be missing but I can't shake off my feeling of deep unease. Perhaps I'm reacting to the close shave, the near disaster of discovery. I look at my hands and they're steady enough but my energy is diffuse and unfocused. I feel I need a stiff drink, just to steady my nerves. A couple of large gin and tonics should do the job, but I have no time left to slip out to the pub. Although I have drunk very little since I became pregnant with Toby my body still feels the buzz of excitement, the euphoric anticipation of leaving all my worries behind for a few hours and slipping into alcoholic oblivion.

A dangerous alternative pricks my brain into a momentary ecstasy as it remembers the chill nasal bite and re-lives the subsequent blossoming of clarity and freedom. There is a man one floor down who works in Corporate Finance who would sell me a line but my heart and mind sink into despair as I recall my previous state of dependence. If I start using again to make me feel better, Toby will certainly suffer badly and I'm not going to let that happen.

I open up the first of the files that Paul considers himself too busy to deal with and begin a painstaking examination of a badly deficient set of cash flow figures. It's good that I'm hard at work as the faint smell of bad breath heralds Paul's looming presence at my shoulder.

'How are you getting on?' he enquires, taking the opportunity to peer down at my breasts.

I turn slightly away from his whiff to reply. 'A couple more days should bottom it, though I do have a lot of other stuff piling up.'

'This is all needed really urgently, Jenny.'

'What about Martin?' I ask bravely. 'Any news? And has he left any notes on this job that might speed things up?'

'No news, nothing at all, at least nobody's told me anything. As for notes, he must have used his laptop for everything, they must all be on his local drive. There's no work of his at all on the server.'

'Well I can't do it any quicker. If you want a proper reconciliation it'll take me at least two more days, longer if I have any queries.'

'Can't you find a way of either speeding things up or else work longer hours until it's finished?'

A pang of panic shoots through my heart. I have to get Toby, I can't stay a minute extra.

'Lunchtime,' I sigh. 'Lunchtime tomorrow, then you can review it in the afternoon and get it signed off by close of play.'

*

Getting a heavy box of folders home on the train is always difficult. My back feels like it has been badly put out. My arms are sore and my shoulders are stiff. I ended up sitting by the doors perched on the damned box, it was too awkward for me to drag down the aisle in search of an empty seat. My kitchen is a mess, crocks piled up in the sink, pans congealing on the hob. It's too late to be clanking around clearing up, it's 1 a.m. and I'm still poring over cash flow information. I'm determined to pass it all back to Paul with a clean bill of health attached. Nobody can accuse me of slipshod work, of not being thorough.

I look with regret at the bombsite kitchen and wonder why I bothered working all these hours after Toby and Tim went to bed. Now I'll be even more tired than usual in the morning, the house will still look like a tip. I've just spent four hours on something a junior could quite easily have done. The time would have been far better used to clean up the house and get some sleep. I resolve to tell Paul to deal with things like this himself in future and I stumble upstairs to bed.

As if sensing my wakefulness as I pass his door, Toby lets out a small whimper and I can hear him turning over in his cot. Freezing, trying not to breathe, I wait for him to settle down again but I begin to feel the tug of his presence and the change in his state. He murmurs softly, calling me to him. My body relaxes and I get back into my breath as I take him in my arms and watch his soft eyes gazing into mine.

8

Four days later I wake up and it is Toby who has died. His little cold body has turned blue and his big brown sightless eyes stare accusingly up at me, asking why I neglected him and allowed this to happen. My whole body is shaking with dread as I heave myself out of bed. The bedside clock glows 3:32 and snores of indifference confirm Tim's supine presence. I shuffle naked through the cold air, not pausing to try to locate my pyjamas, discarded by Tim's passion, and into Toby's bedroom.

The glow of the night light reveals his chubby aliveness. He is lying in an untidy heap at the very bottom of his cot, outside the covers I carefully arranged over him, but glowing with healthy warmth and breathing steadily. It's as if he was struck down with sleep in mid bounce and lay where he fell.

Overwhelming relief settles me into a chair and I hold his hot little hand in gratitude and joy. Martin intrudes. The idea of his own cold lifelessness replaces the dream I had about Toby, but this time it is a waking nightmare. Yesterday shock and fright numbed me after the police came to the office. The worry about what they might ask me had me beavering away, head down, until it was time to collect Toby. He did a much better job of distracting my thoughts than anyone else could and held my full attention from the moment his eyes lit up at my appearance.

Now there's a new day to face and with it the knowledge that I will have to do something, tell somebody perhaps. Oh no, I panic at the prospect of Tim finding out he's been betrayed. I visualise his reaction, the acrimonious divorce, his successful custody battle leaving me ashamed and childless. I look at Toby, my sleeping son, and my heart tells me that he is my only priority. Whatever has happened to Martin, wherever he is, none of that matters compared to Toby.

As I tread softly out of the kitchen with a beaker of water, the soft hum of the computer draws me into the study. Half asleep, I waggle the mouse and squint at the sudden brightness of the screen. 'United to increase bid for Brazilian striker' is revealed, as if I might be at all interested.

I sip my water and feel the cold trickle down my insides. Another chill, a deeper one, joins it as I bring up the browsing history. A long list of items, beginning with 'Blonde has all her holes filled with cock' and continuing in a similar vein of depravation down the rest of the page. Tim often lingers down here after I go to bed, preferring the company of pornographic images to mine. Ever since Toby, he's been like this. Then he comes to me, aroused by the images playing in his head, demanding that I provide a warm receptacle for his selfish ejaculation.

Toby is calling to me and rattling his bars. I hurry back to his room. He's excited to see me. I gather the warm bundle in my arms, feeling the heavy cold nappy that must be making him uncomfortable. An echo of the chilling fear in my dream pierces my stomach then eases as I caress my precious bundle.

Preoccupied by Toby's needs I put any thoughts of Martin at the back of my mind until I am hurrying through Spinningfields, trying not to be late for work. As I walk, a fresh wave of panic causes me to stop and let out a gasp of air. All the possibilities, at least all the bad ones flood through my thoughts, all of them end with Tim prising Toby screaming from my arms and throwing me out of the house. As I try to rationalise away this dreadful result another more certain scenario arises. The Cheshire wife will have me fired if she finds out about Martin and me. I have no doubt she is capable, I am certain it would take only a word from her. Martin was never explicit about his wife's background, but I gather that his exalted and very highly paid position at Landers Hoffman was down to her family's influence.

As I settle down opposite Emma the uncertainty I'm feeling lifts suddenly and my mind becomes totally clear and calm. Nobody, absolutely nobody under any circumstances is to find out about Martin and me. I am adamant now, resolved, final answer. No matter what I am keeping quiet. He may be lying dead or dying somewhere, but that's not my problem. The vision of Martin's cold body lying unidentified in a morgue makes me shudder.

'Are you all right?' Emma's cheery voice snaps me away from the horror film I'm playing in my head.

'Oh,' I gasp, 'I'm a bit tired.'

Emma comes around to my side of the desk and puts her arms around my shoulders. This simple, human act of concern triggers a flood of tears and I find myself crying uncontrollably. Emma stands holding me in beautiful inaction until I try to explain between sobs.

'I had a dream,' I splutter, 'Toby was dead.' I wonder if my dream was really about Martin and the knife of doubt slides back into my solar plexus.

Emma takes me to the toilet like a mother whose daughter has wet herself. She makes me look into a mirror and I see a shining blonde girl, a vision of loveliness, standing beside a small, tired brunette with unkempt hair and crumpled clothes. I look at myself with Emma's eyes and feel pity.

The strong, busy, thirty-four year old has deteriorated into someone who would not look out of place living in a cardboard box under the railway arches. Emma opens her voluminous handbag to reveal a comprehensive stock of make-up, face creams, lotions and scents.

'Here.' She smiles, in obvious relief that I didn't grab a nail file and plunge it into my own heart. 'Freshen yourself up, it'll make you feel better.'

I'm amazed at the difference a comb and a smear of lipstick makes. I can now see something of the feisty femme fatale that would drive Martin mad with desire. A small adjustment to my bra strap gathers what Toby sucked nearly flat into pink swellings that push against the fabric of my blouse. I am beginning to feel better and almost back to balance until I see the uniformed policeman waiting by my desk.

9

'Mrs Jenny Parker,' I reply and watch as he writes carefully in his black notebook.

'When was the last time you saw Mr Youngs?"

There's a flush of guilty excitement coursing through my body as I visualise Martin's nakedness sprawled exhausted on the bed in his flat. I left him there as I hurriedly made my exit, already very late for my lunchtime return.

'A week last Thursday.'

'What time would that be?'

'Lunchtime, twelve thirty, maybe.'

That's when he left the office to go to his apartment – I waited ten breathless and excited minutes before I followed.

'You were here?'

'Yes, sat at my desk. I saw him leave his office. I suppose he was going out for lunch.'

'Did he say anything to you when he left?'

'No.' I'm not going to tell the policeman about the way Martin looked across at me and raised his eyebrows. I shiver slightly at the memory.

'Was there anything unusual about Mr Young's behaviour that day?'

I remember his passion, his magnificent arousal, how his gentle tongue insisted on my own quivering release. Nothing out of the ordinary, nothing he hadn't done many times before.

'No, nothing unusual.'

'The last time you spoke to Mr Youngs, what did he say?'

'We only really talk about work, he allocates projects to me, gives me instructions, that sort of thing.'

'Did he give you any instructions that Thursday?'

I look up at the black garbed man standing attentively by my desk. His eyes meet mine briefly, I detect no real engagement from him, he's only going through the motions, it seems, hardly hearing what I'm saying. There's no active interrogation going on, no careful scrutiny, little chance that he might read my thoughts, thank God. The last instructions Martin gave me were to keep on going, just like that, oh, yes, that's good.

'He gave me some work, that's all.'

'How did he seem to you? Was he happy? Sad? Depressed? Worried about something? What was he like?'

'Happy, definitely happy.' I don't need to lie this time.

'Did you say anything to him while he was giving you instructions?'

Hardly. My mouth was not only full but also busy.

'No, not really.'

Martin had groaned 'Oh my God it's coming,' a completely pointless warning as my mouth was already filling up with his semen. He was always so apologetic about ejaculating. He didn't need to be, whatever he wanted was fine with me as long as he didn't squirt into my hair. One embarrassing afternoon at work with hair stuck together as if with glue is enough for anyone.

'Do you have any idea where Mr Youngs might be, Mrs Parker?'

'No, I'm sorry.' Now the fear comes back. I remember my shaky legs as I tottered down the stairs from the apartment after I grabbed my stuff. Guilty feelings, shame and desperate sadness are crowding in on me now. What difference can it possibly make to Martin whether or not I share our secret with the police? If I knew where he is, I'd tell them, I'd go there myself, I'm so desperate for him to be safe.

But he's gone, I can tell by the emptiness in my heart.

10

I'll give Tim his due, he never fails to bounce back. Despite the really shitty way I have been treating him of late, he keeps positive, keeps on coming back for more. Today he is especially buoyant, today he is being taken by his boss to Hillhead. The way his eyes light up hungrily, it's as if he's about to visit a high class bordello where he'll be invited to take his pick. Instead, at least I understand this to be the case, all it involves is an exhibition of earth-moving equipment, serried ranks of diggers and dozers, all painted the same yellow colour, no doubt. His bullish enthusiasm is infectious, however, and I find myself smiling alongside him, basking in the aura of his fun and excitement.

'It'll give you a chance to talk to Damian about that foreman's job,' I prompt, even though I know how unwelcome my suggestion will be.

Tim clouds over immediately.

'I've told you, I don't want to be a foreman. How many more times do I have to tell you?'

'Well you ought to think again. You can't be a dozer driver all your life. What about prospects, advancement, ambition? Haven't you got any ambition?'

He looks across at me sullenly. I am spoiling his day out already.

'Yes, I want to drive a bigger machine, I want to be the best there is. I want to enjoy what I do. Every day I go to work I can see what I'm achieving. I make a difference, change the landscape. I look around at what I've done and I'm proud.'

I feel myself softening despite the hard knot in my stomach that despairs he will ever grow up and take responsibility for his own life. Not while he has me to do it for him at any rate.

'Okay, okay,' I relent. 'I hear what you're saying. I just don't want you to be passing up opportunities you might regret.'

He brightens up again.

'Anyway,' he says, 'foremen don't get more money, they get less if you take overtime into account. Foremen don't get paid for overtime at all, they're just expected to work late for nothing.'

They do get put on the staff, they do get holiday pay and they do get paid when they're sick, though. I manage to keep myself from pointing this out even though I'm desperate for the flexibility this would bring to my life. As a member of staff, Tim could be much more help with the childcare duties than he is now. Being hourly paid means he gets nothing if he doesn't show up. It's me that gets Toby's sick days to cope with. Even though it's me who has the higher paid job and better prospects.

The twenty thousand pounds in the wardrobe pops into my head. Ten days have gone by since it was delivered to me by Casagrande and I've been reluctant to touch it out of some nagging feeling that it might have to be returned, or handed over to the police.

I have no idea whether the acquisition has proceeded or not, I assume Paul put in a positive report after I'd written up our visit in the warm glow of the money and the death threat. As for the rest of the process, my pretend-casual enquiries have yielded no information at all.

Paul is a dolt. If they've trusted him with any information, which I strongly doubt, he has a smug sense of superiority that prevents him from sharing it. Nor is there anything in the newspapers. There's been no major press coverage involving World Ordnance Systems or whether they bought Associated Composites (Brackley) Limited. A mad, impulsive thought tells me to go for broke, put all that cash in WOS shares and hope they rocket when the takeover is announced.

This excitement soon passes. If my luck is anything to go by, they'll probably plummet as soon as I buy them. Anyway, there might never be a takeover and then someone will be asking me for the money back, or worse, exacting terrible retribution for my botched job.

I can't leave all that cash in the wardrobe, anything could happen. A fire, a burglary or, worse still, Tim might discover it. Leaving Toby strapped firmly in his high chair and busily sucking on a toast soldier dipped in runny egg, I go quickly upstairs. As I open the wardrobe my chest tightens and my heart beats loudly in my throat. I find myself looking surreptitiously over my shoulder as I retrieve the document case. Feeling inside it I intend to take twenty pounds to see me through the day but instead retrieve a whole bundle – two thousand pounds – and then put the case back, burying it deep under shoe boxes. Trembling with excitement and apprehension I carry my swag downstairs to find that Toby has managed to throw his soldier right across the kitchen while jettisoning his egg so that it lies oozing yellow onto the floor tiles.

11

As I queue in line at the bank, an officious lady with hair slightly too blonde and lipstick definitely too pink accosts me. She is carrying a clip board and wearing a navy blue uniform with the bank logo on its breast.

'Can I help you?' she demands busily. Her manner is brusque and unhelpful, in direct contrast to her words.

'Oh.' I am taken aback at first, deep in my own guilty thoughts. Having grabbed the bundle of cash this morning I decide to open a bank account with it during my lunch break, a sole account, one that Tim is unaware of, my account just for me and my future. It seems a safer place to keep the twenty grand and as I stand here excitedly I wish I'd brought it all with me.

'Can I help you?' she asks again and looks aggressively at her clip board as if seeking some justification for all this.

'I want to open an account,' I meekly reply at last.

'An account?' she repeats loudly. 'Do you already have an account with us?' At first hearing, the question appears to be nonsensical.

'No, no, I don't have an account. I want to start one,' I explain.

'You don't bank with us?' she demands, as if I've committed a cardinal sin.

'No, but I want to.'

'What sort of account?'

'I don't know, what sorts are there? Just a normal, everyday current account, I suppose.'

There is a look in her eye that makes me feel even more like a criminal than when I came in here.

She bustles off and returns with some forms.

'Here.' She thrusts them into my hand. 'Complete these then hand them in at the reception desk.' She indicates a large lady in a uniformed blouse that isn't quite managing to contain everything it's meant to.

I breathe a sigh of relief and use one of the pens on a chain to write my particulars on the form. The questions are impertinent, but I persevere and put the thing on the desk hoping to get away in time to buy myself a sandwich.

'Passport, driver's licence and utility bill,' the large lady intones.

'I beg your pardon?'

'Passport, driver's licence and utility bill,' she repeats. 'You need to have proof of identity to open an account, passport, driver's licence and utility bill, that's what you need.'

I fish about in my handbag, pull out my driver's licence.

'Here,' I say, 'it's got a photo and my address. That should do.'

'We need a utility bill and a passport,' she repeats. 'It's money laundering regulations.'

'I haven't got my passport with me,' I say.

'Can't you go back and get it?' she asks.

'No,' I reply. 'I'm only on my lunch break, it's at home.'

'You'll have to bring it tomorrow,' she says.

I take out the money from my purse and put it on the counter with my form.
'Can I pay this in now, then, I don't want to be carrying it around. I'll bring in my passport tomorrow.'

'Oh.' She looks at the bundle of twenty pound notes as if it were one of Toby's soiled nappies. There is a hush. A silence seems to descend on the whole bank. Even the unhelpful lady with the clip board has disappeared, presumably to stalk people elsewhere. The plump lady gives me a conspiratorial look and whispers, 'Not cash, love.' I could barely hear her words. 'At least, not a big wad of cash like that.'

I look puzzled because I am puzzled. This is a bank after all; they should be used to handling money.

'You'll get a visit,' she hisses. 'Does your husband know you have this money?'

I am shocked to the core by her inference and can't think of a suitable response. 'It's all right, dear.' I must look pathetic because she has started to patronise me in a serious way now. 'We're not allowed to tell people,' but she does anyway, 'large amounts of cash get reported, then you get a visit from the police.'

She stops whispering, then shovels the money and the form into an envelope that has the bank's address conveniently printed on it, with a square in the top right corner that helps you to position the stamp in the event that you need to post it back to them.

I get out of there quickly, trying not to run and managing to resist screaming until I'm well away.

12

Roger, two desks away, knows all about the Money Laundering Regulations. He knows pretty much everything about everything, according to himself. What he knows nothing about is personal hygiene and two desk widths are hardly sufficient distance to remain safe, particularly on a warm day. Braving the stench, I ask the question, still worried by my experience in the bank. What was the receptionist thinking? Where did she think I got the money from? Drugs? Whoring? Robbery?

Roger regales me with a detailed account of the regulations and helpfully points out that I should have been on the course, everyone else had been on it. It was compulsory, a part of Continuous Professional Development with which all accountants have to rigorously comply. He expresses horror that I missed such an important element of my education. He can't believe that I'm really not already aware that all suspicious transactions must be reported to the police.

'It's the law, Jenny,' he says. 'Anybody who fails to report suspected money laundering can be put in prison, it's a very serious offence.'

'Yes, but what if I sell my car and the man gives me cash?' I ask.

'Well, if you take over five thousand pounds to pay into a bank they have to report it whether or not they're suspicious. Most banks will report any sizeable cash sum just to be on the safe side.'

'What? Even a couple of thousand pounds? Would that be enough?' I ask. My horrible experience at the bank churns around in my stomach.

'Almost always, unless they know the person paying in the money really well and it's a regular thing that they've checked out before.'

'So if, say, I took the money from the car and opened a new bank account?' I just have to ask.

Roger throws back his head and howls with forced laughter, drawing as much attention to my naivety as he possibly can.

'Well?' I prompt when he stops laughing long enough for me to get a word in.

'Sorry.' He doesn't look sorry. 'But that's classic. Every small time drug dealer there ever was will have tried that out at least once. Surefire certainty that one. Has to be reported by the bank, it's the law, they have no other option.'

'Yes, but if it's my money, if all I did was sell a car?'

'Then you'd be able to show the police a receipt and tell them who you got the money from. You see, it's the person who gave you the cash that the police are interested in. Cars,' he sneers, 'are one of the most common means of laundering money. People buy and sell them for cash, adding some undeclared earnings here and there as they go. It's commonplace, everyone's at it.'

He sits back smugly and gazes intently at me. A sudden wave of nausea greets my suspicion that he fancies his chances with me. He is probably interpreting our conversation as confirmation of my interest in him.

I return to my own desk without spitting at him or kicking him in the groin. It's a close thing, but I have enough to contend with already. I pull out the bank envelope; it contains both the form I completed and the cash. Nobody at the bank has got my details, the receptionist might recognise me if she sees me again, but it was a busy, city centre branch so I doubt it. Thank God I didn't try that stupidity closer to home. The idea that I am a less friendly receptionist away from having the police investigating me is very disturbing in view of the twenty grand in used notes that I can't account for either to the authorities or my husband. I resolve to find a safer place to hide the cash. But where?

13

There is a subdued feeling in the office, worse even than a normal Monday morning. Eyes don't lift to meet my gaze as I walk to my desk, there is no chatter, not even the sound of legitimate business conversations. Even the phones are still. Emma's bright eyes are soft with sadness as she imparts the grim news.

'They found Martin...' She half speaks, half whispers. 'Have you heard?'

I shake my head in denial and prepare for the worst. They found Martin – sounds like they found Martin's body or they found what's left of Martin or they found what used to be Martin. The words give me no hope, only an overwhelming sense of loss.

'He's dead.' Emma confirms my fears with a bluntness arising from ignorance.

As I forgive her for this hammer blow I'm still knocked down and broken. To Emma, the man in the corner office, who waves at her as she walks past, has died. As the tears flow, I begin to heave great sobs that I can't prevent. Emma can have no idea of the reason for my devastation and she looks shocked by the sight of it. She expects me to react the way she reacted when she herself was told the news. To feel the way that she felt, not this way; not a total loss of control, an overwhelming display of emotion.

A small voice tells me that I'm giving the game away, I'm revealing my personal involvement, but I neither believe it nor do I care. Martin is gone; the love, the laughter, the intimacy and the secrets we shared are lost. The weight of guilty excitement lifts slightly now I no longer have an illicit lover. There are fewer opportunities now for my unfaithfulness to be discovered. Shock, sadness, sorrow and relief all mingle in my tears.

Emma watches me recover a little composure before continuing with her news. I know what she's feeling; her knowledge has to be shared while it's new and energetic.

'Are you okay?' she asks. I nod and blow my nose in confirmation. 'They found his body on Saturday. Apparently he had a heart attack or something, anyway they say he died in his sleep. It's just that nobody found him until now.'

'Where did they find him?' I asked.

'Oh in some flat, apparently he'd been there ever since he disappeared. I suppose nothing could be done, even if they had found him sooner.'

'I see.' I feel numb now and very tired. I get up to go to the toilet, there are shooting pains in my bladder.

'Are you all right?' Emma asks. 'Shall I come with you? You look a bit upset.'

'It's a shock,' I admit. 'I'll be fine.'

I hope.

14

From where I sit, almost at the rear of the church, I can see only the back of her black head scarf. I wonder at her sadness, this woman who assumed her missing husband had left her for a mistress. Is this a preferable outcome for her, does it make things less complicated? How had she felt when she heard Martin was dead? Did she feel relief that she'd not been betrayed after all, or sadness that she had lost her husband? There's one way to find out, I can seek her out and ask her. Even the thought of doing this is too frightening and I push it aside and try to concentrate on the burblings of the priest standing beside the polished casket, amid an expensively assembled forest of flowers. Above him, the beautifully preserved ancient vault gives testimony to the wealth and generosity of the local congregation.

The participants in this ceremony are a mixture of local and remote, family and friends, business partners and colleagues. Oh, and one mistress who is racked with grief that cannot be shared.

At the end of the ceremonial discomfort, the coffin is borne aloft and the family head the procession behind it. I stand uncomfortably at the end of an aisle as she passes, unable and unwilling to look at her in case my eyes betray my guilt. An elderly lady follows immediately behind her, supported by two men, one of whom resembles a stouter version of Martin. The woman is his mother, I assume, and my heart goes out to her. The prospect that I might one day attend little Toby's funeral fills me with horror and I fervently pray for an earlier death to deliver me from that pain.

At the graveside we form a sombre queue, ready for the widow to hand each of us a white rose which she expects us to cast into the hole where Martin has been placed. Again, I fail to meet her eyes. I stare down at her dainty feet as she mechanically hands me the flower. As I release it to join the others strewn untidily across the casket, a vision of Martin lying there, cold and lifeless, overwhelms me. It's as if the coffin becomes transparent and I can see his face looking up at me, a slight smile on his face which will now never change.

My legs give way and almost pitch me headlong to join the flowers and Martin, but a steadying hand on my shoulder prevents me from making a disastrous show of myself. Turning, I see the man I assume is Martin's brother; his eyes are kind and soft. I quickly flee to the anonymity of the crowd, stand among Landers Hoffman personnel and begin to recover some semblance of composure.

Emma comes up beside me.

'Are you coming with us to the pub?' she asks. I'm not able to understand her and she explains, 'There is an official do but we don't want to go. We all thought we could get a drink at the pub down the road instead.'

I'm grateful to be taken away by her and half a dozen colleagues. The widow is still receiving people and giving them flowers as we leave. At the gate to the churchyard, I turn for a last look at Martin's resting place to see that his widow is being hugged by a small neat man, the last mourner in the line. Even from this distance I recognise him and my urge to run intensifies. Giuseppe Casagrande, the man who bribed me, is here in Cheshire and attending Martin's funeral.

*

The pub is called the Leigh Arms and it's really a posh restaurant that doesn't normally cater for a dozen or so accountants intent on washing away the sour taste of a funeral. In their concern for sensibilities and out of respect for Martin, Landers Hoffman gave us all the day off to attend the funeral. This has the desired effect of swelling the turnout, but also gives us the rest of the day to get drunk. I'm in no state to resist the pull of the throng and find myself dipping into Casagrande's money for the first time in order to buy a round of drinks. The inevitable consequence of my

41

purchasing intoxicating liquor for half a dozen people is for each recipient to insist on repaying the compliment. This prospect holds no fears for me.

It's late afternoon and my face is numb, my head is swimming, I am becoming nauseous. While the conversation rests on the topic of Martin I have to keep my peace and drink steadily, speaking only the words 'large gin and tonic' when addressed, or nodding to indicate that I do want ice and lemon.

By now, the congregation has thinned out. Two people from my floor remain, Emma and the malodorous Roger, together with three people from downstairs, Bob, Ted and Jeremy. All seem intent on getting even drunker than I am. Roger shifts his position closer to mine, puts a large hand on my skirt and begins to squeeze my thigh. I feel the urgent need to vomit.

By the time I manage to stagger back from the toilet, having violently expelled the contents of my stomach through my mouth and nostrils, only Bob and Roger remain at the table and they greet me with undisguised leers. Being sick has sobered me up enough for me to desperately need to go home. Toby! A thought pierces my stupor and sends a shock through my body. Toby needs picking up from nursery. My handbag is on the bench seat. I rifle through it to find my phone and stare uncomprehendingly at the time display. Seven forty. I don't understand what that means. Seven forty. The phone informs me that I have twelve missed calls. I vaguely remember putting it on silent for the funeral. Twelve missed calls and eight text messages.

'I need to go home,' I keep muttering as I scroll through the messages. It seems that Tim eventually got Toby from nursery but is getting increasingly pissed off with each call. I phone him back and he answers instantly.

'Sorry, I got a bit drunk at the funeral and lost track of time,' is all I can say. Tim has much more to say and when I judge he is mostly done, I hang up.

'I need to go home,' I say to Bob who pushes a drink towards me. The smell of gin makes me want to throw up. 'I can't drink that, I don't feel well.' He gets me a glass of water and puts it in my hand. Even the water tastes horrible, but I drink it down in the hope it will make me feel better.

*

Moving my legs is difficult and painful. Everywhere seems to ache, my head is still swimming and I can hardly lift it. Catching a few breaths brings me round enough to realise I'm in a car, curled up on a back seat made of worn plastic. A man with red hair and a fat stomach is driving. I seem to be the only passenger. I think it must be a taxi. They got me into a taxi, thank God. I sweep my arm in panic, feeling around for my handbag. What remains of one thousand pounds after buying drinks all day is in there. I'll need it to pay the taxi.

I locate the bag in the footwell and my panic fades away. As I try to push myself upright I realise that I'm still pissed out of my head. I can hardly move or think. My bladder signals its intentions to empty itself immediately.

'Stop!' I call out to the driver, hearing my voice in the far distance. 'Stop, I need a pee, I need to pee right now, if you don't stop I'll piss all over your car.'

The car stops, the door is opened and I half fall, half stagger out onto the grass verge. The complete darkness comes as a shock; it must be even later than I think. There is a constant stream of headlights in both directions but I pull down my pants to my ankles and squat. As the flow starts I lose balance and fall backwards which makes me pee into the air. All I can do is lift up my legs to avoid peeing on them as far as possible. The ground is cold and wet underneath my back, I can feel the damp soaking through my clothes. I'm finished peeing now but I can't get up. Rolling over, I try to get to my knees but collapse in a tired heap. I need to sleep. I need to rest for a while and then I'll be okay.

Somebody has got hold of me and is dragging me back to the car and pushing me onto the seat. I'm so grateful. It's much more comfortable here than on the cold wet grass. The taxi

43

driver seems to have got in the back of the car with me which I find a bit strange. He can go now, he can drive me home. Something soft and warm pokes my cheek and I push it away with my hand. The taxi driver is making groaning noises and I feel warm splashes on my cheek and forehead. As I settle down to sleep I feel the car start to move again and hope that I'll be home soon.

15

There's an awful amount of recrimination being thrown in my direction, this constant stream abated only by Tim's need to take Toby to nursery and then go to work. I lie here, still very drunk, still incapable of coherent thought or action. There is nothing I can say or do in any event, Tim has the moral high ground for once and can be relied on to make the most of it. The only thing I can do is sleep.

*

I sit gratefully at my desk, finally re-joining the working masses after two days in bed, recovering from the worst hangover I've ever experienced. There's no prospect of my going within ten feet of a bottle of gin ever again; even the thought of ice and lemon makes me throw up. Tim calmed down eventually but I know he'll raise the spectre of this episode at every opportunity. When he needs a defence against any criticism he now has a cast iron one.

My own sadness is caused by the look on Toby's face as he watches his parents shout and bicker, while he wonders what he's done wrong to cause it all. We've probably traumatised the poor child for life.

There's an envelope on my desk requesting my presence at a meeting with the Managing Partner, Eric Knowles. This isn't a man I normally have dealings with. My contact with him is confined to a few glimpses as he passes through the office. While the partners are the ones who run the business, Eric is the man who runs the partners. He's famous for being ruthless, of being willing to get rid of anyone, including partners who fail to meet his exacting standards. He's also considered to be the reason Landers Hoffman has prospered. He doesn't normally deal directly with staff at my level, though I suppose Martin's absence might have changed that. Whatever he might want me for, I doubt very much it can be good news. Routine work matters are dealt with through Paul; this invite can only mean something else, something non-routine.

A wave of fear greets the word redundancy as it shoulders its way to the head of the possibilities queue. As I stand and face Eric's PA, I wonder if it's a smile of pity on her face as I can't believe she's unaware of the reason for this meeting. She ushers me in, smile unwavering, then returns with a tray containing a light blue teapot, two blue cups, two blue saucers and a milk jug.

'I'll be mother.' Eric reaches over to pour the tea. He's definitely old school, from an era when people used to say that sort of thing. To blend perfectly with the questionable remark he wears a cravat, a shiny maroon silk scarf that pokes out of his unbuttoned shirt collar. His sharp blue eyes look straight into mine as he starts off the conversation.

'Thank you for coming, Jenny.' There's no hint of sarcasm and I wonder if he's even aware of my two days' sick leave. 'As you know only too well, these are difficult times for Landers Hoffman.'

My stomach squeezes into a knot and I feel cold and clammy. Redundancy, I guessed it. That's what he's building up to and not very subtly. Next he will tell me how valuable and special I am and how any other employer would be glad to have me. Then he'll tell me about the need for staff reductions, finally he'll act very sad and give me my notice. I really don't want to be made redundant. I really need this job. It's all so unfair.

'And very sad times too,' he continues. 'Martin will be sorely missed, he was a very special man, I'm sure you'll agree.' As he unflinchingly holds my gaze I'm fearful that he knows what Martin and I were doing. If this is the case then he may be sacking me for sexual indiscretion, clearing out the rotten wood, preventing any possibility of a scandal which would sully the reputation of his precious business.

'So, Jenny, how are you?'

'Fine, thank you.'

'And the family?' He glances almost imperceptibly down at the sheet of paper in front of him. 'Toby must be one now. How is he?'

Now I get it, he's fishing to see if I'm pregnant again. He can't sack me if I'm pregnant. I suddenly wish I was, just to be able to save myself.

'He's growing fast, doing very well at nursery. He settled there right away. It's a very good nursery, very sought after, we were lucky to get him a place.' There you are: I'm a perfect employee, no child care issues, you can trust me to get the work done, please don't sack me.

'Good,' he smiles, 'that's so important. They need a good start in life.' He leans forward slightly in his chair. His small neat hands take the single sheet of paper off his otherwise empty desk and place it in a drawer before extracting a buff folder which has a tag which reads Parker J. He opens it to reveal a letter on Landers Hoffman stationery, presumably addressed to me but I can't make out any details from where I sit.

'I've been keeping a close eye on your work, Jenny.' Here it comes, he's going to make me a liar, tell me all the days I've lost because of Toby and then sack me.

'I'm very impressed. Since you came back from maternity leave your performance has been first class. You have an instinct for this job, you can see past the figures on the page and make sound judgements.'

This is taking an unexpected turn; this last bit is not consistent with being dismissed. On the contrary it seems that Eric is happy with me. The tension lifts and I allow a warm feeling to engulf me. No redundancy, no sacking, and I was so sure. How can I get things so wrong?

'Martin's loss has hit hard. He was an outstanding talent. You might be surprised to know that he thought very highly of you, said you were a consummate professional, recommended you for promotion only a few weeks before he left us.'

I sit upright in shock at the reference to Martin, then feel relieved that Eric seems to have no idea of the background to

Martin's reference. 'Consummate professional' sounds very different when used in a sexual context instead of an occupational one. The warm glow of approval seeps through my skin and into my bones, displacing the doubts and anxiety. My bladder relaxes, stops its urgent prompting, the feelings I'm getting are nourishing and sustaining. Eric seems to be such a kind and thoughtful man, whatever he wants from this conversation I'll be happy give him.

16

Although I shared his bed on many occasions, I can only remember being in Martin's office twice before it became my own. What was his desk faces the city centre, as I sit in his chair I can pick out the line of Deansgate and the spectacular bomb replacement buildings that begin Market Street and house the most fashionable stores.

The rather smart ensemble I am wearing now was recently derived from those very buildings. Stylish and flattering, my new clothes are perfectly suited to a recently appointed Head of Audit. Eric made it quite clear that he's taking a personal risk in propelling me to the dizzy heights of Martin's position. He has several more obvious, safer candidates waiting in the wings but he's given me a three month probationary period. Quarter of a year for me to demonstrate that his faith is not misplaced and that his judgement is sound.

The first two months of this period have flown by on a gale of enthusiasm and energy. Paul is proving amazingly helpful; all my irritation with him as a boss has been replaced by a grudging admiration for his work ethic and dogged determination. He sits in front of me, halitosis diminished by the generous width of my polished oak desk. Behind his shiny head Manchester glistens in anticipation of what another day might bring.

'I've made arrangements for a buffet lunch in the board room to be served at one o'clock. It's the usual thing, laid out on side tables and covered up until the caterers bring in the hot food at one,' he says.

'Won't all the sandwiches curl up and spoil while we're having the presentation? It's all going to be sitting there from when they arrive at ten thirty, why can't they make it all fresh and bring it all in at one?'

Paul frowns. 'That's not what they do. It all gets put out this morning. The only thing they have to do at one is to bring in the hot plates. It means less disruption to the presentation.'

'It means less trouble for them, you mean. When do they make the stuff anyway?'

Paul's answer is to shuffle awkwardly in his chair and look down at his feet. I decide to let it go this time.

'Do you need another run through of your part of the presentation?' I ask.

'No, I'm fine,' Paul says sullenly.

My comments about his slightly shoddy catering arrangements seem to have pushed him into one of his miserable moods. I need him to at least show some enthusiasm for the opportunity that's presented to us. World Ordnance Systems will be meeting us tomorrow, I intend to capture their business and thereby cement my own position as Martin's successor.

The irony that it's WOS which gives me this opportunity is not lost on me. The days Paul and I spent in Brackley seem long ago, when I was a different woman wearing different clothes and with a different mindset. Although my episode with Casagrande still gives me the shivers, I'm certain that whatever that was about has now been resolved. I've heard nothing from the man since my discovery that the proposed takeover took place. It was during the due diligence process that Landers Hoffman attracted the positive attention of WOS and could begin the process of pitching for their business. Tomorrow, I will complete the job and in doing so propel my firm into a new league. It might even get me a partnership.

'You'd better be fine,' I say, 'this is the most important pitch we'll ever do. When we get this account Landers Hoffman will be up there with the big four, on a par with the biggest UK accountancy practices. Having WOS will finally give us the chance to compete for the very largest corporate accounts.'

Paul nods but not very enthusiastically. I let that go. He's heard it all before from me many times. It would be nice to feel just once that he was alive to all the possibilities, though. There's a lot riding on tomorrow's meeting, not least the prospect of an early confirmation from Eric that my position is a permanent one. Give it three months, he said, we'll review the situation after that. I have to keep this job. I am not going back to the way things were before I got it. Now I earn almost three times what I used to and our household income has doubled. My credit card debts are paid off and all without touching another note of Casagrande's money. Harvey Nichols and its ilk are no longer off limits, resulting in the stylish elegance of my new wardrobe. I'm wearing a large chunk of my salary increase and it feels so good. Money aside, I love the job, I'm brilliant at it. I am thriving.

As soon as Eric confirms the job is mine for good I'll get my own place and leave Tim. Even my bladder problems have diminished since I stopped accommodating Tim's sexual appetite. As far as I'm concerned he can indulge himself elsewhere, I've no desire to have sex with him or anyone else for the time being, though the way that Eric looked at me when he saw me in my new outfit leads me to think that he might be in the mood to try to persuade me otherwise. In my present situation, that knowledge is something of a comfort.

Arriving home I find Tim in a conciliatory mood. On the whole, we've been getting on much better since I made him sleep in the spare room. It's seven by now and Toby is already nestled in his cot, fast asleep. I pick him up to cuddle him but he barely acknowledges me, his eyes are heavy and he settles back into slumber. Never mind. I'll get to be with him at breakfast, then he'll be loud and boisterous, full of energetic one-year-old fun.

'How are you?' Tim asks, not bothering to turn off the television.

'Fine, had a good day,' I reply.

'How's your bladder been today?' he enquires as casually as he can manage. What he really wants to know is whether my genitals have recovered enough for him to penetrate them and thrust himself to pleasurable release.

'A bit sore,' I lie, 'the doctor said it would take some time to settle down,' I lie a little bit more. 'At least it's getting better, even if it's going to be a slow process.' I feel like adding that the next penis inside me is not going to be his and that by the end of tomorrow I hope to be a step closer to making our separation a permanent one. If I weren't so stupidly busy and had someone else to look after Toby, I'd have been long gone.

Leaving him to his obsession with men in shorts chasing after a ball, I sit peacefully in the untidy kitchen and eat amid the remains of Tim and Toby's dinner. As I eat, I make a few notes for the presentation, a couple of last minute details that I might need to cover. Tim comes wandering into the kitchen, sees me writing and adopts an air of neediness. He sidles in as if waiting to be rebuffed, but wanting to make the point that my attention should be on him.

'It's okay,' I say, 'I'm finished, only jotting down a few points for tomorrow.'

'Oh that.' His eyes widen in recollection. 'I remember, it's the big presentation tomorrow, is everything going okay?'

'Yes, thanks, it's all fine. I think I must know more about WOS than they know about themselves.'

'This may be a daft question,' Tim asks it anyway, 'but why would they want to change accountants?'

A stab of uncertainty pierces my guts and I am beginning to feel exasperated at his inability to grasp even the simplest concept.

'Well,' I calm myself, moving into presentation mode, 'they currently use the largest firm in the world who are American based and, although Landers Hoffman do operate worldwide our roots are in the UK. WOS are an essentially British company. We'd be able to meet their requirements more closely, more locally.'

'Yes.' Tim appears less than convinced. 'But they already have the biggest and the best. You yourself told me their existing accountants are bigger in the UK than Landers Hoffman, so why should that be a factor?'

'Well, we go further than that. We're essentially a North West business just as they are. We're stronger and more mature in this region than anyone else. Here, where they have their most important manufacturing facilities, is where we are the biggest and the best.'

'Yes, but it's only accounting, does it really matter who does it for them?'

My heart sinks and I fill with doubt. If this happens tomorrow, I won't be able to deliver properly. I have to keep focused despite whatever they throw at me.

'You're wrong.' I try to convince myself. 'Accountants are playing an increasingly important role in the operation of businesses. We don't only deal with the figures, you know, there are all sorts of other vital areas that we get involved with. Taxation, corporate governance, all sorts of things. Since the Enron fiasco, businesses can't thrive without a strong, confident accountant to support them and demonstrate to the authorities that all is well.'

'Sounds like WOS are having trouble getting their clean bill of health then, sounds dodgy to me.'

I flash disappointment at him. 'Don't be stupid. They like the way we work, we're smaller, faster, more flexible, better focused, more attuned to their requirements.' I practise my pitch on Tim with a growing irritation.

'Is that just what you say or do they think that as well?' Tim asks.

'Well, they got a good idea of our capabilities from the due diligence we conducted for them, that's where the relationship started between us. We impressed them and got on very well with their senior management.'

'So you know the guys who are coming to see you?' Tim asks.

'Not exactly, it was Martin who dealt with them originally,' I reply.

'Oh, Martin.' Tim's face lights up as if he's found something interesting to talk about at last. 'What exactly happened to him?'

'He died. Heart attack, quite sudden, no history, bit of a shock for everyone. I don't want to talk about it.'

'But he went missing, didn't he?' Tim persists.

'Yes, he died while he was away on business, it was nearly three weeks before he was discovered.'

'That's really weird, don't you think? People don't usually die and not be found. Where was he? Why did it take so long to find him?'

'I don't really know,' I answer honestly. 'They say he was found in a flat in bed, he must have been staying there when he died.'

'Whose flat, why didn't they know he was there?'

I'm getting a strong feeling of sadness and loss as we talk about Martin. I realise that I don't have any of the answers to Tim's questions. I can only imagine that Martin must have borrowed a friend's flat, yes that must be it. Probably in London, he spent a lot of time there.

Tim comes behind me as I sit and puts his arms around me, working his hands through my armpits, so that he can cup my breasts and squeeze them gently. I shrug him off, tell him I'm trying to eat, and he retreats to his football match.

17

The early morning streets glisten in memory of recent rain. There is a cold harshness in the air as I stride into the building, I feel flat and forlorn when I need to be full of excitement.

The sight of Paul already installed in his office does nothing to raise my spirits. For a brief moment I wonder about his domestic arrangements. He admits to a wife and two young children, but he seems always to be here, working. There's something about him, a distorted male pride that demands that he's first to arrive and last to leave. Is he here because he likes it? Does he prefer to be here rather than at home in the company of his wife and kids? Does he behave out of some misplaced work ethic? Did his father etch this behaviour into his soul before he had opportunity to choose?

I dismiss these thoughts as unproductive, but my lack of sympathy is rewarded by memories of Martin that churn my stomach and make me unsteady. My brusque wave draws Paul into my office and he sits down heavily. His almost complete lack of hair, long face and drooping eyes give him the air of someone much older. As I look at him carefully, the realisation that he's the same age as me comes as a sudden shock. The way that I consciously regard him as an older, wiser head shifts decisively, to be replaced by panic induced by loss of support. Today of all days I need to keep believing in him but now I worry how he will stand up in the presentation when faced by incisive questions from difficult men.

Before I can deal with all this doubt I have to exorcise the haunting thoughts brought on by Tim last night.

'We were talking yesterday, Tim and me,' I start, then something grips my chest as if to prevent the words and keep things unsaid. There's a frightened quality to my voice as if in preparation for the fear and discomfort of knowing. 'He was asking about Martin, where he was found.' My nervousness increases to the point where I can hardly go on. 'I realised I didn't know, not that it matters of course, just curious I suppose, he was asking...'

I finish lamely and watch Paul, his hands pulling at his fingers. I look down to see my own fists tightly clenched.

'Oh.' Paul seemed surprised by the nature of my enquiry, no doubt expecting a hard time over the catering arrangements or some other aspect of the presentation. 'I thought everyone knew. It's common knowledge.'

'Was he in London?' I prompt.

'No.' Paul shrugs apologetically. 'It turns out he wasn't even away. It's a very strange business if you ask me.'

I feel like I'm walking slowly into deep icy waters and my chest is gripped in a clammy chill. I know what he is going to say. There is a feeling in my body that knows where Martin was found. I don't want to make the connection in my head.

'All that time, everyone wondering where he was and it turns out he was right here, here in Manchester, two minutes from this office.'

I wait for the confirmation but already the waters are covering my mouth, preventing me from stopping the conversation and avoiding the knowledge I do not want.

'It was his own flat, as it turns out. He had several of them which he used to rent out. This one wasn't let. He must have been using it to crash after a long session at the office.'

Now I am paralysed, frozen and drowning. I can't even manage to say, it can't be true, I was there, he didn't die in the flat, our flat, it's not possible. Instead I ask, 'Do you know the address of this flat?'

Paul tells me the address as if he has passed on some important news. The waters close over my head with the confirmation that he was found in our flat. My mind screams at me, he didn't die there! I have to face the fact that only I know this. Somebody must have moved him there after my visit. Somebody must have moved his dead body.

I must drag my attention back to the important work I have to do. Today can be the day that brings me freedom, should my new job become officially permanent. But all I can think about are the consequences of the information Paul has given to me. I feel an overwhelming desire to tell somebody about my visit to the flat. The police should be told, of course they should. Moving a dead body about must be a serious offence. I look at Paul and decide he's the last person I would confide in.

Eric will be at the presentation, maybe I should tell him. He was close to Martin and might be sympathetic, even with the knowledge that we were having an affair. Men are notoriously supportive of each other when it comes to having a bit on the side. It may be a way of excusing their own behaviour. Eric won't think less of Martin. What he'll think of me is another matter. Men who stray are Jack the lads, women who commit adultery are sluts. Eric might not think his Head of Audit post should be filled by a slut. Talking to Eric may not be such a good idea; anyway, I can't change anything now. Martin is gone and nothing I do or don't do can bring him back.

*

The presentation is going extremely well, very smoothly indeed. Paul is better than expected, his bumbling awkwardness almost endearing. Even the sandwiches taste like they've been freshly prepared a few moments before consumption. Eric sits comfortably next to me, having said little beyond the introductions. Sir Colin Campbell himself is here, a man more associated with the company of royalty and prime ministers. The discussion can only be described as affable, even during the potentially awkward exploration of our proposed fees and charges. I have a feeling that price has little to do with their consideration of new auditors and wonder whether I might have pitched them more generously. If they want us they don't mind paying for us. If they don't want us they won't have us at any price. It's a situation that seems quite obvious now and I wish I'd realised it beforehand.

'If there's anything else we might help with, any other members of my team you'd like to meet while you're here?' I address the man sitting opposite, who has the soft body of a bureaucrat held in a stiff military bearing. This is Bruce Latimer, Chief Executive Officer and the man I suspect will make the decision that'll determine my immediate future. Latimer glances sideways to meet the eyes of a lady on his left, she of the auburn locks and generous bosom. Sally Mayer, Director of Communications & Public Relations, is a lady whose luminous charms light up any room she enters, together with all the men in it. Poor Paul still quivers like an electrocuted jelly whenever she so much as looks in his direction.

'Well, there is the matter of the OFT investigation.' Latimer speaks softly but there is a tension in his voice.

'I understood that had been dropped, that there's to be no enquiry now.' Paul rather blurts out his words under the gaze of the majestic Sally Mayer.

'We're concerned that's only a temporary respite. There's every prospect that the new government will resurrect the allegations and we'll be put firmly back into the spotlight.'

Mayer speaks directly to Paul, obviously enjoying his complete captivation. It has the appearance of a conversation between a magnificent female cat and a male mouse whose hormones have overwhelmed his sense of self-preservation.

'An investigation will almost inevitably involve a huge increase in workload for our auditors. It would need a thorough review of third party payments, particularly of those made to overseas agents. We need to be certain that Landers Hoffman is happy to be involved in what would be a very public affair, and also that you're capable of working hard on our behalf to ensure a positive outcome.' Latimer finishes speaking and guides everyone's eyes towards me.

More work, more fees, more profit, more bonus: nothing there not to like in my opinion. As for the publicity, Landers

Hoffman could do with it. Obviously it wouldn't be good if WOS were found to have been making illegal payments. Landers Hoffman's reputation might suffer by association but that is a chance I'm quite willing to take. I only need Eric to go along with it.

'Before we made our proposal, we were well aware of the possibilities of the OFT investigation,' I reply. 'As far as we're concerned the OFT can investigate anyone at any time. Our knowledge of your business and the high standards to which you work give us every confidence that the accusations are unfounded. In practical terms, a large global business has to operate in the context of its markets. From what I've seen, the OFT's chief concern is that some countries operate their commercial activities somewhat differently to here in the UK.'

My reply is couched in what I hope are terms which combine reassurance and knowledge. I'm making it up as I go along but continue anyway. 'Landers Hoffman will provide professionalism and a pragmatic approach in the event. Together I'm sure we can demonstrate the integrity of the WOS position.'

Here I am committing us and Eric is showing no signs of contradicting me. I need this account, whatever the risks to Landers Hoffman's reputation. Looking across at Eric I detect no concern at all in his face. Perhaps he hasn't been listening and has transported himself internally to some far off beach hotel and is lying around the pool in the hot sunshine.

A very strange impulse rises inside me and try as I might I can't get it out of my head. In the midst of the most important professional meeting I've had in my whole career, all that I can think of is getting a spray tan. Where I should go, how much it might cost, how deep to have it, whether to get a very light one at first and then gradually build it up over a few weeks. The summer is coming and it would be really nice to have a bit of colour to go with it. There is a place, I remember now, off Market Street, I can't remember the name of the road, perhaps John Dalton Street. Anyway, I could get there in my lunch break. They might be busy at lunchtimes; perhaps I will have to book.

I realise that Sally Mayer has been speaking and I haven't been listening properly and I drag my attention back to the here and now. It would be great to have a tan though. From the look of her, Sally has either been somewhere sunny or has had the same idea as me. Her complexion looks like it would go pink and freckly in the sun, rather than the even bronze that it displays. Maybe I should ask her where she gets hers.

18

The realisation that I'm getting more comfortable at partners' meetings comes with the irritation I allow myself at Alistair's whinging. Once, before my promotion was confirmed, prior to the massive income stream provided by the WOS account, it was very different. Now Alistair's conscience-stricken moaning is not as threatening, though still hard to endure.

I look at the faces around the table and detect a similar reaction to mine with a little more patience attached. It is Alistair after all, the blue-eyed boy, the one who gets all the glory, who brings home the bacon every time. Alistair Mann, despite being ten years older than I am, is still very young to be a full partner at Landers Hoffman. His unkempt appearance belies a sharp and ordered mind which he uses to spectacular effect, or so the other partners constantly remark. As far as I'm concerned, Mergers and Acquisitions are inherently more lucrative than standard audit work and any fool can generate good profits in this area. Add in the fact that his father is a bigwig in Rothschild's and there you have it. That's where most of Alistair's business is generated, crumbs thrown by his dad or companies toadying up to him in order to get on the right side of his father. No wonder he can afford to bleat about ethics and standards, he can afford it, unlike the rest of us.

He is still going on about WOS.

'This latest problem is only the tip of the iceberg. I have it on good authority that the American government tipped Andersens the wink and they dropped them like a hot potato.'

I can't let that pass, even though I still feel like a child tolerated at the adult table. He's undermining my entire position, attacking my right to be here. WOS are mine, they are the badge of my success and the main reason I'm still in this job.

'Hang on, Alistair,' I interrupt, feeling nervous but allowing my anger to prevail, 'World Ordnance Systems are one of the largest and the most important companies in this country, they're our primary defence contractors. The Americans don't like them because they compete with Lockheed and General Electric. And they compete successfully. They'd love to see WOS in trouble and won't miss any chance to give them grief. I would suggest you stop repeating any American-led rumours you might hear and concentrate on supporting what has become Landers & Hoffman's biggest client.'

Alistair sits quietly for a moment, face reddened as if he can't believe that I've finally begun to fight my own corner. There is the beginning of a smile forming on Eric's lips as he supervises the exchange from the head of the table.

'Primary defence contractors,' Alistair mimics me badly. 'Arms dealers, that's what they are, Jenny. Let me tell you about their latest acquisition in the Czech Republic.'

'Did we help them with that?' Eric speaks up at last.

'No, they didn't use us. It was done in house,' Alistair pauses.

'Then we need to push a bit harder, Alistair.' Eric is putting him in his place now. 'International acquisitions can be tricky and of course earn appropriately large fees.' He smiles now. The atmosphere lightens, but Alistair seems bent on making his point.

'I'm glad they didn't use us,' he continues, 'they bought an ammunitions factory.'

'So what? That's the business they're in.' I feel confident I have the upper hand after Eric's intervention.

Alistair leers at me. 'This factory makes bullets and sub-machine guns, AK 47s to be precise. Its primary market is Africa and the Middle East.'

I consider a retort beginning, 'If WOS don't supply them then someone else will,' but I recognise the absurdity of it in time to stop myself. I begin to appreciate what is bothering Alistair. It comes down to the grim truth that my best client makes things that allow people to kill each other more efficiently. There's a massive demand for these products and all Alistair's protestations won't change the world. At least Eric seems to have no big problem with the situation. Without WOS, I can see myself back on the shop floor working for Paul, that's if I manage to keep any job at all.

The discussion moves away from the sale of armaments to third world countries and on to more comfortable ground. For the second quarter in a row my departmental earnings have increased way beyond expectations. At this rate I will soon be leading the highest earning department, overtaking Alistair's Mergers and Acquisitions, despite M & A's apparent ability to make up their own fees as they go along. This goes some way to explain the nature of Alistair's intervention and also accounts for Eric's indifference. As for me, I have a nagging feeling that Alistair is right and I may well have blood on my hands, even if it is second-hand and once removed. The prospect of a healthy year-end bonus does little to dissipate the uneasiness created by this unfortunate reality. Eric decides to recognise my increased workload by transferring some of Alistair's people to me, allocating space on his floor for my work. Worst of all, judging by the look on Alistair's face as Eric gently makes the suggestion, Judith, Alistair's personal assistant, will now be shared with me. While I need all the help I can get, I wonder how it will work in practice. If Alistair continues to feel threatened, having his beloved Judith party to my every thought and movement could be awkward.

My need for assistance more than compensates for that risk. Judith is without doubt the best and most experienced PA in the firm. I find the prospect of her working for me quite daunting, but that's not something I'm going to admit, particularly at this meeting. I smile at Eric and nod my gratitude in his direction while trying not to make eye contact with Alistair.

19

'I know I'm hassling you, I have to.'

Paul sits opposite, his face long and pathetic following my angry outburst. He is hurt and upset but his condition is positively ecstatic when compared with my own.

'At this rate we're going to miss the deadline for the WOS audit,' I continue. 'We set the timescale, they met their schedule and now you're telling me we're so short-staffed we can't manage to do our part. For heaven's sake, Paul, it's a disaster and it's a disaster we can't afford to let happen.'

'It's not my fault,' Paul mutters, looking down at his feet. I barely restrain from hitting him, punching him in the face, screaming out my frustration.

'It's not my fault…' I mimic, 'I suppose that makes it okay, does it? When the Stock Exchange hears the WOS accounts are delayed by audit problems, what do you think is going to happen?'

Paul makes no attempt to answer, despite knowing the consequences as well as I do. WOS shares take a dive, Landers Hoffman lose a client and a reputation. I lose my job.

As if I don't have enough on my plate, Tim is being even more obnoxious than usual. Apparently he logged the last time we had sexual intercourse in some recess of his mind and today turns out to be its half anniversary. All his hurt male pride surfaced this morning in a torrent of abuse that left me shaking and fearful. I can still feel the knot in my solar plexus where I hold the hurt and the guilt. A small voice brings me back to the present predicament. Paul is almost whispering…

'You could sign off with what we have so far.'

An icy cold clamps itself across my chest. If I do as he suggests, there'll be no room for manoeuvre in the future, the decision will haunt every dealing we have with WOS. But if I don't, there may be no future to worry about at all. I make up my mind. I have until Friday, whatever I have by then I'll have to go with, but I'm determined not to give them carte blanche.

'Look, Paul, this is serious. I can't just let it go. If it's what I think it is I need to use it to show them Landers Hoffman are business-like and vigilant. We can't be a soft touch from the word go, we'll lose all credibility.'

Paul seems even more anxious now. My decision has eased the tight feeling in my chest but he's not displaying any signs that he is convinced. Sod him. I need his help but his support is secondary. I certainly don't need his agreement.

'Get Emma in here, I want to know how our old favourites in Brackley look to her.'

A look of alarm spreads over Paul's features, as if I was making him do something dangerous.

'It's not necessary,' he splutters, 'she reported that everything is fine down there, exactly the same as we both agreed after our visit.' He emphasises the word both as if desperate to implicate me.

'I really don't understand how you could send Emma on her own down there. She's far too young and inexperienced for that kind of work; you should have sent someone more senior, someone with a bit of…well…nous. Someone who could make a proper appraisal.'

'Like who?' Paul's anger surfaces. 'Associated Composites are minor fare when compared with the main WOS businesses and didn't we both go there ourselves to check it out? It was her or nobody, we're short-staffed and over-worked. Taking on all this WOS work without dropping any of our lesser clients was a mistake. You insisted we could cope, now look at us.'

My initial surprise at this outburst subsides to reveal feelings of deep uncertainty. What Paul says is right, I have bitten off more than I can possibly chew. No matter how many hours I put in, the mountain of work lies undiminished. Weariness seeps up from my legs and encases my entire body. My brain ceases to function, I no longer have the power of speech. The half formed barbs of verbal riposte stick in my throat. My breath expels suddenly and I realise that this too has been frozen. I fill my lungs with the next inhalation, allow the breath deep into my diaphragm and feel my power returning.

'Just ask her to come in here,' I let out a sigh, 'then you'd better get on with your work.'

Now that he's left me alone in my office I feel the panic returning and struggle to breathe it away. Darkness is descending on Manchester, a sickly yellow glow replacing the grey light. It all seems such an effort and sadly doomed to failure and ignominy. I have no idea why Eric had such faith in me but I know what his reaction will be when he discovers what a terrible mess I'm making of Martin's job.

Emma bounces in, bright, energetic and filled with enthusiasm. My own dim candle begins to glow more vigorously in her presence.

'You wanted me?' She stands expectantly.

'Yes, Emma, sit down. You've been to Brackley, I believe. To Associated Composites. Tell me about your visit.'

'Oh!' Emma seems surprised as she seats herself gracefully. 'Did Paul tell you, he said he wouldn't, that it was best not to. Things like that are quite normal, he said. Forget it, he said.'

'Forget what?' I'm intrigued now but have no inclination to play cat and mouse. Emma looks puzzled. 'Tell me.' I speak firmly. 'Never mind about Paul, tell me what happened down in Brackley.'

She hesitates for a moment. 'He said it wasn't important.' Her voice is thin and plaintive; I can feel her nervousness.

'It may not be,' I adopt a lighter tone, 'in fact I'm sure it's not if Paul says so. Don't worry, you're not in any trouble, you've not let me down.'

I stand up, walk around the desk and place my hands gently on her shoulders until I feel her energy return. I sit in the other visitor's chair, side by side with her.

'Well,' she says, shrugging off her nervousness, 'I didn't like them, you know, the people down there. There was this man, Sullivan, who was rude and unfeeling. He kept saying he had no time for all this poking about, he was fed up of Landers Hoffman. He kept asking if you'd sent me, if you knew I was there.'

I can see this may take some time, Emma is warming to her account and her initial shock has given way to her love of a good story.

'Carry on,' I instruct as I get up and boil the kettle, make some tea for both of us. Camomile seems most appropriate under the circumstances.

'He was a horrible man, I didn't like him. He would look at me in a really leery way, do you know what I mean? Like he was imagining doing rude things to me, not very nice at all. He seemed the sort of man that would go to strip clubs and lap dancing places, you know the sort I mean, I felt really uncomfortable whenever he was there.'

I put her tea down on the desk and sit back beside her. 'Yes, I met him, he gave me a creepy feeling as well. Did you spend much time with him?'

'Oh no, he shouted at me a bit at first and then he went away. The Irishman, the accountant, was a bit nicer, but he had a vacant look, you know like he was never actually in the room. He was like a…a robot, that's it, an auto…automatic thing, you know like in the Stepford Wives, only a man of course, I didn't like him.'

I look at the clock on my bookcase and feel the darkness closing in. At this rate we could be here all night. When Paul was here I could feel the weariness from ten hours in the office, but now Emma's energy is keeping me going. The tightness in my abdomen is eased now.

'There was this nice girl, Mariella,' Emma continues. 'They put her with me so she could find stuff for me. She was nice. She came from Holland but moved to England with her boyfriend who works for Composites. You would never believe it but she's got two guinea pigs like me, they aren't brothers like mine, she got one at first and then the little one to keep the other one company. I showed her a picture of my cage and she was amazed. She absolutely loved it and really, really wanted to make one like it.'

'Emma,' I interrupt gently, 'I need you to get to the accountancy bit now, what did you find out, were there any problems?'

She colours up with embarrassment. I feel compelled to add, 'Look, I love the things you're telling me, they're brilliant and really interesting, I could listen to you all night, you're great to be with, but it's five o'clock already and you'll need to be going home soon, won't you?'

She brightens up and takes a breath. 'Oh yes, thanks. Well I suppose it started when I asked Mariella about some transactions with an Italian company.'

I'm beginning to wonder whether there is any point to all this. Perhaps Paul is right, perhaps Emma shouldn't be bothering me with this. 'Well there's this thing. This Italian company is paying over four million euros for things supplied by Associated Composites and they're not even a defence contractor, they're a racing team, a motor racing team, based in San Marino which is in Italy, I think.' Emma breathes out heavily.

I suddenly become nervous. I get an uneasy feeling that the twenty thousand pounds Casagrande gave me might somehow be involved in what Emma is about to say.

'And,' Emma pauses again, 'I only found out what they did from Mariella. She told me her boyfriend was a racing driver and a famous one, though I'd never heard of him. Ben is quite keen on watching the Formula One on television but I don't take much notice, but anyway, Dirk, that's the name of Mariella's boyfriend, drives sports cars which are different.'

'But I thought you said he worked at Associated Composites?'

'He does, Mariella explained it to me. Associated Composites are his sponsors, they pay for him to drive, they pay money to Crugnolla Racing who are in England. They're on the same industrial estate as Composites, almost next door.'

'How much? How much are Composites paying Crugnolla? Is it in the accounts?'

'Oh yes. It's all there, all recorded. They paid nearly two million pounds last year. I thought you ought to know about that. Don't you think it's a bit weird? I mean they get paid oodles of money for supplying bits for racing cars then pay millions of euros back to the team. Why? That's not a normal transaction is it? Shouldn't we be asking questions about that sort of thing?'

'So what did you do?'

'I told Paul when I got back. He said not to worry. I said that you should be told all about it. He said it wasn't important enough to bother you with.'

It's late, I'm tired, but all I want to do is to get hold of Paul and shake the truth out of him.

'Thanks, Emma. I'll have a chat with Paul tomorrow. I'm sure he's right, but thanks for your excellent work, I'm proud of you.'

She beams back at me. All her cares have lifted and she bounces out of the office leaving me with the lasting impression of her big smile and beautiful wide eyes.

20

I am tired, footsore and my legs are cold and wet. These thin tights are no match for the horizontal drizzle that assails me in the half light. As I stagger ungracefully into the building I am observed by Ian, the night security man and Gary, who I have always assumed to be his boss.

'Morning,' Gary chirps joyfully. 'Bright and early aren't we?'

I can do without that kind of meaningless remark at the best of times, but coupled with my state of agitation it makes me want to scream out loud. After an almost sleepless night, catching the early train was easy, although I had to leave before

69

Toby woke up. I mean to nab Paul immediately he arrives and confront him with the Emma revelations.

I look across at Gary who is still grinning and waiting for a return of pleasantries. He is a short, thickset individual with close cropped hair and a round happy face. At first sight, his bulk might be taken to be that of someone who has a tendency to consume too many burgers and fries for his own good, but that is definitely not the case. Gary has no beer belly, only a barrel of a chest and muscular arms that can hardly be contained by his shirt sleeves.

The sight of his obvious pleasure at seeing me manages to slightly lift my gloom and I walk over to him.

'Needs must, Gary,' I reply, wrinkling my nose to indicate that I don't much like it. 'I've lots on at the moment. How about you, are you busy?'

'Always busy, always grafting, Mrs Parker,' he stares at me with piercing blue eyes. 'You look tired, Mrs Parker, you look like you're over-doing it if you don't mind me saying so.'

His concern touches me deeply and I suddenly feel soft and vulnerable and struggle to hold back my tears. He's right, I am completely spent and the only kind words and support I get are coming from a security guard. This realisation crumples my spirit and robs me of any resolve. Strong hands reach out to steady my shoulders and Gary propels me gently into the chair behind the reception desk. My legs have ceased to function and all I can think about is lying down and crying myself to sleep.

'Get her a nice cup of tea,' Gary orders the tall thin youth. 'Sit yourself down and take a breather, Mrs Parker, a few deep breaths, come on, breath in…all the way…that's good. Now out slowly…slowly, let it all out. Now gently in, that's the ticket, you'll be fine. Too much work, that's your problem – when did you last take a holiday?'

I sit numb and unresponsive. The last holiday with Tim and Toby was much more stressful than working. Spain – sun, sea, sangria and same bed as Tim. Nightly sexual mithering, recriminations, arguments, accusations, sulking, anger, frustration. I look at Gary, his face shows gentle concern and I feel a deep longing to be held and made to feel safe.

Ian returns with a Landers Hoffman mug and puts it down on the desk in front of me. I prefer my tea strong and dark brown with only a tiny splash of milk and no sugar. This is weak, almost white. It's also very sweet, but I drink it with gratitude and relish.

A small trickle of people begins to seep through the entrance and I need to prepare for my confrontation with Paul. The tea and Gary's kindness are restoring the function to my legs, although as I stand I still feel a little shaky.

'Thanks, Gary.' I look at his unremarkable features and feel a huge ocean of calm energy underneath.

'Any time, Mrs Parker, glad to be of help. Now you get some serious vacation time and do it soon, you can't carry on like this.'

There is a truth in his words that reaches deep inside me. He's right. I'm heading for a breakdown, the way my life is. Once the WOS audit is sorted out I'll do something about it. I'll leave Tim or better still kick him out. I'll stop putting it off because I'm busy, stop all the excuses about Toby needing his dad. I'll get back to being a proper mother for Toby. The thought of how my recent neglect has made my poor baby suffer makes my stomach tighten and hurt. How could I have been so selfish?

These painful thoughts are dispelled by the sight of Paul and I call him into my office.

'Can I get myself a brew first?' he asks.

'No, it won't take long,' I lie. 'I only need to check something out with you quickly before I start my day.'

He comes in and sits down.

'Why did you keep important information from me?'

'I don't know what you mean.'

'I'm talking about the things that Emma told you after her visit to Associated Composites.'

'There was nothing to tell, it was a routine audit visit.'

71

'Hardly routine. There are huge sums of money being paid by a motor racing team from San Marino with no obvious justification. She also told me about large amounts being paid back by Associated Composites to Crugnolla's UK company. Didn't you think I should be told?'

'I checked it out myself and everything is fine.' Paul remains calm and shows no sign of discomfiture even in the face of my rather tetchy opening.

'Did you ask Sullivan about this, then?' I ask.

'Oh yes, he assures me it's quite normal. It's all to do with marketing and promotion, Crugnolla are very important clients and the motor racing industry is a big purchaser of Associated Composites' specialist products.'

'Did you ask him what could possibly cost four million euros? I would have thought you could buy a whole fleet of racing cars for much less than that.'

'Sullivan explained that Composites supply a unique exhaust system based on advanced ceramic technology. They developed it originally for jet fighters, apparently all the serious racing cars use it, especially the Formula One cars, he's very proud of it.'

I'm beginning to feel relieved at what appears to be an entirely plausible explanation. I desperately need to sign off the audit, maybe I can take Paul's assurances and get the job done.

'Yes, but so much money?'

'Crugnolla are distributors, they sell on to all the other teams, Composites just supply the parts. It's a very profitable business,' Paul explains.

'Well, what about the money paid back to Crugnolla Racing, what's that for exactly? Sounds like a ridiculous amount of money for a bit of advertising.'

'Not in motor racing terms. They fund the running of the whole team. It's their way of showcasing their exhaust technology and it enables them to develop other kinds of things. Sullivan told me they've made some ceramic engines which are ultra lightweight and efficient. Once they're proven on the racing track, the automotive industry will buy them like hot cakes. It's a huge business opportunity; think of the two million pounds as research and development if you like, that's what it really is.'

'That's what Sullivan told you?'

'Yes.'

'Do you trust him?'

Paul looks down at his knees.

'Well, do you think we should trust his word?'

'Yes.' Paul looks up and his face and head redden. 'He's in charge, he's the top man there, of course we have to take his word. What do you think we are, some campaigning do-gooders? He runs the business, it's his call, not ours. The transactions are all recorded, itemised, explained. That's all any auditor can expect.' His eyes narrow. 'Don't make value judgements, Jenny, it's not your job.'

I'm surprised by his sudden show of vehemence and feel disorientated. This mild-mannered plodder is making an uncharacteristic stand. Pausing for a few breaths, I consider how I feel about all this. The answer my body gives is very clear; I am uneasy, not reassured, I feel panic, not calm, I sense fear, not security.

'Well, I don't believe either of you.' I watch Paul deflate as I speak. 'Sullivan is a liar and you're a fool for being taken in by him.'

'It's not our job!' His protests sound weak now.

'It's my job to sign off the audit. The way things are, I intend to ask for a full investigation of Associated Composites, and until it's completed I won't sign off.'

'You can't do that.' Paul's voice rises in frequency. 'Think what it will do to us, all of us, Landers Hoffman will lose the account, WOS will fire us and make sure we never get another big account ever again. It'll be a disaster. You can't afford that, Jenny.'

'Yes I can, I've got a few quid stashed away. I'm not totally dependent on this job, not like I used to be. Losing it is a chance I'm willing to take.'

Paul sits, hands wringing, shoulders high. He looks around my office as if seeking inspiration.

'Talk to Eric,' he says. 'Before you do anything rash, talk to Eric, see what he says.'

The word rash makes me angry and I feel like screaming. Yet the sense of his words gradually seeps through and I agree.

'Okay, get me all the Composites files, bring them in here. I'll see Eric in the morning when he gets back from holiday.'

21

The terrible banging makes the whole house shudder. Loud shouting drags me awake. The clock says 5:45, I rush in to Toby who stands too bewildered even to cry. As I clasp him in my arms a man appears in the doorway, a huge man dressed completely in black.

My screams scare Toby into his own versions. A woman's face joins the man's and I shout, 'Get out of my house,' and 'Tim where are you?' and 'Leave us alone,' and 'Call the police, Tim, call the police.'

'We are the police.' The woman's face is hard and unfeeling, framed in short black hair under a navy blue baseball cap. My fear subsides a little to be replaced with indignation and anger. All I can think is, what has Tim done? My anger begins to deflect away from the police and towards Tim.

The crashing sounds make sudden sense. I realise they were battering down our front door, but why? What could Tim possibly have done to justify them scaring an innocent woman and her child? The cold seeps through my thin pyjamas, I become conscious of my near-naked vulnerability.

Toby is inconsolable. The black-clad intruders have shattered his trust and given a lie to my constant reassurances. If I can't keep him safe in his own bedroom, he can never trust me again.

Lights are being switched on everywhere and everything focuses into sharp reality. The woman policeman steps forward to take Toby and I cower back against his cot, shielding him from her grasp.

'Get off, you bitch,' I feel like smashing her face with something solid but everything within my reach is soft and cuddly. Hitting her with a Care Bear would not have the effect I want. 'Leave us alone,' I scream at her. 'Get away from me, you bitch.'

'Jennifer Parker, I am arresting you,' she begins.

'No, no you can't, you scared me. You can't arrest me for shouting at you.'

'I have a warrant for your arrest on suspicion of money laundering offences in contravention of Section 329 of the Proceeds of Crime Act. You do not have to say anything but it may harm your defence if you do not mention, when questioned, something which you later rely on in court. Anything you do say...'

The words fade into the background noise as I realise that they haven't come for Tim, they are here for me, to arrest me. All the smashing down doors is to get at me. My legs are weak and won't hold me up any more. I manage to sink down gently to avoid hurting Toby. We half sit, half lie on the floor, he is still crying but a distressed whimpering has replaced the frightened screams.

Tim pushes into Toby's bedroom and stands over me.

'Give him to me,' he instructs and I have no power to prevent him scooping up my child and taking him away.

'You can get dressed before we take you down to the station,' the grim-faced one intones. I obey mechanically, strip off in my bedroom and dress in yesterday's discards. As I walk out I can see several more policemen pulling out drawers, moving furniture, searching. The computer in the study lies naked and skeletal, the innards revealed. Everywhere my home is being violated, dismembered so that choice bits can be bagged up as souvenirs. I realise I'm crying, deep forlorn desperate tears. I know I will never feel safe again and the deep sense of loss is almost unbearable.

22

It is hot in this pokey room. Sitting in here for half an hour has soaked through the armpits of my blouse and left dark stains. If sweating is a sign of guilt then they've an easy decision to make about me. I was told to be at the Court at nine so I made sure I was early, kicking my heels on the steps for ten minutes, feeling the chill of the drizzle on my face. How I wish I could have that cool relief now.

'Sit in here,' the lady in the uniform said. I wonder whether she wore the garb of the prison service or else some similarly attired but less sinister organisation. At least the door isn't locked, I'm spared that. I can walk back out and stand in the rain any time I like. I just want the whole thing to be over and done with. It's taken nearly two months for them to arrange a court hearing. In that time I've been feeling frustrated with an underlying deep despair. At least I've been able to spend time with Toby, lots of time, so much time with him that I've begun to think and feel like a toddler. My mind is a useless mush of meaningless sounds and cartoon characters.

As soon as I was arrested Eric left a message on my phone telling me not to come to work until it had all been cleared up. A formal letter confirming this instruction arrived the next day. When I eventually managed to speak to Eric he sounded cold and unhelpful, despite his reassurances that it was just procedure and nothing to worry about. At least today will provide an end to the uncertainty, though I still worry how my career with Landers Hoffman will be affected. I know that Paul is now sitting at my desk and that vision gives me a gnawing anxiety in my gut.

I put my jacket back on to hide the damp patches. I know I'll sweat even more but I don't want my lawyers to see me in such disarray. I have to be calm and in control and direct them firmly.

One of them arrives. It's Anthony, my solicitor. His thick neck protrudes from a slightly grubby collar that pinches into his flesh like a thick belt.

'Ha.' He flops down opposite me, the flimsy chair buckling under the assault. 'Good, you're here.' He slaps down a lever arch file in front of him and begins to leaf through it, occasionally glancing up at me with an alarming look of puzzlement. After a couple of long minutes he stands, pushing the chair back with his legs so that it makes a screeching noise.

'Sorry, wrong file, I'll get yours from the car.' I wonder if all this haste is a sign that we're going to be late and feel fearful of the consequences of keeping a court waiting. He arrives back, breathless and sweating.

'Okay,' he pants, 'got it. Parked a way away,' he puffs, 'saves the parking charge. Four pounds eighty a day soon mounts up.' He draws a steadying breath. 'No need to pay it when you can park for free a few streets away.'

He returns to his file. I notice that this one is much slimmer than the last and hope that this is a good sign.

'Mr Hunter will be with us shortly, I saw him on his way to the robing room,' he announces.

'Who's Mr Hunter?'

'He's the barrister I've instructed for this hearing. As it's Crown Court, I can't speak on your behalf, it has to be a barrister. Don't worry, I've told him everything he needs to know.'

I look at my watch, it shows nine forty. 'Are we late?' I ask. 'You told me to be here for nine, it's nearly quarter to ten.'

'Don't worry.' He doesn't look up. 'We won't start at ten, the judge is hearing some arguments on another case before he gets round to us. We have plenty of time.'

The door opens and admits a tall angular man wearing a long black gown and a small wig pushed forward over his forehead. The room hardly accommodates his large frame and he has to move to one side to allow the door to close before sitting down. The heat is now almost unbearable and I have sweat oozing from every part of me, my make-up is washing away and is soaking into what used to be my crisp white collar which is getting pinker by the second.

'This is Mr Hunter, he'll be representing you in Court today.'

Mr Hunter's eyes twinkle darkly as he looks at me. I take in his strong presence and feel the authority it commands.

'Mrs Parker, Jenny isn't it? May I call you Jenny?'

I nod. 'Yes, that's fine.'

'Now we need to make sure that we are all comfortable with these proceedings. It's a Crown Court, you understand, Jenny, there will be a judge with a wig and gowns similar to these but,' he smiles, 'much more elegant. Don't let the dress put you off, we're all ordinary people doing our jobs. The gowns are only to distinguish those of us who are acting as advocates.'

'How long do you think it will take?' I ask, warming to this island of competence amid a sea of turbulent fools.

'Now that depends on our plea.' A painful stab of alarm pierces my chest. 'If we plead Not Guilty as I believe you wish…'

'Of course I'm not guilty,' I blurt out, losing what small residue of decorum I have left.

'Quite, quite, I understand. As I was saying, a Not Guilty plea means we'll be in and out in just a few minutes. The Court will adjourn for a trial, the date for which will be fixed later.'

'I've already waited two months, won't I be tried today?'

'Certainly not. Neither side is prepared for trial today. There are witnesses to arrange, statements to prepare, lots of things to do before we can run a trial.'

'So how long will I have to wait?' I'm feeling panicked now. I can't face the prospect of living in limbo any longer, I have to get my life back, I need to work, to progress, to get the hell away from Tim.

'Oh, it depends on the Court's timetable and the judge's availability. I don't think there will be any possibility of getting a slot before next summer and realistically I would expect it to take a fair bit longer.'

'Another year!' My heart sinks at the prospect.

'Unlikely to be less than that,' he confirms.

I put my head in my hands to hide my tears and feel the slippery texture of my forehead.

'However, it shouldn't come to that,' Mr Hunter continued. 'I strongly suggest you consider pleading Guilty.'

'But...' I protest meekly.

'I'm afraid I can hold out very little prospect of success with a Not Guilty plea. With the evidence from your PACE interview, the prosecution have an almost insurmountable case.'

'PACE?' I ask.

'Police and Criminal Evidence Act, PACE for short. It's the taped interview held in the police station on the day you were arrested.

'I tried to explain about the money,' I say.

'I know. You were being honest. However, you did admit quite freely to the charges. You also refused to tell the police where the money came from and who gave it to you.'

'Yes, I know, I told them about the threats, I explained the sort of people they were. They'd do much worse things to me than the police could. They'd probably kill me if I identified them.'

'That is a problem for us. You've effectively admitted guilt, it would be a long uphill struggle to convince a jury of any alternative now. Refusing to cooperate with the police in their enquiries is also unhelpful to your situation. I understand that you're frightened but I suggest that you give that serious thought. It's not too late and it is a major factor against you.'

'No.' My reaction is instant. I can't risk the prospect of putting Toby at risk of losing his mother or even being harmed himself. I felt the ruthlessness in Casagrande's voice, I know he is capable of harming me more than this legal system ever can. I can't believe that all this grief is caused by a man leaving some cash in my hotel room. I didn't rob anyone, injure anyone, burgle anyone, but here I am in court surrounded by bewigged lawyers. It's so bloody unfair. All I want to do is to provide for my Toby, to protect him and take care of him.

'What do you think will happen to me?' I ask.

'Under the circumstances, if you plead Not Guilty and are convicted you can expect a custodial sentence. I don't think that could be avoided.'

Prison! My body goes into shock at the prospect.

'But I can't go to prison, what about Toby, what would happen to him?'

'I'm afraid that cases like yours are dealt with severely. That you have a young child is only a mitigating factor and unlikely to make much difference.'

The door opens and hits the back of the barrister's chair. The female who put me in the room announces, 'The judge is ready now,' and closes the door. Panic wells up inside me. I feel sick, without the energy to retch up my breakfast.

Anthony looks sweatier and more anxious. Mr Hunter is regally unperturbed. It crosses my mind that keeping a judge waiting might not prove as costly to a barrister as it might to a defendant. I'm trying to focus on the calmness in front of me.

'If I plead Not Guilty what do you think will happen?' I ask.

'Nothing is certain, of course. In the event of your being convicted after a trial I would be surprised if the judge didn't apply a custodial sentence of at least six months, it could easily be two years. Indeed your case could be said to require one. If a custodial sentence were not given, the prosecution might appeal and that appeal might well be successful.'

I cannot believe what I'm hearing. Jail, this man is telling me I will be put in jail. Toby will have his mother taken away! What will become of us? I try unsuccessfully to hold back the tears but my envisioned grief pushes them through. Mr Hunter takes a white linen handkerchief from his top pocket and passes it to me. It is much too nice, too clean, too crisp and too perfect for me to soil. I pass it back and fumble in my bag for tissues.

'I can't go to prison,' I manage between sobs, 'I can't leave my child.' I glare at Anthony who keeps his eyes away from mine. 'You told me I'd be OK, that I would probably get off, even if I didn't you said it would be a slap on the wrist, a fine at the worst.'

'Look,' Anthony finally meets my eye. 'I gave you my best advice based on the cases I've dealt with before. It's not a lot of money; I honestly thought you would be fine.'

'Your solicitor's advice is quite understandable,' Mr Hunter intervenes. 'But these cases are viewed very seriously when a professional person is charged under the Proceeds of Crime Act. You are charged under Section 328 for concealing criminal property, under Section 329 for its acquisition, use and possession and, most significantly, under Section 330 for failing to disclose in your capacity as a finance professional. The maximum sentence this court can impose is fourteen years' imprisonment, the least you can expect would be six months. As I say, the law is very harsh in this respect. The Act was set up primarily to combat drugs and terrorism but, as often happens with the law, it is being used much more widely.'

'All I did was hide some money in my wardrobe!' I can't stop the feeling of dread, my body starts to heave and shake.

'There is one ray of hope, perhaps. I spoke with my learned friend in the robing room, purely hypothetically of course, and without prejudice. It seems to me that the prosecution have no desire for a trial. It would mean much effort for them and take up valuable court time. Were it possible to spare them that effort I am convinced they would not press the judge for a custodial sentence.'

My mind unfreezes enough for me to answer, 'So if I plead guilty I won't go to prison?'

'There is no guarantee, it will depend entirely on the way the judge sees it. However with no submission from the prosecution and a decent mitigation from us, I doubt very much that you will do worse than a suspended sentence. You are aware of what that means, aren't you?'

'Yes, it means I don't go to prison as long as I don't do it again. And don't you worry, I won't.'

I have no choice. Not Guilty means waiting a year then going to jail, maybe for a long time. Guilty means I don't get put in prison. I will be out of a job, though, and a convicted criminal.

'Okay,' I gasp, 'I'll plead Guilty if it means not going to prison.'

Mr Hunter smiles and rises in a deliberate manner. Somehow, despite the oven-like atmosphere and the thick wig, he retains an air of cool control as he leads the way out of the claustrophobic hole.

Inside the court I meet an air-conditioned chill which is hugely welcome until the cold begins to penetrate my sodden garments. I am placed in a slightly raised area on my own while the lawyers continue down the steps to occupy the right half of the benches in front of me. The left side is already taken by what I imagine to be the prosecution legal team. Their barrister looks younger than I am, barely thirty at a guess.

There is an order to stand and the judge comes in from a side door and sits down directly opposite me and at my eye level. He looks old and uninterested but he is heavily disguised by a lighter, more generously proportioned wig than Mr Hunter's. His robes are trimmed with scarlet which relieves the uniform blackness of the rest of the legal attire.

The lady who called us in begins to read the charges. I listen to them in disbelief that they apply to me. After each one she pauses and asks me how I plead. Hardly able to speak or stand from terror, I blurt out 'Guilty' each time, feeling a noose tightening around my neck.

Mr Hunter makes an impassioned plea for mercy. When I hear him speak I have no doubt that everything will be fine. I begin to regret my guilty pleas. An advocate of his quality would surely have made mincemeat of any prosecution case. The judge appears to agree with everything Mr Hunter tells him about me, including the bits about being a devoted mother and that unnecessary suffering that might be caused to an innocent child. When he finishes I half expect the judge to immediately let me go with a warning, but instead he asks the prosecution if they've anything to say.

Their young barrister rises to his feet and reads out some sentencing guidelines. To my horror, all these involve long prison sentences. I want to shout out that they aren't supposed to do this, that they promised Mr Hunter, but I am frozen with fear.

Finally, the judge says what a terrible thing I have done, how I have betrayed the trust placed in me, how I have abused my position and that I must serve six months in prison. He then repeats this sentence for each of the remaining charges and says that these sentences are to be served concurrently.

I breathe a sigh of relief at this and wait for him to say that they are also suspended. Instead, he stops speaking and rises. Two women in uniform appear next to me and hold my arms. I look down at Anthony and Mr Hunter who shrugs his shoulders in my direction.

'Sorry,' Anthony says, 'we did our best.'

23

The screaming comes from the Block. Sometimes it consists of a single plaintive howl, mostly there is a cacophony of disturbance. I can hear it as I try to sleep. The anguish penetrates me to the core; I can't help but want to join in.

Here in the cottages there is less noise. Here, we yell and complain. Shout angrily. Cry copiously. But we do little of the really deranged stuff, at least compared to the occupants of the Block.

Alice takes me to one side as I carry my sparsely populated breakfast tray.

'Good morning, Mrs Parker.'

'Hello, Alice.' She has to call me Mrs Parker, it's the rules. I can call her anything I like. Some of the others take any opportunity to be rude and offensive but I prefer to be polite. Being referred to as a stupid fat cow all the time must be very debilitating for the poor woman.

'Don't forget you have another counselling session with Dawn at ten thirty.'

I haven't forgotten, it means me going to the Block, being close to the self-harmers and drug-desperate souls that inhabit it. This counselling business is an attempt to modify the behaviour of the most seriously disturbed by exposing them to long sessions with those of us who are slightly less upset.

'It will look good on your record,' Alice tells me.

The prison officers treat Dawn with great respect, usually three at a time. I don't know if she poses a real threat or it's her size and strength that worries them. When I look into her dull piggy eyes, I can feel only desolation. The poor woman has lost any form of positivity. God knows, I feel bad enough in this awful place. Having to see Dawn on a regular basis doesn't help at all.

After they herd her into the activities room, the officers retreat and leave us to it. I start pushing dominoes towards her, counting them out. When I get to seven and stop, Dawn looks bewildered and hurt so I give her an extra one. She smiles and collects them to her enormous bosom. Even after hours of playing she remains unaware that the more dominoes she has, the less likely she is to win.

'You can start if you like,' I say.

She shakes her head vigorously, unwilling to part with her black oblongs unless I do so first. I place double three in the centre of the sticky table. She shuffles her dominoes, examines each one in turn, then shakes her head.

'How are you today?' I ask.

'They say I can come off the Block and live with you,' she answers.

My breath catches in my throat and a feeling of dread envelops me. Almost everything Dawn says is untrue but this revelation makes me uneasy. It's almost crazy enough to be accurate.

Dawn places an inappropriate domino next to mine.

'It's all because of you. I've told them you're a good influence on me, that we get on really well.' She pauses and leans forward. 'I love you, Jenny. You're my best friend. I'm going to stay with you for ever and be your best friend as well. When we get out of here we're going to find a nice place together and be dead happy.'

'What about your boyfriend, won't you want to live with him?'

Dawn furrows her brow and bangs down a domino. 'He can come for tea. Maybe stop over if he's a good boy and he brings us some gear. It'll be our house, our rules. Only boys if we want them and they bring us nice things.'

'So you're feeling better now are you, Dawn? That's great. I'm really pleased.'

'How much methadone do they give you, Jenny? They only let me have a tiny bit now and then. Maybe we can share when I'm off the Block? You can give me some of yours.'

Alice takes me back to relative calm and sanity.

'Dawn was talking about coming off the Block.'

'Oh, yes. She's much better since you befriended her. Anyway, there's a new intake tomorrow, a rough bunch by all accounts. We need to clear some space for them.'

'You're not putting her with me.' I'm trying not to panic. It's hard enough on my own but the prospect of Dawn's demented gloom makes me want to scream away the injustice.

*

The prison authorities are using me as her unpaid carer, on duty twenty-four hours a day.

'Which one out of Take That do you fancy most?'

'What?'

'Take That. Which one do you fancy most?'

'Oh, the ageing boy band. I don't really like any of them. I find them a bit bland.'

'Yeah, but they're gorgeous, aren't they? Come on, Jenny, which one do you fancy most? You can have first pick.'

I am deep into Thérèse Raquin, and Zola now has the hapless lovers at each other's throats, haunted by their misdeeds, but still having to play out the social niceties.

'I'm trying to read, Dawn. This is a really good book, I'll let you have it when I'm finished.'

'What's it about?'

'Depression, longing, depravation, lies, guilt, all sorts of things. You can read it after me.'

'Who's in it?'

'A French girl is the main character. The book is called Thérèse Raquin.'

'What's her name?'

'Thérèse Raquin.'

'Sounds foreign. Is she foreign?'

'Yes, she's French.'

'Is the book in French?'

'Yes, but I'm reading a translation.'

'I've never read a translation.'

'Then you'll get your chance when I'm finished.'

'I've never read a book. Apart from at school. That was about Billy Blue Hat. There was someone else in the book with a yellow hat as well but I've forgotten his name.'

I put Thérèse down on the table. I'll wait until Dawn's snoring and read it in the night. The noise she makes when she's asleep is even more irritating than when she's awake.

Dawn grabs the book and lets my bookmark fall out.

'Leave it.'

Her eyes narrow, she opens the book and begins to tear out pages.

'Stop that. What're you doing?'

'I don't like your book. You can play dominoes with me instead.'

I reach over to retrieve it but she grabs my wrist and pulls me violently. I topple off my chair; she drags me onto the floor and sits astride my chest. Her weight is preventing me from breathing. I feel a surge of panic. Her hands fasten around my throat and begin to squeeze away my life.

Shooting my arm upwards between hers, I manage a stiff fingered strike to her throat, rotating my shoulder to add power. My fingers are partly absorbed by the fatty folds but manage to connect with something solid. Dawn gasps and holds her neck, releasing mine. I squirm and slither out from under her, she grabs at my leg but I kick it free.

She lets out a deep roar and lunges at me but I'm back on my feet now, back against the wall, looking for something to defend myself with. The chairs are out of reach and too unwieldy. As she rises awkwardly, I venture forward to kick her leg. She absorbs the blow, it provokes her to unexpected nimbleness and she's on her feet and rushing at me. All I can do is sidestep her lunge and allow her to hit the wall with her shoulder and head. The momentum of that huge body damages her more than anything I can manage.

She cries out in pain and slumps heavily to the floor holding her arm across her chest. I slide a heavy chair across the floor and swing it into her face. She keeps screaming and threatening me, so I keep hitting her.

24

'Hello, Jenny, how are you?' Anthony smiles as he greets me then sits in the metal chair on the opposite side of the flimsy table. I sense his nervousness. It's as if he's scared that the women in this place have something that might be contagious.

How am I? Five months on from being abandoned at the court, man-handled into a prison van, locked away from Toby, how am I? Desperate, tired, traumatised, abused, lonely, angry. These are a few of the things I am.

'When can I get to see Toby?' I ask.

'Well, it's up to his father, and he refuses to bring him here, as you well know.'

'All I've had is the occasional phone call, is that all I'm entitled to? He's my son, I'm his mother.' Tears well up again. They render me incapable of anything rational when Toby is mentioned. The pain of separation is too intense for me to endure.

'I've done everything I can.'

Anthony smooths his thinning hair with the flat of his left hand. 'I'm sorry things couldn't have turned out more positively for you.'

'At least I only have a few more weeks, I suppose. Have you been told my release date yet? Even without remission the six months are nearly up.'

Anthony looks down as he speaks, his reluctance to meet my eyes reminds me of Paul Unsworth and my thoughts flicker momentarily to the job I once enjoyed and how Landers Hoffman sacked me almost the instant my sentence was handed down.

'There is a slight problem, a delay, not long I'm sure. I'm pressing them for your release date, but they say that there are other matters that need to be considered.'

'Other matters, what the hell are you on about?'

'Well, there may be other charges brought against you, concerning your cell-mate. Apparently there was an incident. I was wondering if you could tell me what happened.'

'You must be joking!' I feel anger and frustration building. 'They can't be serious. They're going to charge me over Dawn? For God's sake, she nearly killed me. I'm lucky to be alive after what she did.'

'What did she do?'

'She tried to kill me, and very nearly succeeded.' I take a deep breath. 'She's a big girl, massive in fact, most of the time she's quiet, a bit child-like, doesn't really understand what's going on. Occasionally she just bursts, lets rip and attacks the nearest person. Usually it's me she jumps on, as I'm lucky enough to be her room-mate. She hurt me several times but never anything too serious, only bumps and bruises. That is until one day she decided she'd strangle me. I'll tell you it was touch and go for a time, I very nearly died.'

'She tried to strangle you, what did you do to her?'

I suddenly get the picture. Anthony is asking me things he's already been told the answers to. He's getting my side of it, but it's obvious he thinks he knows everything already. It's like he's leading a witness in a trial and trying to get me to admit to wrong-doing. Considering he's my solicitor, I'm getting very upset at his approach.

'You tell me,' I say. 'Tell me what I did or at least tell me what they told you I did.'

He at least has the good grace to look embarrassed.

'She's still in hospital,' he replies. 'Broken shoulder, broken wrist and concussion, they say.'

'It's all bollocks!' I really am getting angry now. 'All this fuss and concern about a murderous psychopath who they should never have exposed me to. They should be protecting me, not accusing me of assault. If it was me lying dead they'd probably say I brought it on myself. They're crazy in here, everyone is mad.'

91

'Whatever the situation I'm afraid Dawn is in a pretty bad way. They say you're a martial arts expert and that's what you used on her.'

'I did do some self-defence classes once, I told them that. It's lucky for me that I did, they aren't concerned about my safety, all they care about is their precious Dawn.'

'What sort of self-defence?' he asks, but I know he already knows.

'You tell me, you've heard their story.'

'They say you're a karate expert, a black belt, and that you terrorised other prisoners prior to injuring Dawn.'

My volcano of exasperation erupts. I can't help bursting into tears and shouting. I know deep inside that none of this will help but the feelings of injustice take over. They're all against me, even this stupid lawyer who is paid to be on my side.

'Poor Dawn, poor everyone, what about me, it's me who's been strangled, it's me who they threaten. It's me they lock away from my son, it's me. Can't you understand it? Can't you see what's happening here?'

Anthony waits for me to sit down and regain some semblance of composure before he replies.

'Take it easy, I'm only telling you what the prison authorities have told me. I know it's their version of events, there are always two sides, I'm only trying to get yours.'

My breath is coming in great gasps now but I manage to slow it down in order to speak. 'Yes, I suppose they're right, I did do karate and I did get a black belt. When you're a vulnerable female you need to be able to do something to defend yourself if you're attacked. My training saved my life, I'd be dead now if I hadn't put in all that time and effort.'

'What were they referring to when they said you terrorised other prisoners?'

'Ha!' I can't help but laugh. 'More the case of me being terrorised by them. As soon as I arrived here they started taking my food and belongings, eventually enough was enough and I stopped being compliant. There were a couple of minor scuffles, that's all.'

25

The temping agency finally came up with something for me. Jervis & Co, Structural Engineers, must be so desperate for a temporary book-keeper and the agency must be so short of staff that they have to send me. Getting a job can be difficult at the best of times. When you are released from prison, having served nine months for corruption, money laundering and aggravated assault, the difficult becomes impossible. Accountancy is not a profession that welcomes dishonesty and violent behaviour.

My CV being fatally flawed means I have to be a little economical with the truth and this is the first agency that failed to make the proper background checks on me. Whether they're lazy or desperate is of no concern. I get to go to work. I get to earn some money, I get to stay in this accommodation a little longer. I get to put off the day I will be living in a Manchester city centre shop doorway.

Tim showed uncharacteristic decisiveness in obtaining the divorce, and immense cruelty when he gained legal custody of Toby with draconian conditions of non-access to his mother. Fortnightly visits are not able to begin to repair the shattered bond between us, only serving to intensify the ache in both our hearts.

Jervis & Co is a step though, the first positive step towards getting Toby back. Alan Jervis is a tall, quietly spoken man with a mane of unruly reddish-grey hair, eyes that twinkle with amusement at the least excuse and a business that is failing fast. The dozen or so engineers he employs are in the main decent, hard-working guys, and everyone seems very busy, but after less than a week I've done enough to know that this welcome position is going to be extremely short-lived.

'How are you getting on, Jenny?' Alan enquires benignly.

'I'm fine thanks, Alan.' I wonder whether to give myself a few days extra employment before telling him there is little more I can do. 'We do need to talk about the cash flow.' There seems no point dragging it out. 'Unless you can get the bank to extend your overdraft or some big payments come in, you're going to find it difficult to pay the wages bill at the end of the month. I'm sorry but that's the way it is.'

His face betrays his worry.

'How much do we need?'

'At least thirty thousand,' I reply. 'You have much more than that owed to you and some of those debts are more than six months overdue, can't you get at least some of those old debts in?'

Alan looks even more glum.

'We have tried, believe me. Most of the money we have outstanding is owed by one property developer. We did a high rise apartment block design for them, they haven't paid us at all. More than sixty thousand pounds is owing.'

'Surely you can't let them get away with that?'

I regret the implied slur as soon as I speak it. Alan doesn't react though, his air of resignation pervades his whole demeanour.

'Oh believe me, we've tried everything, phone calls, letters, even got our solicitors to write threatening a winding up notice. We've done all we can. I have the horrible feeling we'll have to put that one down to experience.'

A prickle of excitement begins in my stomach, spreading upwards as I recognise an opportunity.

'How about if I try for you?' I ask.

'Be my guest, but you won't get anywhere. They say they'll lodge a huge counter-claim if we take it to court. That sort of thing could finish us off, both financially and professionally. Our solicitor says that our legal costs to fight the claim would far exceed the debt – even if we won we could easily end up not covering our costs and if we lost, well, that would definitely be the end for us.'

'I'll have a go.'

My excitement is growing. Somehow my body has recognised something my mind still hasn't worked out. 'But I'll need to agree a success fee with you, you know, a proportion of anything I recover goes to me.'

'That's okay I suppose.' Alan wrinkles his face. 'What did you have in mind?'

'I'll give you a choice. Either pay me ten per cent of what I recover or else I keep everything I get over the thirty thousand you need to pay the wages and keep your business going. You choose.'

'As I've practically resigned myself to getting nothing, and you tell me I need cash desperately, I'll take the second deal. You keep anything over thirty thousand, though I'm afraid we'll both end up with nothing.'

As he answers I feel a pang of disappointment and regret offering him the second option. Ten per cent – easy to calculate and not excessive when you're expecting nothing. Now I'm going for broke. Either I pull off something quite remarkable or he is right. I'll be left with nothing.

Two days of telephoning get me precisely nowhere. The switchboard lady tells me Mr Usman is in a meeting or Mr Usman will ring me back. I decide it's the whole 'Hi, I'm Jenny from Jervis & Co, can I please speak to Mr Usman' thing and decide to change tack.

'Hello, I'm enquiring about your Minshull Street development.'

'Who's calling?'

'This is Rothschild's, my name is Miss Parker and I am the personal assistant to Mr Hugo Mann.'

A brief pause shows me she finally thinks she is speaking to someone worthy of her attention. I have to hand it to my erstwhile colleague Alistair; his father's position always did have that effect.

'Certainly, our Mr Usman will help you, one moment please.'

All the meetings and travel and telephone calls appear to have evaporated.

'Usman.' The curt answer I've been waiting for.

'Mr Usman, Mr Hugo Mann would like to speak to you about acquiring your Minshull Street development.'

'You're Rothschild's, right?'

'That's right.'

'Okay,' Usman pauses, 'What do you want to know?'

'For the moment it's a general enquiry. Mr Mann wants to know if you would consider selling your development.'

'All of it?' Usman's voice prickles with excitement, confirming my suspicion that in common with the rest of the property market, apartment sales in Central Manchester aren't doing very well at all. 'We have some units sold, of course,' he says weakly.

'How many exactly?' I can't resist probing his level of desperation.

'Oh, several,' he gasps, 'I can't tell you exactly as of this moment.'

'Well, our clients are mainly interested in empty properties. We're putting together a one hundred million pound property investment vehicle for them.'

'Ah, yes, that wouldn't be a problem, I could arrange for you to have the whole building if that's what you want.'

'Excellent, then we might be interested.'

'How much…I mean, how much are you expecting to pay?' he asks.

'That's a matter for Mr Mann, I'm afraid.'

'Can I speak to him?' Usman asks.

'That's not possible at the moment. He's in the Middle East now, then he has to travel to New York. I'm not expecting him back before next Friday when he'll finalise the portfolio purchases. If you want your development to be considered, please let us have the details we require before then.'

'What details are those?'

'Oh, details of the building, architect's reports, structural reports, occupation, sales history…' I pause. 'Are you writing these down?'

'No,' he admits.

'Then you need to. It's too late to send you our standard enquiry pack.' I continue to reel off a long list of things then finish with, 'Oh, and you must send letters with each of the reports agreeing to assign them to our clients.'

'What do you mean?' Usman asks.

'We need confirmation that all the reports and the building contract will be assigned, otherwise our clients will not deal. All it means is a letter from each of them, the architect, the builder, the structural engineer and the facilities engineer, stating that they would be willing to legally assign all rights to their reports. They must also state any financial payments they'd require to do this. Of course, the vendor would be responsible for payment of any assignment fees.'

Usman remains quiet. I presume he is still writing. Finally he says, 'I would still prefer it if I could speak to Hugo Mann.'

I pause for effect and lower my voice. 'I'll give you his personal mobile number but you must promise not to reveal it to anyone else and only use it yourself for this one purpose.'

'Okay,' Usman says. 'Thanks.'

'You promise?' I ask.

'Absolutely. I promise, and thanks,' he replies. I give him my mobile number complete with international prefix for good effect, then hang up.

26

'Usman,' he answers immediately, then, 'Good morning, Miss Parker.'

I know he is happy to hear from me. Not from his tone of voice but from the five missed calls on my mobile. It's a simple matter to change the voicemail greeting to one that says, 'This is the personal mobile number of Hugo Mann'.

'Mr Usman, good morning,' I begin. 'Mr Mann is in transit as you know, and regrets he hasn't been able to return your calls.'

'I understand,' Usman says, 'but I need to speak to him, when will that be possible?'

'The next opportunity will be Friday.'

'But you said the decisions regarding the property purchases, whether you wanted to buy my development, you said that would be Friday.'

'That's right.' I'm enjoying his discomfiture. He sounds like a very greedy little man. 'Mr Mann has seen the valuations from our estate surveyors and has asked me to tell you that he will recommend your property to our clients.'

'Yes, but how much, what are they offering? I need to know that, I must know how much.'

'Mr Mann will telephone you on Friday with the offer.'

'Can't you give me an idea? Do you know what the valuation was?'

'Of course, I have seen the report, Mr Usman, but I'm not in a position to divulge that information, I am sure you'll understand.'

'Okay, okay.' He pauses. 'Can you give me a clue, some ball park figure?'

'Look, Mr Usman, all you need to do is get the details requested over to our Manchester office. You have the address? Good, and I must emphasise that all the documentation must be submitted by Friday. Mr Mann made it quite clear that any outstanding issues would mean that there can be no deal.'

Usman is quiet now, I can feel him wondering.

'I can tell you,' I add, 'that our clients are willing to pay a premium to get the properties they want.'

'Okay.' His voice sounds very positive, my pep talk appears to have done the trick. 'I'll get the stuff to you. Should I mark it for your attention?'

'No; address it to Mr Hugo Mann and put the reference HMAD27 on the envelope.'

*

When Usman is put through to me at Jervis and Co I feel an enormous thrill and excitement which almost throws me completely. Alan has kept his promise and is allowing me to deal with him. I have to keep my voice lower and broaden my Mancunian accent throughout the conversation if I am to avoid awkward recognition.

'Jenny Jervis,' I adopt my alter ego.

'This is Usman, I need to speak to Alan on an urgent matter.'

'You can speak to me. I'm the finance director and Alan's wife. Is it about the outstanding account?'

'Well no, err, yes. I suppose so.'

'When can we expect payment, Mr Usman?'

'Ah yes, soon. There have been cash flow problems, you understand. The whole property world has collapsed. I do have some good news though. We may have a purchaser for our development. As soon as we sell we'll have the funds to pay you.'

'When will that be? We've been waiting a long time.'
'Soon, a couple of weeks maybe.'
'Well, that will be good news. Thanks for your call.'
'Wait...'

Usman gets to the point I know he has rung to make. 'Before we do the deal the purchaser wants a Letter of

Assignment regarding your report. If you could let me have that urgently, today if possible, tomorrow at the latest.'

'Let me see…' I pretend to be looking through documents but I already have the figure written in big letters in front of me. 'Ah yes, you owe us sixty-three thousand, eight hundred and forty-two pounds in all. When you pay us that we will let you have your letter.'

'But we have no money. I told you, we have a cash flow problem, a temporary cash flow problem.'

There is no alarm in Usman's voice at my demands. He knows he has to pay up or miss his chance of a sale. After a few minutes of negotiation he agrees to let us have forty thousand on account and I agree to send the letter the moment it is safely in our bank.

27

Angry voices, shouts, threats, crashing and splintering noises.
They are here to arrest me, to drag me away, to destroy what
little hope that remains. Dawn kneels on my chest, hands
gripping my throat, this time there'll be no escape as she
squeezes my life away. I can hear Toby's screams in the
distance. I struggle awake, flash on the light, blink painfully in
the glare. No police, no Dawn, only the usual passing trade,
arguing drunkenly, fighting sporadically, destroying what they
find. For all the attenuation afforded by the loose windows and
thin walls, they might as well be in here with me.

The sheer number of people on the street in the early
hours amazes me. Their unbridled urge to scream and shout
disturbs what little sleep I can manage in this awful place. It's a
normal terraced house in a downtrodden south Manchester
suburb, designed to provide decent accommodation for a small
family. Now it offers indecent lodgings for seven unfortunate
people. I am housed in what was the front sitting room, closest to
the front door and the street. When the people outside are quiet
the other inhabitants seem to take turns to slam the door as they
enter and exit.

The man upstairs, whom I've never seen, provides me
with a deep banging noise at all hours of the day and night, the
remnants of mindless music after filtration through his floor. The
high-pitched screams and shouts attest to a variety of lady friends
whom he entertains on a regular basis. The rhythmic thump of
the bed and the loud groans of its occupants continue for hours at
a time, gradually building up velocity as I lie praying for him to
climax and let me rest.

The noise and disturbances are debilitating. The shared
toilet and bathroom is a source of even greater sorrow. When I
first arrived here I asked what the arrangements were for
cleaning the common areas. The landlord's gruff response was
that it was in hand. My sad experience is that there are no

arrangements and no signs of any change. The dried on brown pebble-dash effect that stretches out of the bowl and up one of the walls gives testament to that. I approach the hideous place with bleach and rubber gloves every time I need to pee.

The lock on my door has taken a gradual journey downwards, currently lodging below waist level. Its previous positions are marked by splintered wood and in one place by a hole you could push a packet of mints through. I cover this with paper and sellotape but some inquisitive passer-by insists on poking it out on a daily basis.

My calves sting where I absent-mindedly scratch the bites. I don't try to visualise what bites my legs in the night, just as I calmly flick away the mouse droppings from my pillow before resting my head. My new-found calm is borne out of the temporary nature of my situation. Today, I remember with exaltation, is the day Usman's money will arrive and with it my share. Tomorrow I'll be able to move elsewhere, I'll be able to rest in peaceful cleanliness without feeling threatened.

*

I'm sitting at the reception desk and have received glorious confirmation that, exactly as promised by the desperate Mr Usman, the forty thousand pounds has arrived safely in the Jervis & Co account. I feel like shouting out with joy and excitement, but feel restrained by the two grim faced men in suits sat in front of me, waiting to see Alan. I feel frustrated that they will have their meeting before I can arrange the payment of my success fee with him. I am a little concerned about the mechanism and timing. If Alan pays me through the books as an employee, Jervis & Co will have to pay employer's National Insurance on the payment amounting to ten per cent or so – one thousand pounds for the tax man, in addition to any personal tax. I can't see Alan agreeing to swallow the whole of the National Insurance and I can ill afford to lose a thousand pounds out of my proceeds. It might be possible to convince him to pay me in full and deduct the National Insurance from the next payment I extract from Usman.

This is difficult for me. Excitement and positivity are unfamiliar feelings and I need some means of release.

Alan comes out and greets his grumpy visitors, I try to catch his eye but fail. Lunchtime comes and goes without anybody emerging, so I nip out to buy a sandwich and a celebratory coffee which comes at a ridiculous cost, way beyond what I could normally afford, but today is special and I drink the frothy, lukewarm, coffee-flavoured milk with slow relish. Perhaps I will buy myself a coffee machine with my earnings, that's if I've anything left after renting a nice clean apartment and buying a new mattress and new bed linen. Oh and some smart clothes, some comfortable shoes, some crisp clean underwear.

The coffee machine seems to be well down the list now and the likelihood of me having available funds when I reach it is very low. If only I can persuade Alan to pay the National Insurance it might have a glimmer of a chance.

Alan's door is still firmly closed. I sit impatiently waiting for it to open and give me the chance to sort things out. I have an almost irresistible urge to barge in, to interrupt the meeting, to claim precedence over the dull men in suits. When three o'clock arrives I begin to get a worried feeling to add to my frustration. Alan only closes his door when he has visitors, but surely they can't still be in there.

The phone line in his office lights up to show that he's making a call; it turns out to be a long call. I wait until he's finished, knock and enter. He sits there alone, visitors nowhere to be seen. Alan looks up at me, his eyes are narrow and his lips pinched. The twinkle has disappeared.

'I need to speak to you about Usman,' I begin.

'It's okay,' he answers quickly. 'I've been sorting that out.'

At first his words sound positive but a feeling of dread crawls up my spine. 'Oh,' I reply, 'you're sorting out my payment, my success fee?'

He snorts, it is a very unpleasant sound. 'Absolutely not, I've been dealing with Mr Usman myself, he's sending us forty thousand pounds on account and I've made sure we'll get the rest very soon.'

'You don't understand,' I reply, 'I got the money out of Usman, just as we agreed. You said I could have anything over thirty thousand, so I'm owed ten thousand pounds.'

'Nonsense.' Alan's words cut to my heart and burn into it.

'Usman explained to me what happened, he has a buyer. It was he who rang us and offered the money on account, it had absolutely nothing to do with you.'

'Yes it was. And you promised.' I feel broken, abused, dysfunctional. I can't believe what I'm hearing.

Alan's body is hunched, defensive, his hands are clasped tightly together, his eyes are cast down at his desk.

'I said you could have something if you got the money. You didn't get it, I don't owe you anything.'

'Listen,' I'm desperately trying to hold on. 'We can get the rest of the money. Don't send the letter, I'll him he has to pay up in full before he gets it. This way you get all the money.'

'Too late,' he smirks, an evil little smirk. 'I already sent the letter.'

'Then you'll get no more from him,' I shout. 'Why didn't you listen to me?'

'Because you don't know what's going on. I sorted it myself, just like I said. What you don't realise is that I put an assignment fee of twenty-five thousand pounds in the letter. Don't you see? That makes sure we get it all, plus a bit extra for our trouble.'

'When?' I am angry now at this stupid man.

'What do you mean, when?'

'When will you get the twenty-five grand?'

105

'Oh, when he sells the development.'

'Ah yes, when he sells. And what makes you think he's going to sell?'

Alan stands up suddenly, anger flashes in his face. 'Don't take that tone with me. Get out. I don't want you working here any more, I'll ring the agency and tell them. Now go.'

I stand my ground.

'Usman has no buyer, nobody wants to buy his poxy development. I pretended there was a buyer, so he would pay us. It's all my doing. It was me that got you your money, it was me.'

He is coming towards me to physically throw me out, his face is relentless, he no longer hears me. I am lost. My dreams are shattered. I walk out of his office and keep on going.

28

I find myself in the centre of Manchester, walking aimlessly in the early evening dark, unwilling to return to my cockroach-infested and shit-spattered accommodation. Looking down at the Irwell from Blackfriars Bridge I wonder for an instant what that cold oblivion might taste like, then anger swells up and heats my spirit. I am not finished yet, I tell myself, and start to believe it, at least enough to avoid clambering onto the slippery stone parapet and plunging to my death. There is no joy in my surroundings, the scurrying people hardly glance at my unremarkable figure trudging the streets they use as thoroughfares. The Deansgate bars and restaurants bristle with the recent discharge from nearby offices. I long for a decent meal and a strong drink but even more for sympathetic and supportive company. The first two longings are beyond my financial reach, the last one is made a mockery of by the brash louts who inhabit those places.

Bereft of any sense of purpose, I slip away from the bustle by taking a familiar track down Spinningfields. Peering through the Landers Hoffman glass doors I see the lone security guard seated at the reception desk and my thoughts turn to Gary. The last time I entered the building was the day I confronted Paul, but my lasting memory is the calm comfort that Gary's presence brought.

My heart leaps with hope as I imagine him being there now, a safe haven among all this turmoil. Someone to tell my troubles to, someone who will listen and understand. Strangely, because that last morning was the only time I exchanged more than a good morning or a wave with the man, I know next to nothing about him, only that he has something to do with the security company that guards this building. There is a sticker on the glass door which reads GOD Security and GOD is Watching over You.

I remember now, Gary O'Donnell, that's his name, it must be his business, either that or someone else has a wicked sense of humour. The lanky guard sees my nose pressed against the glass and waves me away as if dispersing some disagreeable smell. This upsets me; after all, I used to be quite an important person in this office. I rattle the doors angrily, completely out of nervous reaction. He ambles across to dismiss me more effectively, but before he can speak I shout,

'Gary, I'm looking for Gary, is he here?'

Slowly, painfully, a look of understanding creases the long face. He reaches down and lifts up a bunch of keys hanging by a chain from his belt.

'Come in.' He looks up and down the street as if anticipating a horde of the unwashed racing to take advantage of the slight opening he is offering me.

'It's Mrs Parker, isn't it?' he asks.

'Yes.'

'Haven't seen you about for a while.' He states the obvious.

I don't bother with the explanation he's expecting.

'Do you know where Gary is?' I ask.

'He's doing the football,' he answers enigmatically.

I stand and look at him waiting for a better explanation, glad of the warmth inside the building. After a minute or two I realise that this is the best explanation he can offer.

'I need to talk to him.'

He picks a mobile phone sheathed with a rubberised protective case out of his pocket, presses two buttons then hands it to me.

'Hello,' I say.

'Hello,' Gary answers.

I feel small and pathetic, close to bursting into tears. 'I need to see you,' I blurt, 'I need to talk to you about something.'

'Who is it?' he asks gently.

I colour up under the unremitting gaze of the thin security guard, turn away and walk deeper into the building.

'It's me, Jenny Parker.'

The silence on the other end confirms my worst fears; that he doesn't know me and doesn't want to.

'Mrs Parker, I used to work here…er, at Landers Hoffman, that's where I am now, with your man.'

Of course I am; I wince at my inadequacy and wish I hadn't started this conversation, or at least that I'd started it differently, been authoritative, precise, clear and all the other attributes I once associated with myself but now lack.

'How are you?' Gary's voice is warmer now.

'Not too good,' I reply honestly.

'What can I do to help?' he asks.

The list that flashes through my mind is long and comprehensive.

'I need to ask your advice, it's urgent. I don't know what to do. I've been walking around all afternoon.' I stop before the tears make me stop.

'Well, you can come out here if you want.'

'Where are you?'

'Near the Manchester United ground, we do some parking here on match days. I'll be here till about eight o'clock.'

He describes the place, I am to look out for a man in a high visibility vest waving, he says.

It takes me almost an hour to walk there. Gary is standing at the entrance to a car park belonging to a large office block. Men in yellow jackets are taking money off motorists, I see ten pound notes being pushed through windows and no change given. The car park is vast and filling up rapidly. He greets me warmly without removing his hands from the pockets of an olive green, waxed cotton coat.

'I wondered where you'd got to, I presumed you were in a car,' he smiles easily.

I try to send a smile of my own back but it feels tight and despairing. 'You look like you could do with a cup of tea.'

He leads me through a gate in the fence and we emerge alongside a burger van where three ladies are dispensing greasy food to ravenous football supporters.

'Hi, Gary,' one of them beams. 'Can I tempt you with anything tonight?'

'A couple of teas please, Andrea.' He turns to me. 'Are you hungry, Mrs Parker? Do you want something to eat?'

My stomach churns in anxiety, saliva collects underneath my tongue, but I find myself weakly refusing. At last count, unless I have a hole in my purse, there is less than two pounds there. I have half a box of porridge oats at the apartment, unless the insects and rodents have scoffed it. I have to wait for that.

Two plastic cups are proffered. Gary passes one to me. No money changes hands. I reconsider my refusal, the frying smells are overwhelming my senses, fixating them, robbing my awareness of any sensations that are not hunger. I sip the tea gratefully, remembering the previous weak and sugary brew I enjoyed in his company. It seems that's how people make tea when Gary is around.

'Tell you what, Andrea,' Gary says, 'I'll have a couple of your bacon baps to keep me going.'

Andrea obliges, stacking four rashers of bacon in each bun then squashing the tops on with industrial force. She finishes the procedure with an elegant flourish, wrapping a white serviette part way around each sandwich before handing them over. Gary, bless him, hands one of the beautiful creations to me and to my intense shame I wolf it down so quickly I am certain it looks like I inhaled it rather than chewed and swallowed. Gary, twice blessed Gary, passes on the second, over which I try to exercise more decorum.

'Let's go and sit in the car,' he suggests. 'It'll be more comfortable.'

He installs me in the sumptuous leather passenger seat of a huge black Range Rover. Tim's ambition was always to own a Range Rover. Any sort, any age. Here I am sitting with Gary in what appears to be a brand new one, complete with personalised number plate. My original impression of Gary as a lowly security guard now seems shamefully inaccurate.

He waits until I have finished the second bacon sandwich then asks, 'What did you want to talk about, Mrs Parker?'

'Jenny,' I insist through a full mouth.

'So how can I help, Jenny?' he asks.

Take me home with you, hold me, protect me, feed me more bacon sandwiches. All these answers occur to me at once but I swallow the last crumbs and embark on my story about Jervis & Co, about Usman's debt, about Alan welshing on our agreement. I feel so much the naive fool as I tell him; the narrative has an inevitable outcome which I feel ashamed I didn't anticipate myself at the time.

Gary, surprisingly, looks increasingly excited and impressed, rather than critical and dismissive.

'So you conned this Usman into parting with forty K,' Gary grins. 'Brilliant, amazing, you did very well.'

'But I didn't get paid. I need that money, Gary, I need it very badly. The place where I'm living is so disgusting I can't bear to spend another night there. Jervis's money would have got me out of there, put me back on my feet. Can you help me get it off him, beat him up or something?'

I sound pathetic, weak and desperate. I am all of these, close to abandoning what vestige of self-worth I have left. The exultation and excitement I felt at Usman's capitulation to my imaginary pressure is only a distant sour residue, buried by piles of frustration and disappointment.

Gary smiles, 'I'll be glad to help.'

'You will go round and bash him up?'

'No way, but I will help you. Do you fancy working with me?'

The question leaves me stunned. I look around at the burly men collecting money, I imagine the others sitting alone in empty premises waiting for trouble.

'I don't know what I can do.'

'You're an accountant, that'll do for a start. Then there's this debt collecting talent you've demonstrated, that'll come in handy. We could offer that as part of the business. When all else fails GOD will get your money.'

'What?'

111

'Oh, don't you like it, Gary O'Donnell, GOD Security, GOD Debt Recovery, GOD is Watching over You. Get it?'

I get it but I have no comprehension of what he is saying.

'This job,' I ask, 'where is it, when would you want me to start, how much is the pay?'

Gary is resting his arms gently on the steering wheel and is still smiling.

'So you are interested?'

'Gary,' I reply, 'I'm out of work, broke and desperate. Of course I'm interested, even if you wanted me to clean toilets I'd be interested.'

'Good.' He reaches down and opens the glove compartment above my knees. 'Here.' He passes me a white envelope, unsealed and stuffed with ten pound notes. 'Take this, advance payment of wages. We're going to be business partners. Don't worry, there'll be plenty more like this.'

He glances down at his ornate watch.

'Got to go now.' He fires up the engine. As if on cue a hand passes wads of notes through his window and he stuffs them inside his jacket.

'I'll drop you off at the Campanile, you'll be best in there for tonight.'

29

Lying back in the soft warmth of the scented bath water I begin to feel human again. Small beginnings of positive thoughts are released by my return to a safe and clean environment. There is no hole in the sturdy door, only a strong lock. This bathroom is spotless and fragrant and mine alone. It's been a long time since I felt secure enough to relax while vulnerable and naked.

The familiar way that Gary negotiated the room rate down to thirty-five pounds including breakfast makes me doubt that I'm the first woman he's brought here. The thought crossed my mind that he might expect some sexual compensation for the money he was paying out, but when this didn't materialise I felt relieved rather than disappointed. This bath is more comforting, more pleasurable and more nourishing than anything Gary might have offered.

When it cools I replenish the warmth with the endless supply of searing water, each time pushing the threshold of my heat resistance. The only thing in the world that might tempt me to get out of this bath is the crisp coolness of the pristine bed and the prospect of undisturbed sleep for the first time since before prison, before Toby even. So long ago that the possibility makes me excited.

*

An urgent need to pee tips me reluctantly out of bed, the air in the room is chilly compared with the soft warmth I am leaving. I close the bathroom door and lock it before sitting on the toilet, then smile grimly at the reflex that makes me do that. Shivering I crawl back into bed, wrapping the still warm duvet around my naked body. The red numbers below the television screen tell me I've managed an unbroken nine hours' sleep. Although I feel I could do with dozing for a few hours more, I know it's breakfast time. That it's available, paid for and close by. My reluctance to leave the bed is overwhelmed in turn by hunger.

It's a revolting thing to have to take yesterday's discarded clothes from a heap on the floor and put them on again, all that bathing I did loses its edge and I feel disgusting and filthy once again. Once dressed I begin to feel regret at leaving this room and dread at having to return to my own apartment. The thought of the crawling things there makes me nauseous.

Gary finds me half way through my breakfast, having already eaten enough for two large men; I am intent in getting him full value for his all-inclusive room rate. As I splutter my thanks through a mouthful of toast he puts an envelope and a mobile phone on the table.

'Sorry,' he says, 'something's turned up and I can't spend any time with you today.'

My heart sinks. I begin to wonder how I'll get home. I feel desperate that I won't be warm and safe.

'I've booked you in here again tonight, hope you don't mind.'

Relief spreads like warmth through my body, I find myself grinning so wide that crumbs and pieces of egg are dropping out of my mouth.

'Here's a phone, so I can call you to make arrangements for tomorrow. My number's in it already, so you can get me any time.' He points to the envelope. 'I have a mate with some empty flats in Salford, his number's in there, take a look and let me know what you think.'

I don't care what it's like, I know I will want it but be unable to afford it, so what's the point of all this. I realise too late that my thoughts have escaped and Gary can hear them.

'Don't worry, as I said, he's a mate, and they're empty. He'll do you a good deal. Call it part of your remuneration package.'

'What will I be doing,' I ask, 'what's the job you want me for?'

'Accountant, finance director, business partner, whatever you like, call it what you like.'

'How do you know I can do it, this job? I don't know anything about your business, I don't really know much about you.'

'Listen,' Gary's eyes are soft and comforting, 'things don't just happen, everything happens for a reason. I've been needing someone like you for a long time, someone I can trust, someone who is strong and capable, then you just turn up – no job, no money, nowhere proper to live. Don't you see, this is an opportunity for both of us, one that is meant to be.'

I can't possibly agree with what he's saying but I can at least understand where he's coming from.

'Fair enough.' I don't exactly have any other options at present. 'Thanks,' is all I can manage before he leaves me to continue my quest for cholesterol poisoning.

30

Gary's office consists of one room and a portacabin in a yard filled mainly by untidy heaps of broken concrete. The only occupant is a twenty-year-old with a shock of pink hair whose name is Carrie, she acts as the telephonist, receptionist and office clerk; her job consists mainly of explaining to people who ring in that Gary is not available and she will give him a message. The other part of her job seems to involve searching in vain for documents she knows were received but can't quite remember where she put them. The easy, over-familiar way she treats Gary leads me to suspect that she might be the reason he is so familiar with the Campanile Hotel, now that my first guess that she must be his daughter proves to be mistaken.

Gary has no desk, not even a seat in the office. It seems he just isn't the office type. The remainder of the portacabin houses a ladies' toilet, clean and fragrant, a gents' toilet, not clean, not fragrant, a kitchen and a large room apparently used for discarding old clothing and dirty overalls. My desk is next to Carrie's, an arrangement made compulsory by the geometric restrictions of the space. At least it's warm and dry and not far at all from my new flat.

There is a theory put forward by Gary and adopted by myself that Carrie now works for me. After four weeks I'm still waiting for her to grasp this new arrangement. I swear she gives a visible start of surprise to see me every morning, then treats me like a visitor, even to the extent of showing me the way to the ladies' toilet in case I forget it's next door and start peeing in the untidy room at the end of the corridor.

Today Gary, unusually, is in the office, sitting on the corner of Carrie's desk while she rummages uncomfortably for something she knows in her heart will never be seen again. He is telling me his life story, this in response to my casual enquiry as to how his business has ended up in this state. I have a feeling he's taking my question as a compliment.

116

'I came over from Ireland when I was sixteen and stayed with a mate of me Dad's in Salford. I got a job as a lorry driver, tipper lorries they were for shifting muck – earth and soil and stones and such like.' He pauses proudly and admires the concrete piles that threaten to engulf the office.

'Isn't sixteen a bit young to be a lorry driver?' I ask. My understanding of the haulage industry is by no means complete, but I'm feeling certain that someone would have to be at least twenty-one to drive a big lorry.

'No, I'm a good driver. I already drove big things in Ireland so there was no problem, at least not for a year or so. Then they started to get a bit fussy about it all.'

'Fussy?'

'Yes, like they wanted to see my licence and such, red tape, that's what it was.'

'And did you have a licence?' I ask, knowing the answer already.

'No, of course not. How would I be getting a licence at sixteen? You have to be twenty-one at least.'

'So was that the end of your lorry-driving career?'

'No, absolutely not. I bought my own truck. It was a bit of a scrap heap of a lorry, always breaking down.' Gary grinned. 'That's how I got into the security job. I was driving for a mate of mine and he asked me to keep an eye on his machines and stuff – ended up driving during the day and mending my wagon while I was security-guarding. After they confiscated my lorry I gave up the driving.'

He pauses to drink his tea, giving me a chance to ask for more details, things like 'Who confiscated your wagon?' and 'Didn't you get into trouble for driving without any form of licence and presumably insurance?' I'm sure that these details will emerge at some stage, but I have caught his drift, I understand his casual attitude towards rules and regulations.

If I'm to do the things he has hired me for, I'll have to somehow legitimise what he does. This process will take time, lots of time. It's no use my complaining that things are not as

117

they should be; if they were I wouldn't be needed. I wouldn't have the nice flat where I can bring Toby to sleep.

31

Toby is trying to climb over the balcony railings; his little feet are scrabbling for grip on the decorative glass panel. I realise that if these had been unprotected he would have been over them in a flash and plunging eight storeys down to the street. My heart leaps in painful fear and I call him inside. When he fails to respond I pick him off the parapet and deposit him on my lounge carpet, firmly closing the door behind me. He runs past me straight to the window, and tries to prise it open with his little fingers. He then complains loudly at his confinement.

'Come on, Toby,' I cajole, 'we'll play inside. It's cold and dangerous out there on the balcony.'

His face puckers in displeasure, then he demands to watch television, pointing and yelling 'CBeebies, CBeebies,' at me. The bitter truth is that I'm glad of the television, grateful for its absorptive capacity. What I imagined to be a reunion of sweet loving pleasure is turning out to be a sad disappointment.

I have spent countless nights enduring tortured visions of Toby's anguish over our separation. Now I see the strength and resilience in him, I recognise his capacity to cope is greater than my own. This should warm my heart, ease my suffering, but it fails. Instead I feel empty and cold inside. A panic wells up that tells me that I've lost him, that he's no longer connected to me in the way that I'll always be tied to him.

Internally this apartment is smart, clean and comfortable, apart from the balcony Toby is safe in here, but outside the streets look grimy and feel dangerous. As a consequence, my daily run has to be performed while it's still light and I feel safer. I can only guess about the schools close to here, but can't imagine they compare favourably with the one he's due to attend next year. Bringing him here permanently would be folly. I need to make a proper home near a decent school, a place with grass and trees and room for him to bounce around. I have to face facts; it will be hard to prise my son away from his father and even more difficult once he's settled down at school. This place is a big step out of the gutter but I have to keep climbing quickly.

At least my arrival wiped the usual smirk of that bitch's face. I shrivel up with horror at how she must treat my precious son. Alison, the woman Tim has replaced me with, is a thin-lipped, miserable looking female with long slender legs and disproportionately large breasts. The sight of me pulling up in the black Audi A8 limousine kindly lent to me by Gary for the weekend did nothing to improve her normal sour expression. There's even a car seat in the back, the perfect size for Toby, courtesy of one of Gary's sizeable brood. Whatever awkwardness exists between my child and me, however unfamiliar our feelings might be, this weekend is a wonderful improvement over the couple of awkward hours I've occasionally spent in Tim's front room with my Toby. Now he is here with me, only me, I have his full attention and he has mine. There will be no heads around the door constantly interrupting, asking if he's okay, reminding me I have to leave.

As he munches through his pizza fingers and alpha-bites, generously garnished with tomato ketchup, I detect his increasing ease with me and the situation. He is calmer now, less demanding, willing to connect with a look and even a smile. We sit together, close, touching, watching the multi-coloured brightness of impossible creatures that strangle their speech. I have less than twenty-four hours, then he has to be delivered back to Tim and his unfeeling female. Make the most of it, that's all I can do for the time being. When I have a suitable home for him I can get custody, all legal and straightforward, then his father can ask me for permission to see him. He can turn up and play for a couple of hours. By then, maybe, my new partner will scowl and grimace at him, show Tim how it feels to me now. In the meantime, I keep an unblemished record of punctuality, co-operate to the full and betray none of my feelings or intentions to Tim.

As Toby sleeps, vulnerable and trusting in the corner of my bed, I am overwhelmed by tearful emotions. My heart is filled to bursting point with love for my beautiful child. My body aches with the sadness of our separation and my whole being wallows in the darkness of the guilty knowledge that it's all my fault.

32

Gary keeps repeating his mantra, 'I'm not so good with the paperwork.' He uses it as his stock excuse for just about everything. I tell him in return that Her Majesty's Revenue & Customs will have no problem in filling in the appropriate paperwork which will confiscate all his possessions and send him to jail.

'We need to sort things out, Gary, it's only a matter of time before they come and investigate you. When that happens we need to be able to show them lots of paperwork, all filled out correctly.'

'I'm a great believer in not bothering them if they're not bothering me,' he replies. 'But you're the boss, that's what I hired you for. To do the necessary.'

'It'll mean declaring income, paying tax, you understand that?'

'We already pay tax,' he protests.

This is true, there is an elderly lady in Eccles who does all the wages and sends in the income tax and National Insurance deductions. Gary thinks this constitutes the limit of his liability, even though he pays his workers half their wages in cash and only half through the books. He made the same arrangement with me. I get an envelope every week containing three hundred and fifty pounds in cash. My problem is that when I need to get a mortgage that will be based solely on my declared earnings. Telling the building society not to worry, that I get enough cash to cover the repayments, just won't do the job.

We agree to set up a limited company and trade through this. To my surprise Gary insists that I become an equal shareholder and act as both director and company secretary. Once again, he pleads his lack of interest with paperwork. He also adds that he trusts me and that we need to look out for each other. There's little I can say about this other than to agree. The thought crosses my mind that somehow Gary is being smarter than his disarming manner portrays him, but I let that go under the plaintive look he gives me.

'I'll need to make a list of all the assets you intend to put into the company, like the yard and the offices. When did you acquire the land here?'

'Ah,' Gary wrinkles his brow, 'that'll be about six or seven years ago, that's when I acquired it.'

'I'll need details of the transaction, how much you paid, ownership plans, that kind of thing.'

Gary looks even more puzzled. 'There's none of those things,' he admits.

'You've lost them? Don't worry, I can get the information from the Land Registry.'

'They won't have it either,' he says.

'Look, Gary, if you bought land there will be a transfer document lodged by your solicitor with the Land Registry.'

'There's the thing,' Gary says, 'I never bought it, I just acquired it so to speak. It was a rough piece of land, nobody seemed to want it, so I put a fence round it and waited. I put up my security notices all around and nobody ever complained, so I started using it for bits and pieces of storage. Then I put the offices here. I spent good money on electrics and drains and stuff. Anyway, it's no problem, it's sound. Nobody bothers about it.'

I'm disconcerted but not very surprised by this account. All Gary's dealings have a great deal of informality in common. I have to admit that his approach to business seems much more successful than many others I've witnessed.

33

I'm allowing the unusual indulgence of tapas in a heaving
Deansgate restaurant when he announces his interest by sending
a drink over to my single occupancy table. I wave my acceptance
and meet his eyes. I decide I will go to bed with him. He looks
wholesome enough, my age or even a little younger, out with
four male friends and brave enough to risk a knock back.

'Andy.'

He sits down opposite and holds out his right hand.

'Jenny,' I reply.

He can't resist a triumphant look back over his shoulder.
As we share a bottle of house red he reveals himself to be a
policeman, his friends are all policemen, they're having a lads'
night out. I assume he's married or at least spoken for, but this is
information that I've no need to confirm at this point in our
relationship.

Small talk and comfortable pleasantries soon lead to his
gallant offer to walk me home. I offer in return to make him a
coffee and his quick, eager acceptance reveals the self-indulgent
nature of his gallantry.

Coffee forgotten, Andy soon has his hand inside my
knickers. I am glad of it and getting more grateful with each
passing moment. We move to my bed. He gently parts my legs
then my lips and pushes himself inside me.

I am moist and agreeable as he sinks into me. As he
thrusts I feel the condom scratching my insides, as if he's
wearing a crinkly crisp packet and the salt is inflaming my
internal wounds. I flinch in pain but he pushes harder and faster.
I try to push him out of me but he grips me more tightly by my
buttocks. My moans of discomfort and anguish are increasing in
volume. He mistakes this for my passion and is now hell-bent on
his own. I am being impaled by shards of broken glass; my
agony is emitted as screams. He makes low pitched animal

noises and shudders to a halt. I feel him becoming limp, eject him with my hand and stagger into my bathroom.

For fifteen minutes I am peeing dribbles of acid, the pain is intense, and my disappointment is unbearable. Even with Tim, it was never this bad.

I return, unsure and embarrassed, to find Andy snoring and indifferent. He lies on his back with a self-satisfied look that I want to cut off with a knife. As I stand over him, he snaps into wakefulness as if somehow heeding my violent thoughts.

'Wow!' he spurts, 'you were great.'

No, I wasn't great, it wasn't great, it was horrible and it made me ill. I'm in agony and all you can feel is the end of your dick. Before I can say anything, he gets up and begins to dress, no doubt worried his wife will be wondering where he is by now.

'Got to dash,' he manages. 'Sorry, on earlies tomorrow, I'll call you.'

I think of Martin, his gentleness, his connection, his sensitivity. I remind myself of his death and how I let him down. The tears begin before Andy has let himself out.

34

Gary is suggesting that I leave early today. He stands in uncharacteristic agitation, the doorway framing his taut body. Outside, the half gloom reveals several unfamiliar faces, blank and unflinching, attached to large figures. When I look at them they turn away quickly and pretend to be more interested in the nearest pile of broken concrete. I turn to Gary but the questions die in my throat. Now is not the time for answers, my concerns are not relevant. Nothing I say can change things or influence events. Gary's energetic state is shocking to me, a glimpse of the powerful man that is usually masked by easy-going deference.

Even though it's barely four thirty in the afternoon, the gloom is descending rapidly. It has become one of those sad winter days when the sun never manages to pierce the dark blanket. Light drizzle speckles the yellow haloes around the street lights; soft drops, almost like snowflakes, drift gently on the still air. The rain is the only thing in motion; the men in the yard are immobile, frozen in attitudes of unconvincing informality.

As I allow myself to be ushered out of the gate, I count four more burly individuals squeezed into Gary's car. I catch the eye of the swarthy man with thick black hair sitting in the front seat. A shock of recognition changes his neutral expression for an instant; this scares me as I've no idea who he might be.

There are two more men outside the yard testing the supporting qualities of the perimeter fence. A frisson of sharp fear pierces my stomach as I glimpse a polished wooden gun stock protruding below a coat and understand the look in Gary's eyes.

*

Sleep is impossible after a whole evening of worry. A hundred times I pick up the phone to call Gary for some reassurance but each time I replace it carefully on the table. The eerie atmosphere

I experienced at the office has transposed itself to my apartment, carried in on my waves of anxiety. Now I lie here alert, nerves jangling, mind racing with dire possibilities. The man who recognised me in the yard haunts my thoughts. His expression when our eyes met was one of surprise followed by intense dislike. At least that's my memory of it now.

My speculation about him has turned into an endless recurring loop that can only be severed by answers. Gary may have these but I judge his attention is firmly fixed elsewhere at the moment. Best not to disturb whatever he's doing, I only hope he's safe. The idea that an army of gun-toting thugs is needed to protect him puts me in a sad, doomed mood. My life is picking up again, thanks to Gary and his job; this situation can't be anything other than a turn for the worse.

There could quite easily be no office, no job and even no Gary come morning. Then I face the prospect of a return to unwaged squalor, shared toilet and cockroach-infested lodgings.

Something wakes me from a nightmare where a sinister man is grimacing with the effort it's taking to expel dribbles of semen which trickle down my cheek. I have a rock of tension in my stomach and flaring pain between my legs. A deep sadness chokes the breath from me. I'm certain that my life will become even more painful and distressing.

My phone says seven eighteen, and one message. Perhaps the short vibration woke me up, in which case I'm grateful to be spared further abuse. The text is from Gary, it says 'stay off tdy don com wrk' and fills me with alarm. He answers my call immediately.

'Are you okay, Gary?' I ask.

'Yes, fine.'

'Is the office okay, what happened?'

'All fine.'

'Isn't it safe to come to work?'

He hesitates before he answers.

'Oh, not a problem, it's just that I don't want you there, I don't think we can work together any more.'

He hangs up leaving me frightened and confused in equal measure.

35

The frustration is driving me crazy. Sitting here in the apartment, warm, well-fed, clean and safe, should be a welcome respite from my busy and often uncomfortable life of recent times. Instead it feels worse than prison. Three days have gone by since I last spoke to Gary when he told me we could no longer work together, whatever he meant by that. Every attempt to call him fails. My messages are ignored. It's as if I am abandoned and forgotten. Today is Friday and despite his clear instructions to the contrary, I've decided to go to the office and hope to confront him there.

Toby is mine this weekend. I need the loan of a car from Gary, otherwise I'm back to train ride, bus ride and two hours in the front room being supervised and feeling unworthy. My frustration and fear is turning to anger and resentment. How can Gary treat me so inhumanely now? To go from gentle kindness to complete rejection is surely a cruelty beyond forgiveness.

My long walk in the chilly dampness is unrewarded. The yard is replete with piles of rubble, there are bricks and earth and window frames and glass and plastic everywhere. Entry to the office is blocked by unstable mountains, dumped indiscriminately. Nobody is about. The gate is closed and padlocked, as if to protect the deposits inside against theft. Now I wish I'd spent my money on a taxi, I could have saved myself the twenty minute walk through the Salford wastelands and be whisked home now in speed and comfort. Instead I trudge away, empty of ideas.

My phone complains that it's low on battery, as if to prompt me to try one more time. A speck of hope remains on the surface of my despair. Stopping, pressing the buttons carefully, lifting the phone to my ear. Ringing, ringing, no answer, no answer. Yes an answer, only the voicemail. A disembodied female inviting me to leave a message then wasting my time with complex keyboard instructions in case I want to edit or repeat the things I have to say. There is no 'scream' button, no mechanism for reaching down the phone and grabbing Gary's attention. Nothing. Only despair and silence now.

*

Tim is scornful when I tell him I can't take Toby this weekend. Any thoughts of asking him to bring my son to me and pick him up again are dispelled by his unsympathetic coldness. Better to give up my child's company than beg favours from that man and give him the pleasure of seeing my discomfort when he rejects me. There are sores remaining from our relationship that Tim is intent on keeping open and suppurating.

*

Every night the dream returns, the same man, the same grimace, the same degrading and disgusting finale. Sometimes, there are other men, also snarling and sneering. Every time the knot in my guts gets tighter and the pain in my groin stings. When I awake I feel sick and ashamed.

*

The television shows scenes of a major accident on the M6. There are lorries and cars in twisted heaps. Flashing lights and cones across the carriageway prevent progress, a view from a helicopter shows mile after mile of stationary traffic. The newsreader expects the northbound carriageway to be closed for some time and advises travellers to take an alternative route. My efforts to feel grateful to be alive and to rejoice that I've not been crushed to death in one of those mangled vehicles fail completely. The incident has no interest for me until I hear that thousands of Arsenal supporters may be unable to get to the match with United. An electric energy snaps me out of my torpor. I stand up and dress quickly. This time I will take a taxi.

36

Gary is standing in the same place as he was the first time I sought him in desperation. Although I felt my misery was complete then, I believe this time it's even worse. My spirits are even lower, my need is even greater. Last time I had nothing and expected nothing, now I feel deprived of something very valuable. The car park remains empty, apart from a handful of cars, the lights are on in some of the office windows, the football parking has not begun in earnest. Gary watches me approach, shoulders hunched, hands in coat pockets, face blank.

'Gary,' I begin.

'I can't talk now, things to do, I'll call you tomorrow.' He interrupts me and turns dismissively. A twinge of fear and disappointment knocks me off balance and I stand transfixed as he shuffles away.

'Wait.' I summon up enough anger to shout. 'You owe me an explanation, I've been chasing you around for days, we have to talk *now*!' My lips are quivering and I want to run over and grab hold of him, make him listen.

'It's no use.' He turns to face me. 'You've not been straight with me. I can't be having that.'

His eyes glint strangely yellow in the street lights. My bladder spasms, a sharp pain slices my abdomen.

'What's the matter?' Gary asks.

'I need to pee,' I explain, doubled up and fighting the pain.

He leads me across the car park to the corner made by the tall L shaped office block. After sifting through an enormous bunch of keys he bends down and releases the lock in a glass door.

'Over there on the right.' He points to the Ladies sign beside the staircase and I half run, half stagger into darkness. The light switch is elusive. My gropings fail to locate it and I re-emerge, embarrassed, into the vestibule. I prop the door half open with my foot to let in some light from the hallway and find the switch.

Despite the urgent feeling, despite the cramping pain, despite the bloody inconvenience, it takes several minutes before the stinging trickle begins. My frustration overwhelms me, tears are welling up at the realisation that Gary doesn't trust me and I'm losing the one chance I have of changing this because of my faulty bladder.

As the seconds tick relentlessly by and I sit powerless, I convince myself that Gary will have disappeared by the time I finish in here. This thought brings panic which stops me from peeing.

My body relaxes slightly at the sight of him sitting in the foyer, still waiting for me. I realise he needs to lock the door and this forces him to hang around. Now I have my opportunity to get to the bottom of his antagonism.

He stands up immediately I sit beside him.

'Sit down, Gary,' I order.

'I'm busy,' he complains, but sits back down on the plush visitor's chair.

'Five minutes, that's all, we need to sort out what's going on. I need to know what's caused you to stop trusting me.'

He looks down at his toes. 'As I said, you've not been straight with me. I can't have that, that's all there is to it.'

'But I have been straight with you, Gary, what makes you say I haven't?'

He sits silently for a few moments, then shifts uncomfortably as he speaks.

'You should have told me, I can't be getting that sort of information from someone else.'

'Told you what?'

'About you being in with a bad lot, dealing with very dangerous people. I can't afford any trouble, not from them sorts of people.'

'What bad people? It's not true. Who told you this?'

'Never you mind who, it comes from a reliable source.'

'One of your mates, I suppose.'

'Not really.' He looks around the empty building as if expecting some sudden intervention. 'It was the man, Popov, the one who supplied some guys to protect the yard. It was him that recognised you.'

My mind flashes back to the eerie atmosphere and the look in that man's eyes as he sat in Gary's car.

'I saw him in your car. I didn't recognise him, I've never seen him before.'

'But he knew you. He warned me off, said you were in with a bad crowd.'

'Popov? Who is this Popov anyway, why should he say such a thing?' I want to ask why Gary should immediately think the worst of me, but I stop short of this.

'That's not his real name. It's what we call him – you know – if you want someone taken out, popped off – see.'

There is a cold reality to his words that brings everything into sharp focus. The phrase it takes one to know one runs through my head.

'He's wrong, he's mistaken. If he's seen me before I have no idea when or where. I am not in with anybody. Not connected with bad people, not trying to hide anything from you, Gary. We work well together. Don't let a bit of hearsay come between us.'

My own words have a strengthening effect on me, I feel more resolution and energy than I have for days.

'He says he knows you from a couple of years ago, you were involved in something heavy and the people that hired him were pretty scary, even to a man like him. That's all he said, but like I say I can't afford any trouble, especially from the likes of them.'

'Two years ago I was an accountant, going about my business, involved with normal companies and ordinary people. Then I got sent to prison because the police found some money in my house and I was stupid enough to tell them where it came from. That's it – that's the whole of it. No gangs involved, no mafia, no dangerous criminals. A sordid little crime, that's all.'

'There must be more to it.' Gary's face is softer. He seems more receptive, less adamant. 'If Popov was involved it's likely there was someone killed.'

The words hang in the air and I receive a blast of fear from inside me. Martin's face, smiling, kind and loving comes into my mind. The fear is replaced by sadness, then by anger.

'Martin.' I manage to speak his name. 'He died. There was some mystery about his death, but they said it was a heart attack.' This time I look down at my feet. 'We were having an affair, they found him dead in the flat we were using but I knew he hadn't died there, someone had moved his body. I didn't have the courage to tell anyone.'

'Okay, sounds like that might be it, that could be the job he's thinking about, no doubt he'd have seen you with the target if that's the case.'

'So now you know. What about us? Can't we carry on as normal? I have a lot to do, you need a lot of work on the business if you're going to avoid big problems. Come on, Gary, look at me, do I look like a gangster? Have I ever given you reason to doubt my word?'

'Fair enough.' Gary's face crinkles in a half smile. 'I suppose I was being too careful. That guy Popov is big trouble, I wouldn't want him on my case. Maybe he's worried you might finger him, that you saw him then. Okay, let's put that behind us. I'm all right with that if you are.'

My relief is so intense I can hardly prevent myself from reaching out and hugging the big lump. When we walk outside there's a steady stream of cars disgorging men full of excited energy and alcohol-fuelled enthusiasm.

Gary rings his mate to organise a car for me to collect Toby. I listen to the conversation.

'Something nice, with a child seat. No not far, twenty miles or so, that's all. What have you got in?' He nods and looks at me. 'Yes, she'll be fine with that, nice one.' Gary ends the call and looks at his watch.

'Hang on here,' he instructs, 'my mate's bringing you a car.' He winks. 'I think you'll like it.'

'Your mate?' I ask. 'Is he a car dealer?'

Gary smiles. 'No, not exactly. He does the parking at Manchester Airport.'

37

Gary's peace offering is a yellow Porsche, complete with carbon fibre child racing seat in the back. Alison looks like she is licking piss off a nettle as she stands gripping Tim's arm tightly in case he abandons her for a woman in a shiny car. Toby shows no signs of excitement at the vehicle, only a rewarding beam and a big hug for his mother. I breathe deeply for the first time in days.

As we whoosh down the motorway, my little boy's chatter enchants me. All his news since the last time we met has been stored up to burst out in a jumble of thoughts and ideas. Although I can make little sense of most of it, I feel delighted at the sound and energy. My longing grows for the opportunity for us to be together on a permanent basis, so that I can understand the words and references he's making, so that I can be the origin of his experiences rather than the second-hand recipient.

At the flat he leaps upon his Fisher Price garage with the air of a business proprietor anxious to re-establish trade after a holiday. Cars are carefully crammed into the lift, then released down the ramp to speed off into the distance. My apartment is alive again, occupied, animated by childish noise. Suddenly it's a home and not just a borrowed place to sleep in. Most importantly, Toby settles here instantly. He feels the homeliness as well. My heart and eyes fill up at the sight.

The weekend with Toby has left me feeling even more determined to make a home for us as I make my way to work. Because I now know its origins I'm doubly scared about damaging the Porsche as I manoeuvre through the thick Manchester traffic. Buses make collision paths towards me as if instinctively knowing I will back off and allow their brutal passage. Other cars herd me into a lane I don't want, forcing me to make double circles at the big roundabout then hold my breath as I creep apologetically onto the exit for Trafford Park. A new day at work is ahead, but this time in a new place. Gary tells me he has abandoned the yard; 'let a mate have it for a bit' were his exact words. After the frightening display of armed men, I wonder if the opposing threat is too much even for Popov and his Eastern European army.

This is another question I have for Gary which I might never feel sufficiently comfortable to ask. I park the Boxster and, as instructed, hand the keys to a man who emerges from a van marked 'Valet Parking', then watch as he carefully covers the seat with plastic before clambering in and driving away. The van follows behind at an unsafe distance. There is a great deal of relief for me in its departure, more than I realised there would be. I appear to have been obsessed with anxiety for the wellbeing of that bloody Porsche and I'm disappointed that I have room in my life for such relatively trivial worries.

Carrie greets me with a slightly puzzled smile. This time there is more justification as she must have spent a few days here alone and become used to it. The new offices are on the ground floor of the large block where Gary took me to pee. Carrie has a small reception desk in the foyer while I occupy an office behind her to the right.

The seven battered, rusting, unmatched filing cabinets have survived what must have been a rough trip from Salford, as have my old desk and threadbare chair. I arrange myself so that I can see Carrie through the open door, and even call cheerful encouragement to her if I can be bothered. Gary visits mid-morning and sits on the edge of my desk.

I tell him, 'These bills came to the flat,' and pull out a sheaf of envelopes which he quickly passes to Carrie for her to lose.

'Don't bother about them, I'll sort them out. Anyway,' Gary continues, 'I've got a new place for you. It's nearer, you'll like it.'

It's hard to stop myself feeling upset and resentful. Despite Gary's obvious good intentions and generosity, the flat I have is perfect. Toby is familiar and comfortable with it, why change? Again I don't want to ask this question, suspecting there

137

may be an arrangement even more informal than that involving the cars he loans me.

'I've sorted a van to get your stuff this afternoon, I'll take you over there and show it you.' He points. 'It's only a cock-stride across the bridge, near the Lowry. It's sound, you'll like it. Anyway, what was it you wanted to ask me?'

My job is to formalise the informal, to account for the unaccountable and to regularise the irregular. It's a long process, made more difficult by the evasive nature of Gary's answers to even the most basic questions.

'How much do you charge for this job?' My question ought to be answered succinctly and numerically. Instead, Gary wrinkles his brow, scratches his head, details the family history of the client, explains all his other businesses, tells me about things they've done together in the past, and becomes puzzled by my frustration and dissatisfaction.

It's not that simple is his mantra. In this respect he is absolutely one hundred per cent correct.

I would rather question him about Popov, about his part in Martin's death, but I have a feeling that bringing these matters back into his consciousness would have only one result. The prospect of being cast adrift again daunts me. Time is needed for me to gather strength, accumulate funds and find my independent streak again. Only then will I be able to face the dangers my enquiries will bring.

38

'My mate is owed money, I want you to work your magic.' Gary hands me a thick sheaf of papers. 'Here you are, all the details and invoices and such are here.'

'Magic?' I ask.

'Yes, you know…what you did last time with that Usman fellow.'

'It might not work again, I might not be able to help.'

'Oh, you'll think of something.' Gary beams with confidence. 'Anyway, I told my mate you're the best, leave it to Jenny I said, she'll have your cash as quick as Flash Harry.'

His confidence is touching but I feel too weighed down by grinding detail to be buoyed by it.

'Make this your number one priority,' Gary orders. 'If you need any help just tell me what you want and I'll make sure you get it.'

A vision of Popov and his armed gang dragging out the reluctant debtor with a bag over his head fills my thoughts. A pang of worry accompanies the knowledge that if it were that simple a job it wouldn't need me.

After Gary breezes off about his business I settle down with the file. Carrie, bless her, brings me a cup of tea, probably out of boredom and possibly to open up the opportunity of a gossip. I sip the weak, sugary liquid gratefully, it reminds me of everything about Gary and his staff, everything comforting and everything irritating. I've lost count of the number of times I've told her strong, not much milk and definitely no sugar.

My original inkling that maybe Carrie was Gary's bit on the side proved wide of the mark. Without my asking, the story emerges that she's the daughter of a mate of his who was killed while trying to free a prop shaft on a piece of soil screening equipment. His success led to him being caught up in the machinery and torn to pieces, at least that's how his daughter describes it. She goes on to reveal that she lives with Gary and his family since her mother was sent to prison. The man her mother murdered was living with them at the time and the look on Carrie's face when she talks about him leaves me in no doubt what he was forcing her to endure at the age of twelve. As far as I'm concerned they should have given her mother a medal for what she rid the world of.

Anyway, Gary remains high in my estimation. I'm glad that his relationship with Carrie is both generous and benign. There is also the comforting thought that her lack of competence is not my problem and that Gary expects as little from her as she delivers. She's telling me about her latest boyfriend and I'm tempted to give her my opinion on him. Based on the brief description she gives, I'm convinced he's a thug and likely to do her serious harm. Obviously, she doesn't share my judgement and seems delighted and amused by the hooliganism she's describing. I remain silent, comforting myself with the thought that Gary will no doubt deal appropriately with him if there becomes a need to.

While Carrie is distracted by her phone, I begin to look through the documents Gary has given me. The sums are significantly large, running into tens of thousands of pounds. After a quick tally I reach a total of £256,722.36, excluding VAT. The invoices in dispute are from an earth works contractor, O'Shaughnessy, to a housing company, Monton Homes. The bills relate to a large housing development in North Manchester where O'Shaughnessy was contracted to prepare the ground that the homes were to be built on. It seems that the earth they used was unsatisfactory and had to be replaced by another contractor. At first sight I can't see how O'Shaughnessy can expect to be paid, having made a right mess of the job in the first place. Flicking through the rest of the correspondence I'm tempted to tell Gary to forget it, that his mate is lucky not to be sued.

39

Michael O'Shaughnessy is a short, balding man with a voice that's too high-pitched to emanate from such a portly frame. The words he utters are simple and clear but are made almost completely incomprehensible by the way he speaks them. I've been listening to his account for half an hour now, but feel little wiser.

Gary, bless him, appears to understand every syllable and, as if seeing my bewilderment, is attempting to provide a partial translation.

'So there then, it's them what said what stuff to carry and I did.' O'Shaughnessy pauses as if to recover from his own verbal stumbling.

'The whole contract was directed by Monton Homes, all Michael did was to pick up earth at one place and deliver it to the housing site. He wasn't responsible for the quality of the material.'

Gary's version has a clarity which I'd not associated with him before now. Thanks to Gary's interventions I'm beginning to get the picture.

'Let me see if I understand what happened,' I intervene. O'Shaughnessy shows no sign of wanting to end his garbled account and I'm in danger of becoming mesmerised by my efforts to follow his speech. 'Your lorries removed contaminated soil from the housing development site and then replaced it with clean material.'

'Yes, that's right so we did and it was...'

'Okay,' I continue, 'but the clean material wasn't clean and this had to be removed as well?'

'Absolutely, we did the job twice...well nearly three times it was. All the cost was on us, two lots of tipping costs, the last stuff was bad gear, had to go to a proper tip.'

'Yes, I see. There're some invoices for disposal in the file of papers that you sent me. Is it normal for you to pay for all the tipping?'

O'Shaughnessy looks at Gary in a conspiratorial way.

'Oh yes, that's it, we give a load price to the customer, we sort out the tipping, that's what we do, it's part of it, so to speak...'

'Tell me about Monton Homes, it was their site you got the earth from, wasn't it?'

'Ah yes they were building houses where there used to be a big factory, that's why the contamination and such like. Needed clearing up... We did a great job, so we did. Clean as a whistle when we finished hauling out, all the tests, everything tidy.'

'Then you were told to bring in earth to raise the levels so the houses could be built?'

'That's right it needed a lot of muck so it did, ten thousand cube, more even, lots of muck.'

'And then they built the houses?'

'Yes, well...most of them by the time the testing and such was finished. It was the gardens, they were no good, dangerous, might cause sickness and things.'

'I see here that the Environmental Health insisted all the garden areas were cleaned up by removing the soil you had put there.' I wave a letter at him then push it towards him. He looks down and nods. 'Okay.' I am at my most business-like now and enjoying it. 'So the problem lies in the stuff you brought in and you're saying this came from the other Monton Homes site?'

'Yes, from Oldham. They're building some new offices there, so they are.'

'Who was it that told you where to get the soil?'

'That would be Jackson. He works for Monton Homes. It was him who arranged everything. We were loaded from a stockpile, we didn't worry about anything, it wasn't our stuff this time. Normally we would find the clean stuff ourselves, and it would have analysis and tests and paperwork, this had nothing. It was Jackson that decided it was OK, it was him who organised the stuff to be put on the housing site.'

'And now they refuse to pay you?'

'Yes, that's right and we aren't doing any more work for them, they're big customers of ours, it's a big problem.'

Gary leans forward. 'Michael is having to lay off drivers, he's short of work as well as short of cash.'

O'Shaughnessy nods in appreciation of Gary's summary.

'Can you help?' O'Shaughnessy asks.

'Of course she can!' Gary confirms before I can speak. 'She'll get your money, just you wait and see, I guarantee it.'

All I can do is mutter, 'Leave it with me,' as Gary shows a smiling, hopeful O'Shaughnessy out of the building.

40

Gary's new legitimate business is now set up and trading nicely. Although I'm doing what's best for him and what he says he wants me to do I still feel very insecure. The first VAT bill is due and it's a hefty amount. Added to this, Gary is having to fund much increased PAYE and National Insurance costs. He may just decide I'm not worth keeping on. The cost of legitimising his business is high and hard to justify without any threat of enforcement action from Her Majesty's Revenue & Customs. One or two of his mates have been in trouble but this might not be enough incentive for Gary to continue with the expensive option I represent.

All I can do is try to sort out the O'Shaughnessy problem and fulfil Gary's promises. Unfortunately this is not going well. If truth be told, it is not going at all. Every enquiry, every stratagem has met with a blank. This is my one remaining ploy and I don't actually understand how it might work. All I know is that O'Shaughnessy's money might be the thing that keeps me in a job and a home.

Toby is as unimpressed by the new flat as I am. Given the choice, I would have stayed in Salford. There is no choice though, considering whatever arrangement Gary has for my apartment is likely to be as informal as the other deals he does. There's some doubt in my mind as to whether the actual owner knew I was living in the previous flat. My best guess is that Gary provides security for it while the owner is away and would call me the night watchman if ever questioned. The flat on the docks is new, never been occupied and consequently unfurnished apart from poor quality grey carpets which don't allow Toby's cars to run freely. He gets so frustrated as they pile up in a heap at the foot of his garage ramp. The old flat had smooth wooden floors on which every car was a racer, running fast and free until it crashed into a wall or table leg with a satisfying smack.

I spent the first two weeks assembling Ikea furniture to provide some sparse comfort. Although Gary lent me Ian and the van to visit the shop he assumes I'm capable of putting it together myself. Still, beggars can't be choosers, I haven't enough money to rent somewhere even this nice.

*

The industrial estate at Walton Summit proves more complex than it appears on the map, with featureless roundabouts lacking any direction signs adding to my confusion. All I have is an address and the hastily fingered route I plotted in Gary's offices. However straightforward it appeared then, finding the Environment Agency is proving to be a frustrating business. I'm criss-crossing beneath the marching pylons festooned by thick cable that overwhelm the entire area. I decide the place is either underground or non-existent and follow a tiny sign for the M6.

As I turn I catch a glimpse of a building on the right with the logo I'm searching for. This is round, green and has a white stick figure seemingly fleeing from a nuclear explosion. I'm almost sure that this isn't what the designer had in mind, nor is it what the Environment Agency meant to choose to represent them.

The car park is crammed full to overflowing, all the marked spaces are taken and cars are parked on kerbs, on grassy verges, anywhere they can be abandoned without completely blocking up the access. I tour around the office main entrance where I find two possibilities. There is a single disabled space unoccupied. My alternative is an area hatched in yellow directly outside the doors which is clearly marked 'No Parking Deliveries Only'. The disabled space is beckoning to me when I hear an engine start up and decide to investigate.

The small Toyota contains a weary looking man with sandy hair, whom I greet as I pull alongside.

'Have you left a space?' I smile my most friendly smile as I lean out of my window. As he stops to answer, I read the badge on his green fleece: 'John Johnson'.

'At the back, over there.' He indicates with his thumb.

'Thanks, how long will you be?'

He looks puzzled but answers nevertheless. 'Only an hour. This place is a nightmare for parking.'

I squeeze into the Yaris-sized space with some careful to-ing and fro-ing. Inside, the reception area is cramped and already has five out of six visitors' chairs occupied. This is where I must prepare to play it by ear, but my car park encounter has given me an idea.

'I'm here to see John Johnson,' I announce. After two telephone calls and a lengthy consultation with her computer she replies, 'He's not in, can anyone else help?'

I look her in the eye and whisper softly, 'No, it's personal, I need to see John. He said he'd be here this afternoon. I might be a bit early.'

The receptionist softens slightly at this and invites me to take the remaining seat. From its relative comfort I watch her struggle to cope with the rising levels of exasperation around her. She looks experienced and her manner remains friendly, caring and anxious, a vestige perhaps from a previous profession where people actually mattered.

Taking my cue from the angry man on my right who seems about to explode into violence, I gently approach the poor, besieged, possible ex-nurse and ask for the toilet. She points to the door on her right and has to press a release under her desk to admit my entry. Once inside, I have access to the staircase as well as the Ladies. As I climb the stairs glancing quickly to make sure the kind receptionist is not watching me I am propelled by desperation. It would be nice to have a clear idea of what I should do now, a plan, something to work to, but desperation is all I have.

At the top of the stairs my progress is halted by a closed door with a keypad, presumably to keep out people who can't find the toilet. Two men in deep conversation start to climb the stairs behind me. I scamper down towards them and smile as I pass. I shout 'bugger' as I reach the bottom, trying to appear as if I forgot something important, and turn around. Adjusting my speed carefully I run back up the stairs in time to catch the door before it closes, smiling at the men as I push past them into a large open plan office.

Some people look up as I walk past but none of them are at all interested in me. A thick-set woman with curly grey hair comes out of an office in the far corner and walks towards me. As we pass I detect the stench of tobacco and guess that she might be heading outside for a smoke. I watch her exit the way I came in then walk quickly into her office and close the door behind me.

In front of the small beech veneer desk is a round table with four chairs. Next to the table four coat hooks are fixed to the wall. Hanging from these are a brown corduroy coat, a high visibility jacket of the type used by Gary's parking team and a green fleece with an Environment Agency logo on the breast. The fleece fits me, it would fit perfectly if I were taller and fatter, but it will do. Leaving it on, I open the top right hand desk drawer. Here I find, among a collection of pens and salary slips, three boxes of business cards from which I extract a few. I also take a badge bearing the name Annie Osborne and the now familiar Environment Agency logo.

A sudden panic grips me as I leave with the stolen items. I feel sure I will be apprehended, that the police will be called and they will put me back in prison to be beaten and strangled by psychopaths. My legs become weak, my knees are buckling under the strain of keeping me upright.

Pausing at the office door, I suddenly become aware of the baleful glare of a dozen pairs of unfriendly eyes. The temptation to drop everything and run, to try to reach the exit before they catch me, is hard to resist. The prospect of doing anything other than run is daunting. I need something to help dispel my air of panic and guilt. I need to look like I have a purpose other than robbery.

The door leading to the stairwell is the whole length of the building away. Half way stands a large photocopier. Quickly I grab a sheaf of papers from Annie's desk and brandish these protectively as I walk steadily towards the exit. At the photocopier I load the paperwork and press the buttons which give me the most satisfaction. Twenty copies of each on A3 paper feel good. The big green start button begins the noisy

147

process but this ends almost as soon as it begins. The feeding mechanism does not handle stapled items well at all. The whole sheaf bunches up and crinkles to a messy halt. I let out a genuine moan of frustration and disappointment as I stand transfixed, unable to move, consumed by a certainty that now I'm bound to be caught. My thoughts turn to the disappointment that Toby will feel and that stinging loss bites through my stomach. My bladder tightens and drills pain into my lower body making me double up and whimper.

A male hand steadies me. I turn to look into his eyes. They are sunk deep into a round hairless head that merges into a ridiculously rotund body by way of a thick neck wrinkled by fatty waves. There is no malice in his gaze, only mild concern and a hint of amusement. He begins to pull shards of paper from the feed mechanism. His only introductory words are 'Bloody useless.' I have no idea if he means me or the machine.

'I need the loo.' My reply is entirely truthful and I stagger off leaving him with the paper jam.

Downstairs the urge is so insistent that I almost take refuge in the toilet I'm supposed to have been in all along. The prospect of sitting there in jeopardy, waiting for the bogus photocopying to give me away, anticipating the security guards outside the door, is not one I can entertain. Given the choice I would rather pee in my pants while fleeing. In the event it doesn't come to that. I manage to hold it in as I move briskly past the besieged receptionist and into the car park. Once in my car, engine running, gear engaged, the urgent feeling subsides and I make my escape.

41

The road through the half-built housing estate is slicked with brown mud which is resisting removal by the persistent rain. As I approach the site office, the terrain changes from muddy road to a road of mud. My car skitters and slides as I bump it through the giant puddles. Gary offered me a giant four wheeled drive vehicle for today's visit, even brought it round to the offices. The mission I'm on is stressful and dangerous enough without the added prospect of having to blunder my way around in an enormous pick-up truck that is almost certainly stolen, despite Gary's protestation to the contrary.

'I'm supposed to be an Environment Agency officer, my car is much more in keeping.'

'It might be a bit muddy, I thought this would be better,' was all Gary could reply as we stood dwarfed by the enormous beast.

My Corsa is old, battered and not as red as it ought to be. The paintwork might have lost what little shine it had, but it is mine, paid for by me, taxed and insured by me and with a valid MOT certificate. Gary's discomfiture at all this unnecessary paperwork is nothing compared with his shocked disposition when I refuse any more of his airport cars on the basis that they are stolen. 'Borrowed' is the word he prefers, but stolen is how their owners would see it. My newly acquired moral stance only serves to put even more pressure on me to keep delivering what Gary wants.

My doughty car brings me safely to an island of rough stone where a dozen vehicles are parked above the sea of mud. Two grey portacabins sit proudly in supervision of the brown morass all around them. Hopping out of my seat, trying to avoid wetting my feet in a puddle, I'm startled by a huge yellow dump truck, even taller than the portable offices I am cowering by. My discomposure is multiplied by the name on its side. A brief glimpse of the name is all I need for my legs to turn to jelly and be gripped by an almost irresistible desire to flee. 'O'Brian' is written in big brown lettering underneath the familiar OB logo. Raising my eyes to rediscover the landscape beyond the cabins I recognise three large bulldozers, all liveried with the OB sign.

It's not fair, I have enough on my plate without being surrounded by Tim's workforce. I am pretending to be an Environment Agency officer but now have the prospect of someone recognising me as Tim's ex-wife, or ex-convict ex-wife to be exact. It was a long and difficult job to obtain an audience with the busy and self-important Mr Jackson and I'm reluctant to cut and run, especially with so much at stake. Even the sight of Tim's battered Ford Mondeo parked two spaces away from my Corsa fails to deter me. It does nothing to improve my nerves though.

'Hello, I'm Annie Osborne.' I press the business card into Jackson's hand and sit opposite him. He is a short man, hardly taller than me, and exhibits a sallow unhealthy complexion. His mouth curls in a permanent sarcastic smile. There is nothing about him to like; this suits me fine.

My nervousness threatens to betray me. It's hard to think clearly, to adopt the Annie persona, to act as if I don't care. *It's only a job, it's only a job*. This mantra has a grain of truth, enough to stop most of the trembling. Wriggling my toes seems to help, even if it fails to ease the discomfort of my tight shoes.

Despite the hours I've spent in preparation, the legislation I'm supposed to be using remains largely impenetrable. There seems to be an awful lot of rules and regulations, advice, best practice notes and statutory guidance involved when dealing with waste of any description. The man sitting sneering at me is experienced in the practicalities of it all, deals with the Environment Agency on a regular basis and might even have come across the real Annie Osborne.

At this thought, my blood runs a little cooler despite the intense heat inside the protective green fleece I stole from Annie. It's my main weapon, my camouflage, my impenetrable armour. It makes me who I say I am. I can't afford to remove it, however hot it gets in here.

O'Shaughnessy has been next to useless. He did make great play out of having all the paperwork as he called it. Transfer notes was another epithet he applied and his assurances about his possession of these gave me the idea that set me on the path to becoming an Environment Agency employee.

I explain in what I fear are quivering, nervous shrieks how the Agency is concerned regarding the whereabouts of dangerous polluting and poisonous soils that were removed from his Oldham site by O'Shaughnessy. The look on Jackson's face tells me that it's not going well. I can hear myself gabbling too many words. I am trying to be convincing but failing even to convince myself. He isn't taking any of this with the seriousness I need. The growing compulsion to leave, to get the hell out before I'm completely unmasked becomes almost irresistible.

My mouth closes at last, the gibbering ceases and I allow the silence to build. His eyes dart around the office, shifting and dancing, staying loose and refusing to be transfixed by my stare. It is my best stare, my strongest, most powerful one and eventually pins him to me. He has to look back at me and I have to show him I am real.

'What has this got to do with us?' He eventually breaks the silence and looks away. My silence continues. 'Everything we do is documented, the Agency already has all the reports,' he tries again but I am steadfast. 'Look, the consultants have signed off the site, it's clear, all the contamination has been removed in accordance with the method statement. You have all the reports already.'

Much of what he's saying is meaningless but the way he's speaking is changing. The cockiness is disappearing. He's getting increasingly agitated now that I have shut my mouth.

I wait until his protestations diminish and then, mindful that Tim could make an appearance at any moment, try to press home my attack while I still have the courage. All I have to arm me are a few bits of information gleaned over hours of talking to O'Shaughnessy.

'Let me get this straight.' I have to get this right otherwise I'm in danger of revealing the ignorant impostor I am. 'Monton Homes own the site where the soil was dug up, and taken to Eccles where you were building houses?'

'Yes, we're a major land owner and have an exemplary track record in cleaning up contaminated sites.'

'So the site was contaminated?'

'Yes. It used to be a factory. Our consultants wrote procedures for the clean-up. You agreed to them, everything was agreed by the Environment Agency, by Darren Gilbert.' Jackson looks at me as if I should be familiar with the name. I feel myself floundering again but before I can speak and reveal my ignorance he helps me out.

'Your boss.'

His pomposity sends me a lifeline and I breathe deeply with relief.

'Everything went through Darren, he's happy, he's got no problems with any issues at all,' Jackson continues.

At least I now know who he's talking about but I've no inkling of how significant this information might be.

'In fact, I rang him earlier. He was surprised to hear you were coming to see me, very surprised.'

My blood freezes in my veins, this is bad. Just how bad remains to be seen. All I need now is for Tim to poke his head around the door. It feels like my chair is absorbing my body, I'm slipping into oblivion. My thoughts veer wildly towards the possibility that my cover is already in shreds. Even if I get out of here without being arrested, it's all too clear that nothing I say is going to help matters. Jackson is not going to take seriously any threats I make on behalf of the Environment Agency. All he has to do is ring up his pal Darren and his mind will be put at rest.

'Of course he didn't know I was coming.' I listen to myself speaking clearly and authoritatively. 'Mr Gilbert is under investigation himself. These are serious allegations, very serious. Contaminated soils were taken from your site to a housing development. People could have been poisoned. I had hoped you might have been more cooperative today but under the circumstances I've no alternative but to arrange for a formal PACE interview.' I stand up and before I turn to leave have the satisfaction of seeing Jackson's worried look. All his cockiness has evaporated.

Outside my close calls continue when I see that Tim's car has gone. A few moments earlier and we might have met and he would have discovered his former wife had not only joined the Environment Agency but also changed her name to Annie Osborne.

42

'Listen carefully. I've been to a lot of trouble to get this far, a lot of trouble. I've put in a lot of hard work and plenty of personal risk.'

I'm looking at O'Shaughnessy and O'Shaughnessy's son whose name astonishingly is Sean. Gary is sitting beside me, all beaming pride at what I am about to say.

'I've just left Jackson and I think he'll call you very soon. As far as I'm aware the Environment Agency has no interest in the job you did for Monton Homes. They've raised no concerns. All the reports were accepted and both sites were given a clean bill of health. I am hoping, though, that Jackson thinks he's in trouble. I may have convinced him that he is going to end up in court and that the Monton Homes name will be dragged through the mud unless he can come up with some documentation that gets him off the hook. That's the documentation that you have, the transfer notes.'

Gary smirks a little more but I remain unconvinced by the blank faces in front of me. I need them to understand what's going on if they're to have a chance of getting their money back. Even the slightest confusion on their part might give the game away. Unhappily, the men sitting opposite seem more than slightly confused already.

'Jackson will need the transfer notes to show the contaminated soil went safely to the landfill site, that's the only thing that will get the Agency off his back, or so he believes.'

'I thought the Agency were happy.' O'Shaughnessy senior confirms my worst fears.

'They are,' I say, in what I trust is a patient voice, 'but I pretended to be an Environment Agency officer and told him otherwise. Unless he gets the tipping tickets you have he thinks he has a big problem. I'm hoping that you're his only way out of this, that way he'll have to settle up with you.'

'How did you do that?' O'Shaughnessy the younger appears slightly less bewildered than his father.

'I dressed up, you know, disguised myself, then I went to his office.'

Eyebrows are raised in tandem at my tale of bravado. A sudden thought occurs to me and I'm prompted to ask,

'These transfer notes, the ones for the contaminated soil, all properly signed up by the landfill site. You do still have them, don't you?'

The two men look at each other. 'We'd have to look, they'll be somewhere, we just need to see where.'

This answer does not fill me with confidence. 'Look for them, find them, if you can't find them, somehow make some more. Those tickets are worth a lot of money.'

From the look on their faces, I get the feeling that they'll have a really good look for them when they get back.

'Now, when Jackson gets in touch you need to tell him that you have the tickets and you'll send them to him once he's paid. Do you understand?'

'Perfectly, he gets the tickets when he pays the bill.' O'Shaughnessy senior responds.

'Good, now this is very important. If Jackson asks you about the Environment Agency tell him the truth. Tell him that nobody from the Agency has been in touch.'

'Shouldn't we lie a little though, tell him there's big trouble, that we'll all go to jail and such like?'

I shake my head vehemently and am still shaking it long after they have gone.

43

Carrie is telling me a long involved story about a man who was unhappy with his marriage and had his wife put in prison. She arrived this morning wearing a bright blue top and a yellow skirt. This combination, together with her shiny black hair, has me thinking that an ugly old crone with a poisoned apple is heading her way. When I ask her how her seven tiny housemates are she wrinkles her face and laughs in a way that tells me she's missing the joke entirely.

I'm only half listening. Nothing has happened that suggests my elaborate scheme to get O'Shaughnessy's money is working. Jackson hasn't been in touch with him and I'm beginning to despair. All my effort and risk seems to have been in vain. Worse, I feel Gary will suffer a big loss of face in front of his mates. My customary feelings of anxiety become even more intense at this thought. I need to keep Gary happy.

'Apparently he hid some money at home and told the police it belonged to his wife,' Carrie is explaining. A sudden thrill of recognition spears through my chest and she has my full attention. 'The police came to the house and took her off to prison.'
It sounds like my situation but expressed in terms simple enough for Carrie to repeat.

'When was this, do you know?'

'Oh,' Carrie replies, 'I don't know, years ago maybe.'

'And who was this scheming man, what was his name?'

'Oh, I don't know his name, he was an ordinary guy, nothing special, not a clever lawyer or someone like that. He drove a bulldozer.'

It's me she's talking about, it has to be. 'So a dozer driver decides to get rid of his wife by planting illegal money at his own home?'

'Yes,' Carrie's face twists, 'that's what he said.'

'Who said?' Her features contort further as she thinks hard, I get the impression that she's been told not to reveal her source and I have put her in some difficulty.

'Who said, who told you the story?'

Carrie sits red-faced, unable to reply.

'Gary asked you not to tell me, didn't he?' It had to be Gary.

'He said to tell you the story but not who told it to me,' Carrie nods.

'Do you know that I was married to a dozer driver and I was sent to prison when they found money in the house?'

Carrie looks shocked enough for me to need no answer.

'No!' she gasps. 'It was you he was telling me about, I'm sorry.'

'There's no need to be sorry. It does sound like my situation but that's not what happened to me.'

'But you said...' Carrie looks eager for further explanation and I'm happy to get it off my chest.

'There's no way my ex could have done that. He didn't know about the money and I'm sure he wouldn't have told the police about it, even if he had. It was all my own fault I went to prison, nobody else's. I admitted to taking the money as a bribe.'

'Yes, but someone shopped you, told the coppers, it had to be him – your husband, didn't it?'

Carrie's words sit uncomfortably on my long-held conviction that Casagrande or his henchmen were responsible for my fate. I can't believe that Tim did anything, apart from take his chance to dump me when it came. At least that's what I believed until now. When I recall those horrifying moments I get a feeling that Tim's composure was remarkable under the stressful circumstances. Could he really have engineered the whole thing?

None of this is making much sense to me. Only Casagrande knew I had the money, only he could have informed on me. That's what I think, it's what I've always thought. I took their money and they made sure I didn't enjoy it, that's what it's all about.

157

The version being offered by Carrie is a harder, more hurtful one. What if Tim found the cash then used its presence to get rid of his troublesome wife? That would make him a cruel, cold-hearted monster, with no regard for anyone's feelings but his own. He would be the one responsible for making Toby suffer so badly. That is not the action of a loving parent. Quite honestly, in my heart, I don't believe that Tim would do such a thing. I can ask Gary, but I know his ways. If he'd wanted me to talk to him about it, he wouldn't have used Carrie as a conduit. I'm sure he's trying to be helpful but chasing him about it will only lead to him clamming up entirely and not bothering to pass on any information in the future. There's no point in even telling him I know he set Carrie up to tell me. I have a simple way of clearing up the whole affair, I can ask Tim.

44

The painted sign on the door says 'O'Shaughnessy Group Head Office' and is clearly meant to impress. The letters are clean, precise and white as if recently retouched. Inside the door any positive effect of the sign rapidly disappears.

My first impression of a collection of huts, garages and sheds pushed haphazardly together is confirmed as I crunch my way along the corridors caked with dried mud before O'Shaughnessy senior ushers me into a side office. He offers me the choice of a disparate collection of broken chairs. I am about to lower myself into the most stable-looking when I notice the ominous dark stain across the plush seat. I abandon that one and perch instead on an olive green typist's chair which lurches crazily beneath me, a reaction to one missing wheel.

Young O'Shaughnessy joins us and the two of them crowd around me, standing as if they know too much about the pedigree of their chairs to take a chance on sitting down.

'What would you like?' Old O'Shaughnessy asks.

My puzzlement provokes the additional words 'to drink' after a long pause.

'Tea, please,' I answer automatically.

Both men shuffle out of the office as if making tea needs as many hands as they can muster.

If this is their best office, the one they receive visitors in, I don't want to see any of the others. A trail of ubiquitous dust has followed me through the door, stacks of beige folders lean halfway up the walls, their contents turned a matching yellow by passage of time. The small table jammed between two pock-marked metal cabinets wouldn't look out of place supporting a fixed line telephone in some domestic hallway. Dust and grime are everywhere, a faint smell of decomposing refuse is in the air.

The O'Shaughnessys return, proudly bearing a mug of tea which is placed on the little table but not before a beer mat is found to act as a coaster to protect the precious wood on the scrap table. There is a disconcerting sheen on the surface of the dark tea, not so much rainbow oily as white and scummy. I regret my automatic request and notice that the O'Shaughnessies seem to view the quality of their own tea in much the same light as the safety of their chairs.

'He's been in touch, so he has,' O'Shaughnessy senior begins.

'Yes, you said on the phone.'

'Ah, yes, you've done the trick, I think.'

'Has he sent you the money?'

'Ah, no. Not yet. He's saying he needs the tickets first.'

'Good, have you got the tickets?' I can feel the level of frustration building inside.

'Ah, yes. We sent them already.' O'Shaughnessy smiles proudly.

My breath flies out in exasperation.

'Why did you do that?' I don't need an answer but I ask anyway.

'So he'd send us the money. That's the arrangement.' O'Shaughnessy junior chimes in. Both men are smiling proudly.

I take a deep breath and my chair capsizes, almost pitching me onto the floor.

'Let me get this straight. Jackson asked for the tickets, you sent them to him and you don't have your money. What made you think that was a good idea?'

'Ah, no. That's where we've been a bit crafty, like. Jackson doesn't have them, we sent them to the Environment Agency, to that Annie Osborne. That's the arrangement, Jackson says if she's happy with what we sent we'll get our money.'

'But Annie Osborne knows nothing about all this. She's not at all interested in the tickets, she's nothing to do with any of this.' My patience is just about spent, I feel like giving up and walking out.

'That's where you're wrong, Jenny.' Old O'Shaughnessy calling me Jenny in that patronising way isn't helping matters one bit. 'Jackson told us she visited him and demanded proof we tipped in the right places. He's a worried man is Mr Jackson.'

160

I am Annie Osborne, it was me that put the fear into Jackson and I must have told this to O'Shaughnessy a dozen times. It seems they are incapable of grasping the situation. I should have devised a plan that kept them out of it. I point to the phone on the chintzy desk.

'Ring Jackson now, tell him you have Annie Osborne from the Environment Agency here. Then give me the phone, I want to talk to him.'

O'Shaughnessy senior's eyes widen and furrows appear on his brow. 'But...' he says.

'No buts. If you want your money do as I say. Ring Jackson now.'

He pulls a grubby notebook from his jacket pocket, licks his forefinger and leafs slowly through the pages. I wonder how his contacts list is organised, obviously not alphabetically. Maybe it's in the order that he met people, a cast list in order of appearance. Finally, he sees what he's been searching for and dials.

'Mr Jackson, please. O'Shaughnessy here. He knows what it's about. Thanks. Ah, there you are. It's O'Shaughnessy. There's a woman here wants to speak to you. Hold on.' He thrusts the receiver into my hand and retreats into the doorway.

'Good morning Mr Jackson, it's Annie Osborne from the Environment Agency, we met last week.'

'Is everything OK?' Jackson asks.

'That's what I wanted to tell you. My investigation has brought me here to Mr O'Shaughnessy's offices and he has been very helpful. He has provided me with access to all his records and from what I have seen so far it appears that all the waste transfer notes relating to Monton Homes are in order. I haven't completed my investigation but I can tell you that I'm satisfied with everything I've seen so far. Mr O'Shaughnessy wanted me to let you know, he insisted on telephoning you to put your mind at rest.'

'Oh, thanks. So we're in the clear, so to speak.'

'That's right. Goodbye Mr Jackson, thank you for your cooperation.' I put the phone down and feel the excitement and nervousness in the room.

'There,' I address O'Shaughnessy senior. 'That's the best I can do. Let me know if the payment arrives.'

I alight unsteadily from the crooked chair and walk out.

'You've not drunk your tea,' I hear O'Shaughnessy calling after me.

45

It's one of those days where a little sunshine would make all the difference. Instead, the greyness matches my mood and does nothing to help my state of mind. When I woke up this morning I realised that I hate the crappy flat, I despise everything about it. I despair of my separation from Toby. I detest the haggard, scared face I see in the mirror.

Even Gary's message telling me that O'Shaughnessy has been paid has not prevented me from feeling ineffective and vulnerable. I need to be strong and resourceful when I face Tim, I need to be able to take whatever answers he gives me without collapsing.

One cheerful glimpse of sunlight, one tiny sparkle on the red bonnet of my car wouldn't solve anything, but it would help. The clouds ahead to the north as the M61 swings away from Manchester are slightly less grey, a little brighter than those behind. I take what comfort I can from that.

She has gone out, taken Toby to the park. At least the rain is holding off long enough for her to do that. Tim is very nervous as he admits me into what used to be my house as much as his.

'You sounded upset when you called.' Tim sits me down in the lounge, still littered with Toby's familiar toys. There are breakfast dishes and cups lying uncollected. The paint on the walls is still that hideous shade of brown I originally thought cool and chic.

'I want to know what happened to me,' I begin.

'Oh.' Tim looks surprised. 'I thought you were coming to talk about Toby.'

At the mention of Toby I soften and push my own needs away. I should be here to talk about Toby, about his happiness and welfare.

'Later.' I swallow the feelings of selfishness. 'Tell me the truth, Tim, did you call the police, was it you who had me arrested?'

'No,' Tim answers quickly. He relaxes slightly, shoulders lowering, head retreating; it's as if I asked the right question, one he's happy to answer truthfully.

'But you know who did, don't you?'

This time he stiffens.

'No. How would I?' he answers quickly and untruthfully. His eyes evade my gaze, he puts his hands on his thighs and looks down at them.

'You tell me, Tim. Tell me who you think it was, then. I won't blame you, it's all in the past now, what's done is done, just tell me what happened. Please.'

He stands up slowly and walks over to the chest of drawers where we always kept important household documents. A large envelope is fished from the bottom and he places it on the coffee table in front of me.

'One of the lads at work downloaded these off the internet. Everyone could see what you were up to. It's no wonder you never bothered with me.' His face twists with genuine hurt. 'All that time you were denying me you were enjoying yourself, getting your pleasure with someone else.'

Martin's face, Martin's soft voice, Martin's loving touch flashes back into my awareness. I look through the envelope and imagine photographs of Martin, of me and Martin together. I visualise what hidden cameras in the flat might have captured. The scarlet heat I feel in my cheeks must be betrayal enough, even to Tim's inattentive eyes. Before I can gain enough composure to reach out and prevent it, Tim opens the envelope and spills out the dreadful images. I gasp in horror at the naked flesh, engorged organs, obscene couplings. My stomach churns as I recognise none of the faces except my own.

Tim is staring at me, his expression is vacant, his body twisted and taut. I feel too sick to speak; words mean nothing in the face of this depravity. Drugged, raped, abused, photographed, exposed, defiled, defamed. I want to tell Tim I'm innocent of all this, that I never betrayed him with these men, that I'm not like that, but I can't say anything. I am guilty. I did betray him and in

164

a much more complete way than these depictions of semen being squirted on me by anonymous miscreants can ever represent. I am worse than it looks, not better. Silently I gather up the photographs and replace them in the envelope.

'So then what did you do, Tim, why didn't you confront me then?'

'It was after some men visited me at work. They said you'd taken large amounts of money in bribes, it was something to do with your job, you'd taken the money but not done what you'd promised. They said it'd be in the house somewhere. If I found it, I was to leave it where it was and ring them.'

'And you believed them?'

'I found the money in your wardrobe, exactly as they said. Of course I believed them, who wouldn't? Anyway, by then I didn't care what happened to you.' Tim's defiance is not convincing.

There's nothing I need say to this hollow man, whom I once loved enough to gladly have his child. Anything I might say now can only make him feel better about his role in my distress. Comfort is a commodity I need to reserve for myself. I might understand what Tim did and admit the damning circumstances he was faced with, but I have no sympathy, no shred of compassion, no forgiveness, no understanding to offer. As far as I'm concerned he can continue to suffer what little remorse he feels. He's not getting my permission to feel all right about what he did.

I take the photographs and stand up ready to leave.

'One thing,' I ask, 'these people, the ones who told you about the money, who were they, what were they like? Were they Italian?'

Tim's face tightens, perhaps he expected some sort of apology or explanation and is disappointed.

'I didn't know them. Two guys came to me at work. They weren't Italian, I'm not sure I'd even recognise them if I saw them again.'

Clutching the photos I hurry out to my car, holding back the tears long enough to park safely out of sight where I sob my heart out at what has been done to me.

46

The creased brown envelope containing the photographs of my violation sits on my table, demanding my attention. I can't bear to look at the envelope, let alone the contents. At Tim's house I felt shocked and numb, the numbness has gone now. I am raw and desolated. My hand trembles as I reach out to take it. Vague memories surface of Martin's funeral, the pub afterwards and disorientation that lasted for days. I wonder how many people have seen these photos, how many were present while I was being raped. A small voice inside me is whimpering and making me cringe, but a flush of anger propels my arm forward and I scatter the disgusting contents. They are even worse than my first look led me to believe. I know I was unconscious throughout, but from the way these photographs have been taken it's so easy to imagine I'm participating willingly. The closed eyes and soft smile seem to indicate compliance and even pleasure.

There's no point in feeling sorry for myself. No matter how distasteful I find it, I need to study these carefully if I'm to find my attackers. My mind goes into furious overdrive as I imagine what I will do to these men when I catch up with them. There is a lot of cutting, slicing, castration and maiming going on in my head. It's horrible and satisfying and justified. I know I can do all of this and more. I pray to be given the chance to have even one of them begging for my mercy.

The backgrounds to the pictures are featureless white walls, with the exception of one photograph which reveals part of a window with familiar rounded corners. The glass is criss-crossed with reinforcing wire similar to those in the portacabin I previously occupied as Gary's office. I was abused at a site using portable offices but there are no distinguishing features and no clue as to its location. There are thousands of these dotted all over Manchester.

There are three different men in the photos. I have a side view of one of them, the bottom half of another face and the full face of the third. I also have a lot of pictures showing abdomens, legs, arms and, of course, penises. These may include distinguishing marks if I look closely but I am loathe to do so. The one full face is my best piece of evidence. As I look into his wide staring eyes, I wonder about him. Does he rape defenceless women as a day job or is he only doing it as a side-line? His hair is black and close-cropped, nothing remarkable. He might be Eastern European, though I wonder if I'm imagining this because of my encounter with Popov and his thuggish entourage. Could Popov be involved, did he organise and orchestrate the whole procedure? That's a question I know I can't ask Gary, if he thinks that I'm delving into Popov's business he'll drop me like a shot and make himself scarce.

The disgusting display still haunts me even though I've stuffed the offending items back into their envelope. The urge to destroy them, to burn them, is almost overwhelming, but I'm determined to keep this evidence and one day use it to get revenge. Perhaps I will use them to show the man with the grimace why his genitals are being hacked away.

Throwing the envelope into a drawer, I strip off and stand in the shower, scrubbing the shame away, weeping quietly. As I wash myself, the cold chill of fear douses the fire of my determination and I suddenly realise I could be contaminated, fatally diseased, terminally infected.

47

Gary is sitting in the office talking to a large man with long white hair that has thinned to an alarming extent. His prominent nose is decorated with a lattice of blue and red veins giving him the look of a bird peering from a gossamer nest. I know this man, he knows me and neither of us is acknowledging the fact. It's rare for Gary to conduct his meetings indoors and even more unusual for him to do it in my presence. This gives me an uneasy feeling that he is busy making promises for me to keep.

Peter O'Brian is Tim's employer. Every time he looks at me I feel more uncomfortable. He knows me, knows I am Tim's ex-wife, knows about my past, my prison sentence, my circumstances. He may even have seen the photographs. Tim is not a reticent kind of man, he tells everyone about everything in my experience. The thought increases my uneasiness, though O'Brian's calm blue eyes transmit only kindness and good humour. O'Brian is the proprietor of a huge construction group and he is one of the wealthiest and most influential men in the Manchester area. There is plenty of time for me to speculate about why a man like O'Brian needs to visit our office, while the two men talk about various things including a mini-digger that was stolen and the merits of things they refer to as gypsy buns. Carrie brings in three mugs of tea and shakily places them in front of us, managing to dribble brown liquid across my clean white pad of paper that I have readied for note-taking. As the men chat, I take a sip of tea and almost spit it out in disgust. It is so sweet as to be undrinkable. By now Carrie knows I don't take sugar, she must have mixed me up with O'Brian.

'This one's got sugar in it,' I break into the conversation.

O'Brian looks at me and smiles. He picks up his cup and tastes his tea. 'This one has none,' he answers, then exchanges it for mine.

'Gary tells me you're doing a great job for him, transformed his business, he says.' O'Brian looks at me and allows the silence to build until I feel compelled to answer.

'It's just a question of getting the books right. Gary is the one doing the business, I only do the accounts.'

'Peter is considering investing in our business,' Gary announces excitedly. 'He's wanting to inject substantial amounts of capital so we can expand, take on more staff, get involved in other types of work.'

O'Brian smiles benignly at Gary.

'You're doing a good job, with my help the business can grow considerably. There's things you can do for O'Brian's for a start. I also have in mind some new areas of business for you, good prospects. Things that I don't have time to do justice.'

My heart is sinking. My ex-husband's boss is about to take over Gary's business. It could end up with both of us working for O'Brian, a prospect that fills me with alarm. In O'Brian's organisation I would be one of many accounts staff. I face performing some sort of subservient role. That's if he keeps me on. All this joviality and positivity is only the courtship phase. Once we are absorbed, reality will set in.

I don't want to work for O'Brian, even if he does turn out to be telling the truth when he says he values me. Perhaps I should say something now, put my position firmly on the table, tell them how I feel, that I'm intending to be no part of this. Resign, walk out, quit. Fear rises in my throat and stills my voice. I'm in no position to do that. Whatever crumbs might fall from this rich man's table I need to harvest them with care and gratitude.

'How exciting, that sounds really good.' I try not to sound flat and worry that I have over-compensated and my response is much too gushing.

O'Brian reaches beneath the table and produces a black leather holdall. He pushes it towards me then rises from his seat.

'That's the first tranche, I'll bring you the rest as we go along.' He looks at Gary. 'There's no need for our relationship to be formalised.' He turns to me and smiles. 'In fact I will be very appreciative if we could keep it to just the three of us.'

O'Brian has not even reached the door before the import of his words hits home and I suddenly realise what he is really up to.

When Gary returns from the car park his grin looks like it's been painted on.

'Great that,' he enthuses, 'O'Brian and me, business partners, great isn't it. We'll do very well you and me, very well.'

'What's this?' I point to the case.

Gary grins even more widely. 'Investment money, it's O'Brian's stake. Plenty more where that came from as well, so he says, plenty more. I said we'd do well.'

I open the bag to reveal the contents. It's crammed full of fifty pound notes in tight bundles.

'It's cash,' I point out unnecessarily, 'cash, what are we supposed to do with cash?'

Gary looks puzzled for an instant then the smile returns wide as ever. 'Ah, you're joshing me aren't you? Pay it in, put it in the bank, it's O'Brian's investment money.'

'Is that what he said, is that what he told you to do, Gary?' I watched the smile fade away.

'Err, no,' Gary wrinkles his forehead, 'not exactly. He said to keep his involvement a secret, just you and me have to know.'

'So,' I'm starting to feel like a nagging wife, 'if I go to the bank and say this is O'Brian's cash, his investment money, they'll know as well, won't they?'

'Yes.' Gary's expression shows he now sees what I'm driving at. It won't be a secret any more. Slapping the bundles onto the desk I make a large pile, counting as I go. Two hundred bundles, fifty notes in each bundle, half a million pounds exactly. It reminds me of Casagrande's gift, but makes that pale into insignificance. A hot flush seizes my upper body and suffuses my face. Quickly I shove the money back into hiding and clip the bag shut.

I push it towards Gary. 'What are you going to do with that?'

Gary pushes the bag back at me. 'You need to put it through the business, that's the plan, put it through the business, you're good at that sort of thing.'

48

The driveway up to the house twists through trees and bushes
which part briefly to give views of sweeping lawns and
manicured flower beds. The house itself appears vast and
ancient; an enormous door studded with iron at the side of the
building provides the obvious main entrance.

Peter O'Brian instructed me to come round to the back
door to avoid him having to make the considerable trek from one
part of his mansion to another. A narrow passageway between
the side of the house and more shrubbery eventually reveals a
paved courtyard on which several cars are already parked,
including one monster that could easily accommodate my Corsa
in its boot.

'Knock on the back door and I'll let you in,' sounded
simple, but I can see four candidates from where I'm sitting. As I
lug the heavy case towards the nearest and most obvious
prospect, a large Rottweiler raises its predatory head and looks
unconcernedly at me. Although the dog makes no attempt to
intercept me, I'm grateful for the heavy chain that tethers it.

The door is a disappointment, it is solid, black and firmly
locked; as I beat weakly on it I'm discouraged by the thick
cobwebs that are testament to the infrequency with which it is
opened. Ah well, one down, try the next.

I turn to see the Rottweiler at the full extent of its chain
sitting malevolently in my path. As long as I stay in the alcove by
this door I'm perfectly safe. Unfortunately, in order to get back
to my car or knock on another door I have to negotiate the dog.
Brandishing the case I try to exude confidence and casual disdain
as I approach it. As a child my mother told me that dogs can
smell your fear and when they do they attack.
Whatever this one can smell, it greets me by showing its yellow
teeth and emitting a snarl that could have been the prelude to a
major earthquake. It's quite clear that getting within biting
distance will result in being bitten, probably to death. It starts to
rain hard, my coat is in the car, my phone is in its pocket. I am

dressed for sitting inside. My blouse is getting wet. My hair is losing its shape. At the risk of becoming entangled in cobwebs and devoured by spiders, I shelter in the disused doorway while the dog sits untroubled by the water streaming off its head.

The intensity of the downpour increases and I become more concerned at the cash becoming water-logged. Returning a runny mess of paper pulp where there once was half a million pounds is not a good start to the difficult conversation I'm anticipating with O'Brian. 'Sorry your money is ruined, I was scared of your dog' sounds a feeble excuse but the massive jaws, slightly open in readiness, provide plenty of justification from where I'm cowering. Whether this will stand up later remains to be seen.

The wet is seeping through my clothes, my skirt is sodden and little droplets shower from it if I swing my hips suddenly. The cold is beginning to bite, particularly in my lower back and the tops of my thighs. My situation has gone beyond a joke, it's become a nightmare, a disaster, an embarrassment and now it's becoming funny again. No part of me has escaped the drenching, I might as well have laid down in a pond or jumped in a river. Moving about within the confines set out by the dog's reach does nothing to dispel the cold and I'm beginning to make the dog nervous. It keeps giving a little pull on its chain as if checking to make completely sure that it's still firmly tethered. The low growl comes and goes like a passing motorcycle.

Banging on the door and shouting brings no response, but I keep it up, gradually releasing any idea of dignity and allowing the full force of desperation to give vent. Enough time and rain has passed for me to seriously worry about dying from exposure and hypothermia and that sort of thing, though I suspect I'd have to be trapped here at least overnight for that to happen. Even so, I'm suddenly excited by the appearance of the man in a voluminous green coat and wide brimmed hat who is walking slowly towards me carrying a duck. As he draws nearer, the prominent nose and wisps of grey hair identify him as the man I'm supposed to be meeting, Peter O'Brian.

174

The dog acknowledges his presence by ambling back to the shelter of its stable-proportioned kennel.

O'Brian greets me with a smile and says, 'You'd better come inside.' He gently places the duck on the ground and walks towards the kennel.

'You come on now,' he says, 'I'll hold the dog.' As I make to follow, the Rottweiler senses my movement and intention and re-emerges from its lair. Immediately O'Brian grabs its metal studded collar and is carried towards me, clinging on, lying across the dog's back to try to slow its progress.

'It's okay,' he pants, 'I've got hold of it.'

Despite the doubts I harbour about the outcome of the contest, I make faltering progress in the direction indicated, all the time fearing for both our lives. This door is unlocked and I pass gratefully inside to stand in the relative warmth. A small puddle forms on the tiled floor.

O'Brian joins me, panting with effort. 'He's really quite soft when you get to know him.'

All I can think is that I don't know him at all and more importantly he doesn't know me.

We travel through a series of rooms stacked with old furniture. Desks and tables are interleaved, alternately inverted, forming piles that reach into the high ceilings. In one room there are marble slabs, placed like playing cards, in the next the contents of a church complete with a wooden pulpit. Eventually, we turn right down a carpeted corridor, passing open doors which reveal more utilitarian items, sinks and washing machines among them, until we emerge into a large kitchen. Steps lead down from here to a glass roofed conservatory which commands a spectacular view of rolling lawns, majestic trees and flower beds in riotous colour.

There is a lady standing in the kitchen, she is thin and elegant with flowing curly, golden hair and blue eyes. Her face is fully made up as if she was about to attend a formal event, her cheeks rouge red in contrast to the almost white pallor of her foundation which ends in a line at the base of her chin. O'Brian hands me over to her without any introduction.

'She's been standing in the rain,' he says simply. 'She's got a bit wet.'

'Come with me.'

She leads me into a hallway with the heads of dead animals protruding from the wooden panelling. In the centre of the hall is an ebony grand piano with a scarily lifelike dummy of O'Brian sitting at it. Mrs O'Brian, I am happy to make the assumption, points to a door.

'There's a shower in there. Let me have your wet things and I'll see what I can do about drying them.'

She has a soft voice with the accent of a newsreader. My reaction to the thought of stripping naked in this house and handing my clothes to a stranger must be written all over my face. Mrs O'Brian smiles gently and hands me a white towel that would double as a bed sheet.

When I emerge from the grateful warmth of the shower, protected by my massive towel, I find a small pile of clothes outside the bathroom door. I put these on and a check in the steamy mirror reveals that I look better in Mrs O'Brian's clothes than I did in my own.

White jeans, green blouse and pink sweater are not items I would normally consider wearing, but I have to admit that they do lift the drabness I've been carrying around for many a long year. The old Jenny might have strutted out looking like this.

Mrs O'Brian, presumably hovering close by in case I needed assistance, appears immediately I open the bathroom door for the second time and whisks away my wet clothes. Downstairs, O'Brian is watching two small dogs chasing each other across his garden. The briefcase is on the floor by his feet, its presence triggers feelings of anxiety as I remember why I'm here. The glossy wooden floor is stained slightly darker by the run-off from the sodden case.

'Ah, there you are,' he smiles. 'How do you like your tea?'

'A little milk, no sugar please.' He pours a lot of milk into a cup and follows this up with a pale yellow trickle from the porcelain teapot. I'm glad I didn't mention that I like it strong as I peer into the still almost white drink.

'Help yourself to sugar.' He pushes a sugar bowl towards me and I feel obliged to put a spoonful into my tea. As I stir I feel diminished. If I can't muster the strength to insist on a decent cup of tea, it's no wonder I'm in the state I am. My only excuse is that I need O'Brian to remain calm and happy, to accept the return of his money and forget all about investing in Gary's business. Antagonising him over something trivial like a cup of tea is not the start I wish to make.

'I've brought your money back,' I begin, feeling nervous and glad of the tea despite its sweet pallor. 'I'm sorry we can't do anything with it without involving you in some way. The regulations and procedures are very tight nowadays, we can't bank a large amount of cash without being able to account for it and that means being prepared to tell the authorities where we got it.'

O'Brian smiled sadly. 'I'm well aware of the problems, Jenny, my own accountants are well versed in all these things. It's just that Gary told me he needed some cash, some investment money and that you were able to sort it without any comeback to myself.'

'Why don't you put it in your own business?' After what seems an age of silence I find myself answering my own question. 'I suppose that wouldn't make any difference, the source of the cash would still have to be identified.'

A phone rings distantly for a while then stops. Mrs O'Brian materialises at the top of the steps and speaks softly.

'It's Irene.'

O'Brian clambers out of his chair and sets off in search of the telephone. Mrs O'Brian dematerialises as quickly as she appeared and leaves me alone. I try to pour more tea from the pot but only get a sludgy trickle of tea leaves. A peacock wanders into view, dragging its tail as if intent on sweeping the grass. The vision of a many-eyed semi-circle that impressed my childhood self brings back longings for the time I felt safe and cared for. It seems so long ago and gives such a false impression. My father mocked me even then, saying the bird had taken a fancy to me and that's why he was aroused. The significance of that word has been lost until now. The deep anxiety returns, pressing me into the chair. The brief excitement at seeing the magnificent bird is gone.

There are forty-eight panels of glass in the conservatory roof, twelve paintings hanging on the walls, ninety-six tiles on the wall behind the sink. I'm trying not to think about my father and what he did to me. It's the betrayal that cuts deeply into my heart and that is placed firmly with my mother. How could she let that happen to her child, why didn't she protect me?

The peacock has waddled away now, relieving me of the desire for it to flaunt its magnificence and for me to return my thoughts to O'Brian and his money. He is not a stupid man; on the contrary he must be remarkably clever. Nothing I came here to explain is news to him. He knows the score as well as I do, maybe even better. My mind is going round in circles, if I put the cash in the bank I will have to reveal its origin. 'A man gave it me to look after' is not a valid reason for having money. It was less than twenty thousand pounds that got me locked up. Half a million would tempt them to throw away the key. Proceeds of a sale would be a better line, but then what has been sold and to whom? Why was I given cash? More questions that can't be answered. The best way would be to sell lots of things for small amounts, real items so they could be identified and accounted for but products with a big mark up. Nothing that Gary does even comes close to helping here. The way the rules are now, it's almost impossible to create legitimate earnings out of illicit cash. If you're caught with a bag of bank notes you're guilty unless you can prove your innocence. I should know.

O'Brian is taking his time, I wonder if he's forgotten me and consider leaving my seat to go and look for him. At least I can make myself a cup of tea, after all I am practically sitting in the kitchen. There are three steps up to the kitchen. As I put my foot on the first one there is no-one to be seen, the place remains deserted. As I reach the third step Mrs O'Brian is standing in the doorway.

'The toilet is through here,' she points helpfully. 'I'll make us some more tea. Peter is still on the phone.'

The toilet is the size of a decent lounge, festooned with flowers and trailing greenery. The long window is frosted in a diamond pattern which dissects the light into a hundred tiny rainbows. I feel like sitting here in peace until they forget about me then slipping quietly away. This prospect, remote as it might be, is rendered impossible by the inevitability of that dog sitting next to my car. I need safe passage out of here and only O'Brian can provide that. The conundrum in my head stops turning round and round and settles on a vision of Emma, my young colleague from Landers Hoffman. I see her sitting in Martin's office explaining to me how she had got on at Allied Composites. It didn't strike me at the time but she could have been describing the perfect money laundering set up. It doesn't help me with O'Brian but at least it makes me realise what a huge issue this has become.

Back in my seat, the conservatory windows are beginning to reflect more as the light fades outside. He makes no apology on his return, murmurs, 'Where were we?' and expects me to answer.

'Cash is a big problem to us all, Mr O'Brian,' I begin. 'The penalties for undeclared earnings are bad enough, but the possession of large amounts of money without a documented reason leads to severe legal penalties. I should know.'

O'Brian looks straight at me, meets my eyes and remains silent.

'Gary has promised to help, though to be fair he doesn't understand the implications of his promise. My job is to honour that commitment without putting us all in jail.'

O'Brian smiles gently. He likes what he is hearing now.

'So this is what I propose. You keep the money, apart from fifty thousand which I'll take with me. When I've invested that I'll come here and collect some more. It will take time but I'll be building up assets in a business that you and Gary can then argue over. As I say, it'll take some time and until then, you must keep the cash.'

'Okay.' O'Brian nods. 'What about you, what do you see yourself wanting out of this?'

His gaze is unrelenting and I feel myself wilting slightly and colouring up. What do I want? I want nothing to do with his dirty money. I want Toby, I want a nice place to live, an honest job, an honest, kind man. That about covers it.

Instead I say, 'Ten per cent.'

O'Brian nods. 'Ten per cent it is. You need to be motivated and rewarded. Ten per cent of what I get back, that's the deal.'

I had in mind ten per cent of the capital, fifty thousand pounds, but I can see his point, and nod my acquiescence. He pushes the bag towards me with his foot.

'And you take the bag with you, that's the deal. I don't want it here, you take it, I trust you.

49

Gary is still grinning. I'm not sure if it's the return of the money or the story of the dog and my embarrassment that he's enjoying most.

'He's a big softy,' he says unhelpfully. 'He wouldn't hurt a fly.'

It was so late by the time I left O'Brian's house I was able to wear my own clothes which had been washed, dried and ironed to look better than they ever had, even when new. Too late to meet Gary, I spent an uncomfortable night semi-sleeping with half a million pounds under my bed. Every creak was an armed robber, every car was a police van coming to take me away.

'He's a persuasive man is O'Brian.' Gary likes stating the obvious. He is happy to do it all day.

'We need a business that takes cash to run this through.' I pat the travel-weary bag.

Gary nods. 'What do you have in mind?' He's positively gleeful at my entrapment in O'Brian's steely web.

'It was your idea, you promised O'Brian in the first place. What do you think we should do?'

'We can use the cash to pay the lads,' Gary suggests.

'Not a good idea, I've only recently stopped the cash payments, the risk is too great.'

Gary is still grinning though. He knows I have a plan. He's relying on it.

'Well?'

'I have an idea. It came to me while sitting on O'Brian's toilet.' This is making me feel superior for a change. Gary really needs reminding just how bloody good I am. Maybe he'll stop whinging about tax and VAT long enough to be grateful he's still in business.

'Caravans.' I am almost bursting with excitement at my own cleverness. 'We are buying a caravan park.'

'How does that help?' Gary asked.

I spread out the full colour prospectus I obtained from the agents. 'Look.' I point to serried ranks of neat shacks all bathed in sunshine. 'These are residential caravans. They rent for five hundred pounds a month. If they were holiday lets they earn that much a week.'

'How does that help with O'Brian's cash?'

'We buy the place then we convert it to a holiday let. We use O'Brian's money as if it came from the holiday makers.'

'What about the residents, do we chuck them out?'

'No need, they stay put. I'll just account for the place differently. It only needs to be a paper exercise.' I put the figures down on the table.

Gary's grin gets wider.

'How many can we buy?' he asks.

50

I can't look Tim in the eye. My defiance is spent, dissolved, evaporated in the glare of those photographs. She is standing by his side oozing malice, resentful of every moment I spend in his presence. Toby is bouncing with excitement, grinning with mischief as he flings himself at me. A nugget of satisfaction glows inside me at his display before the desolation bites as I release him back into her influence. I miss him already, even before I leave.

'I hear you've been to see Peter O'Brian at his house?' Tim's words betray his insecurity rather than revealing superior knowledge. If O'Brian told him he saw me, there is no doubt in my mind that the reason for our meeting was kept firmly under wraps. For Tim, knowing that his ex-wife is having meetings with his employer is bad enough, not knowing why is another reason for him to worry. The advantage I might gain from having O'Brian's ear is not something I appreciated until Tim spoke. Our dealings over Toby may take a more even aspect in the future.

'Don't forget I'm taking Toby on holiday with me next week.'

'I hadn't forgotten.' Tim looks sideways for approval. 'Hope the weather turns out nice for you.'

She gives him a look that says being pleasant to his ex-wife will bring punishment and I take some consolation from her display of irritation. As I look away I retain the image of her hands positioned protectively over a slightly swollen belly. A jolt of excitement flares inside me. If she is pregnant that can only help me with Toby. It will be a consolation for Tim when he loses custody.

The short trip down the M61 is filled with alternating hope and fear. Hope that I will soon have a place for me and Toby, fear that it will all be made impossible by my failure to deliver what Gary expects. Hope that I stay feeling strong and healthy, fear that tomorrow will bring news of terminal disease and contamination.

*

The hospital waiting rooms are filled to overflowing. Everybody is here to see the same consultant, everyone has the same appointment time. Everyone is told to turn up at 10 a.m. and wait. Although I insisted on being referred to a female gynaecologist I have been leered at, prodded and poked by a succession of sausage-fingered men. Today, for a change, I am assured I will actually meet the woman herself, today is the day I get my results.

At 1.48 p.m. my name is called by a nurse who ushers me into a tiny room dominated by a complex metal bed with long protuberances, designed to spread your legs the required amount and hold them open while you are tinkered with. Mercifully the small Indian lady points to the grey plastic chair in front of her. She squints at ragged sheets of paper hanging out of a manila folder. She looks up at me then back at this file. I begin to fear the worst. How many of the diseases do I have? Are any of them curable, how long can I expect to live with HIV?

She leafs through a few more pages, from my vantage point I can see a few lines of typescript in each but not decipher any of it.

'You have been screened for the common STDs.' She looks up. 'All the tests are negative.'

My brain fails to understand and my body goes into panic mode.

'You are clear.' She explains and I begin to recover. 'There are no infections identified.'

'What about AIDS?' I ask.

'You are HIV negative, you need not be concerned about AIDS.'

'What about the pain, I can't have intercourse, it's too painful.' I feel unworthy sitting here, taking up this important

184

doctor's time. It's only about my pleasure or lack of it now. It's cosmetic, unimportant. I can manage without.

'There are a variety of conditions that cause discomfort. Dryness can be helped by using plenty of lubricant. Let me have a look.'

The bed with the leg irons and stirrups beckons to me and I have been through this often enough to remove the appropriate clothing and assume the position. She is gentle and respectful, her touch warm and soft in contrast to previous rough manipulation. When she is finished delving around inside me she waits for me to dress and resume my seat.

'There are signs of some damage, a little scarring, but this does not look recent and should not be causing any problems. As I said before, dryness is the probable cause of your discomfort. It is very common, more so as you get older. There are proprietary lubricants you can use, I could prescribe one for you but I think it is cheaper for you to buy them yourself.'

Nothing wrong with my body, nothing to stop me having a life, a relationship, love, passion, joy. All I need is a bottle of lube. I should be happy, ecstatic at the relief, but I'm not feeling anything other than sadness and rage. I've not been infected, I'm not contaminated, but I have been horribly abused. All this doctor can offer is a physical solution, a slap of ointment, a squirt of grease.

The injustice of it all overwhelms me, my sadness wells up and overflows. My arms and legs are shaking. Gripping the chair hard I try to control it but can't prevent the scream. It is a low guttural sound, frightening in its intensity. The doctor's face contorts with shock and fear, it has to come out, it can't be held back any longer.

Two men burst in and stare uncomprehendingly at me. I scream back at them louder, more powerfully than ever. Before they can touch me I am suddenly spent. All the air is gone, all my energy expended. Their hands manage to prevent me from slipping to the floor then place me on the examination couch and hold me there. Two female nurses enter, the room has become overcrowded, they can barely push their way inside.

The kindly Indian doctor asks them to help me over to the Psychiatric ward and tells me I will be taken care of there.

51

Coincidentally it's the same court where I was convicted, in the same cavernous unfriendly building. My knees turn to jelly as I mount the steps and submit to the airport style search and metal detector.

'It's going to be fine,' Maurice, my solicitor, soothes. 'Just routine, these things have to be ratified in front of a judge. Procedure, you understand.'

Maurice is reputed to be the best family solicitor in Manchester. The ridiculous amount he charges is testament to his high regard but my previous experiences still weigh against trusting any lawyer. The last time I walked into this building I was full of hopes that were dashed. This time I don't dare to be so presumptuous.

Since I filed for joint custody, Tim has been frosty and uncooperative. Picking up Toby for weekends suddenly became an issue. Nothing was ever convenient. Now all that awkwardness should be at an end, at least according to Maurice.

'You're his mother and you have a perfectly good home for him. He can stay at the same school, it's not going to be a problem for the court.'

Maurice's slicked back, receding hair gives him the look of a portly vampire. There is an air of authority about him, though, and I cling onto this with both hands. As we wait outside the courtroom, Tim and that woman, Alison, wander in and sit opposite. These pre-hearing seating arrangements are disconcerting. I wonder how many fights have to be broken up and whether I should start one just to wipe that nervous smirk off her face.

Tim refused my request to share Toby equally, an unreasonable act which he compounded by contesting my legal application. They have their own daughter now, so Toby is bound to be neglected. She will favour her little princess in every way she can. Sole custody is what I really want, it's what we both need, but Maurice dismissed this as going too far for the courts to agree.

'Take this big step forward first,' he counsels, 'get this under your belt, ratify your position, then we'll see what can be done next.'

When I think of Toby with me every day my heart leaps with joy before descending into a morass of fear and doubt. Today is the day the doubts are going to be settled.

*

Tim's lawyer is a fat, balding man with an air of indifference; he is asking me about my past, my conviction, my prison sentence. Maurice's preparation helps me to remain calm and truthful, exactly as he advised. There are no nasty surprises, I have the feeling that everyone is just going through the motions. The three magistrates, two women and one man, sit stony-faced and watch. Even though it goes as well as can be expected, my legs are weak and unsteady as I resume my place next to Maurice.

A young man with red hair and a freckled face replaces me in the witness box. This is the Family Court Advisor, Graham Watts, who visited me at home to look at where Toby would be living. We got on very well then. I'm certain he's happy with the arrangements and expect him to tell that to the court. Instead, he is spouting a poisonous litany of speculation and scandal about me. I told him about my conviction and time in prison, now he's making out I'm a violent criminal. The shock of hearing him distorting the truth stuns me at first but I recover quickly and begin to try to defend myself.

'That's not right,' I shout.

Maurice leans over and places a restraining hand on my shoulder, trying to make me sit down again.

'It's all lies, I'm not like that,' I insist. People are telling me to sit down and be quiet. I have to put them right, make sure they hear the truth, not some distortion made by a spiteful youth.

The catalogue of misdemeanours continues. I can hardly believe my ears when he says,

'The most recent episode of violent behaviour occurred only two months ago when Mrs Parker assaulted a female doctor at Hope Hospital. She had to be restrained and committed to the Psychiatric ward for sedation.'

I am pleading with him for the truth.

'I only screamed, I only screamed once, I was upset. It was only a scream. I didn't touch her...' but strong hands are pressing me down, holding me. The man on my left arm smells disgusting, his body odour engulfs me and I need him to move away. My arm shakes free and I use my elbow to push him aside. He stumbles and hits his head on the corner of the bench. More hands, more smelly men. I need to get out into the fresh air. My screaming is having no effect on them, nobody believes me, nobody cares.

52

This is the least appealing café I have ever been in. The staff, in starched blouses and black pinafores, are cold and aloof. Stodgy cake and pretentious teas and coffees seem to be their idea of sophistication. I sit looking at a charcoal-backed teacake with enough butter on it to soften a piece of roofing felt. My tea is weak and insipid, even though I have left it to brew for a good half hour. Despite the hideous décor, despite the frosty atmosphere, this place is heaving with clientele, ladies of a certain age, class and disposition. I had to fight to get a cramped table, hardly the size of a dinner plate, and now I'm struggling to keep it.

Next to mine is a table for four, quite empty despite the crush, a modest 'Reserved' sign sufficient deterrent. I am hoping that Miriam Youngs, Martin's widow, is the beneficiary of the table's protective sign.

I have to start somewhere. There's no need for me to continue to act with restraint now that Toby has been denied me. It all started with Martin's death and being too scared and weak to stand up and tell what I know. I was scared it would inconvenience me and I'm now able to sneer at myself in the knowledge of what being inconvenienced really feels like. Somebody killed Martin, the man I loved; somebody raped me; somebody had me put in prison. Keeping my head down only brings frustration and anguish. Now I need answers. Now somebody is going to pay for what they did to me.

She is barely recognisable from the brief glimpses I had in the church and by the graveside. She sits with her back to me, close enough for me to be enveloped in a cloud of fragrance. Her hair is a light golden colour, cut shoulder length and to perfection. Each hair looks like it has been interviewed for its part and given detailed instructions on how exactly to behave. The idea of accosting her when she sits in regal splendour with three equally impressive friends seems like a bad one.

The envelope I extract from my bag is slim and white, addressed simply to Miriam Youngs. Inside it reads:

Dear Mrs Youngs,
I am sorry to be bothering you but I feel compelled to write this letter. Your husband was a work colleague of mine at Landers Hoffman. At the time of his death I was unable to bring myself to speak out but I am absolutely certain that Martin was murdered. Although I do not have conclusive evidence, I believe that Giuseppe Casagrande was involved, together with a gang of Eastern European thugs controlled by a man nicknamed Popov. I realise this will be a shock to you but I want to bring these criminals to justice and you are the only person I can turn to for help. Please contact me on 0783 492 1472 so that we can speak privately.
Yours sincerely,
Jenny Parker

Heart pounding, legs shaking, I stand and touch her shoulder deferentially. She half turns and looks at me without any sign of recognition. Quickly I thrust the envelope into her hand.

'Please read this, it's important.' Then I turn and walk quickly out of the café without a backwards glance.

Sitting in my car, it takes me several minutes to compose myself enough to drive away. The Knutsford traffic system has other ideas and ensnares me. I find myself in thick traffic, crawling slowly past the last place on earth I want to be. Miriam Youngs is standing outside the café, mobile phone to her ear. Instinctively, I reach down to my bag and take out mine and put it on the passenger seat. It remains silent.

*

If it was hard to face Mrs Youngs, telling Gary what I've done is even more difficult. A terse text, 'we need to talk', drags him reluctantly into the office.

'You're not going to like this, Gary,' seems an honest opening.

'What's up?' he replies, 'are we in trouble?'

'I've been to see Miriam Youngs, Martin's widow.'

Gary's face betrays his lack of understanding.

'I told her what I know about Martin being murdered, I put it in a letter. Let me read out what I put.'

As I read, his eyes flash at the mention of Popov and his face takes on a worried look. He lets me finish before speaking.

'You shouldn't have mentioned Popov, if he finds out you're accusing him he'll turn nasty.'

'Listen, Gary, I'm sure Popov is involved in Martin's death. You have to realise that I can't just let that lie. Someone killed Martin, someone moved the body and someone had me assaulted. Whoever they are, I'm going to find them and make them sorry.'

The fact that Gary is still listening tells me I have his support. The caravan site business is going very well. A second bag of money arrived yesterday from O'Brian, he is so pleased with the returns he's getting from his investment. Gary is getting rich from my efforts now and grants me the attention and consideration I deserve.

'You never said you were assaulted,' Gary said.

'It was after the funeral, Martin's funeral, they spiked my drink, gang-raped me and put the photos on the internet.'

Gary's face widens with the shock of my words.

'Bastards!' A low growling emits from Gary's throat. 'Bastards!'

Relief sweeps through my body, the tension of the situation evaporates. It's me and Gary talking honestly and openly at last. I can feel his supportive energy holding me. I realise how great that tension was as it releases. Without Gary I am lost. If he rejects me I am cast adrift, to starve and die in a sea of monsters.

'What do you want me to do?' Gary asks.

I am so happy at this outcome I throw my arms around his thick shoulders and hug him hard.

53

My phone whirrs and tinkles into life, flashing urgently at me as if the sounds it makes are not enough. Judith. The PA I once shared at Landers Hoffman, someone I haven't spoken to since, well...since I worked there.

'Hello,' I answer tentatively, not sure if my phone is mistaken, if her number has been taken over by someone else.

'Jenny Parker?' It is Judith's voice, I recognise it, but the chill in the words freezes my response.

'Yes,' I say.

'Mrs Youngs will meet you at 8 p.m. on Thursday at the apartment at Spinningfields. She says you know the address.

'Yes, I...' She terminates the call, leaving me with a very bad feeling, partly confusion, partly distaste. I am frozen by the indifference in her voice. She knows me. It may be a long time since we spoke, but surely I warrant more consideration than a few terse instructions. Apart from the discourtesy, there is also the unease I feel that Miriam Youngs chooses to deal with my revelation through a third party and at a place that has deep significance for me. I wonder whether she chooses the flat out of convenience, it is hers after all now, or because she is aware of its connection to me. Is there some spiteful intent here? What would I do in her place? I'm certain that I wouldn't keep the letter to myself, that I would enlist help and advice from people close to me. That's if I had anyone to turn to.

This thought brings with it a sense of abandonment and loss. She has lost Martin, I have lost him too and he loved me in a way that he never loved her, of that I'm certain. Now I have nobody, not even Toby to comfort me.

Thursday it is then, two days to wait, two days to prepare myself. If I'm to face her, to do what I need to do, to find out what I need to know, I have to be strong. These feelings of guilt, betrayal and unworthiness have to be overcome. My rights and needs have value. I have to be able to look her in the eye. I'm not sure that when it comes to it I can be strong enough.

An unfamiliar female voice answers at Landers Hoffman after I press various options on my keypad.

'Judith Mears,' I say simply, 'is she still working at your Manchester office?'

There is a pause, then, 'Yes she's here, shall I put you through?'

'No, that's okay, don't do that. Tell me whose PA is she now?'

'Oh…' The girl is caught in the act of automatically transferring me. 'Let me see…ah yes, Mrs Mears is PA to one of the partners, Mr Unsworth.'

'Paul Unsworth?' I can't help the query. 'A partner, since when?'

I put the phone down before I get a reply. The news of Paul's elevation leaves me angry at what might have been and was so cruelly denied me. There is something deeply unsatisfactory about this whole Judith issue. Paul's PA is acting as Miriam's go-between, but why? The only answer I can think of is that she's a personal friend helping out, Miriam's confidante, someone she can turn to. The idea that Martin's wife has such a close connection with Judith alarms me. The Judith I worked with prided herself on knowing everything about the Landers Hoffman staff, especially their personal lives.

As for Paul, I suppose he filled the gap I left, despite his lack of talent or imagination. I could have done so much had I been allowed. The horrible feeling I have has nothing to do with Paul, only Judith. She is the type of PA that you tell everything to. I remember welcoming her support and interest. What did I say about Martin to her? How much of my feelings did I reveal? I told her about my problems with Tim, a daily catalogue of frustration and irritation, but did she guess Martin's part in my life? The query hangs like a beckoning gibbet.

*

Carrie has a ring. She displays the sparkle of the single stone which seems much too large to be anything other than crystal.

'We're getting married,' she oozes. 'Justin proposed, went on his knees in front of everyone in the pub, gave me this.' She waves her finger about some more.

Justin. I've seen him and I don't like what I see. Worse, I've seen his handiwork on Carrie's bruised face and arms. He's a thug, but she won't listen to me. My only consoling thought is that she's under Gary's protection. She's not my responsibility but she is young and vulnerable.

'Very nice, must have been expensive.' My words sound mean and spiteful, even to my own ears. 'I hope you'll be very happy, at least you and Justin must be getting on a lot better now, that's good.' I try hard to recover and put kindness into my voice.

'That's the thing.' Carrie speaks wide-eyed. 'We weren't getting on at all. He was being horrible, but now he does this, isn't it great? He's more than made up for it.'

My own loveless marriage began much more auspiciously and I want to tell her, warn her, make her see sense. She should tell the brute to piss off and leave her alone. She is buzzing with excitement, happy beyond reason. I return to the caravan site accounts. At least these provide positive news. Gary is intent on buying a third site now that the first two have performed so spectacularly well. The money is flowing back to O'Brian more freely than even he could have hoped. He has extended our line of credit so that acquiring even the largest sites is well within our reach. Most importantly, I have the residue after tax of a £50,000 bonus nestling in my personal bank account. But as I evaluate the latest prospects, my nagging disquiet about Carrie's brutish boyfriend refuses to die.

Gary arrives breathless, hurrying as always, reluctant to spend time indoors.

'There's a match tonight, I need to get out there and make sure the lads are sorted.' He has one foot in my office and one poised to make an escape.

'This is more important.'

His nose wrinkles at my comment. O'Brian's money has transformed the business; earnings from football parking are now almost insignificant in value. To Gary who worked hard and long to establish himself, the football parking is still the single most important activity in his life.

'Won't it wait? I must get on...' He continues to insist on his own priorities.

'I need you to read these agreements and if you're happy, sign them. There's also a new loan agreement for you to look at. O'Brian has increased the rate of interest and taken on part of the loan personally. That means we're now officially linked with him, although this is entirely above board and legitimate. We need to decide if it's what we want, whether we should take on the added cost and the increased risk.'

As I speak Gary thumbs through the thick legal papers until he finds his own name. As soon as he does, he scrawls quickly underneath and pushes the document aside.

'There.' He looks up. 'Done, signed and sealed, sorted. All it needs is for you to read it and sign if you're happy, I'm happy if you are.' He looks at his watch. 'Got to go.'

'Wait.' I need to tell him about tomorrow evening.

'What is it?'

I can see his distraction is almost complete and give up. 'Oh leave it, I'll talk to you tomorrow. Make sure you come in here first thing.' I give him my sternest look then release him to his football parking.

54

Mrs Youngs herself answers my ring and admits me to the all too familiar apartment. The glass coffee table is still framed by two black settees set at right angles; one is occupied by an elderly gentleman dressed in a dark blue, pin-striped suit and sporting a florid pink tie. The creases on his face and the slack jowls on his neck give him a withered look. It's as if his body was once inhabited by a plumper, more vigorous person and is trying hard to adjust to a new lodger. He is leaning back, almost lying, chin pressed into his chest as he looks at me with apparent distaste.

'This is my father.' Mrs Youngs perches on the edge of the seat beside him. He makes no attempt to rise or any other sign of greeting. Mrs Youngs is dressed in a black and white checked jacket with matching skirt, the fabric shimmers and glistens as if lit from within and programmed to enhance every small movement of its wearer's body. Her hair is coiled and severely swept back from her angular face. I feel very uncomfortable, but it's nothing compared with the tension I detect from these two.

I concentrate on maintaining my own equilibrium, feeling down through my feet to the floor, flexing my toes, helping my awareness to stay with my body and not fly out of my head with needless speculation. The two figures in front of me maintain a stony silence, no greeting, no pleasantries, no softening of the hard ice.

'Thank you for taking the time to speak to me,' I begin, faltering as the words spill out. Coughing, clearing my throat, trying to plaster over the crack in my voice. They look blankly at me.

'Listen. I came to this apartment a week after Martin went missing. He wasn't here. But about ten days later his body was found here. Someone must have moved him after he died and that someone must have killed him.' The urge to justify my cowardly inaction rises in my throat, but the wall of indifference prevents this indulgence.

'It all has something to do with World Ordnance Systems, I'm certain of it.'

The mention of the company name prompts a slight shift in posture from Miriam's father. His face takes on an even more malevolent look.

'Casagrande gave me money to smooth through WOS's acquisition of Associated Composites, a business in Northamptonshire.' I persevere with my exposition but with a growing certainty that what I'm saying isn't welcomed by either of them.

'That business is a front for money laundering activities. I felt real disquiet when I conducted the due diligence exercise and I realise now that it was justified. The operations carried out by Associated Composites are designed to take in cash from criminal activities and make it look like legitimate earnings from the business. Casagrande is the man responsible. He's the one that set me up and had me arrested.'

'How much do you know about this man, Casagrande?' The father speaks for the first time. His voice is surprisingly deep and resonant coming from such a withered frame.

'I only met him once,' I admit. 'Down in Brackley, that's where he gave me the cash. And I saw him at Martin's funeral talking to you.' I look at Mrs Youngs and watch her face change colour slightly underneath the cosmetic perfection. She looks quickly round to her father then back to me.

'There were many people at the funeral, I didn't know all of them.'

'But you did know Casagrande, I watched you greet him,' I press home my point and she allows it in silence.

'You mentioned another name, Popov.' He pronounces the name with disdain, as if it were a cartoon character.

'He's implicated.' I state calmly, refusing to give any further justification.

'How do you know?' he insists.

'I just know.' It's true, I do know. My information is a look and Gary's reaction. 'I just know it was him,' I insist back.

'Where can I find this Popov?' he asks.

'I don't know.'

'Why didn't you go to the police?'

The old feelings of shame push me off balance for an instant.

'I came to you first, I wanted to speak to Mrs Youngs before I did anything. I suppose I was hoping for your help.'

'Help?' The word suddenly bursts out of Miriam's mouth. 'Why would you come to me for help, what help could you possibly expect? You of all people.'

The last words are spat violently at me, leaving me in no doubt that she is aware of my part in Martin's life.

His voice takes over, carefully modulated, very upper class, commanding.

'You have made some serious allegations, young lady, tell me what leads you to them. Is it pure conjecture or is there more to it?'

The numbing effect of Miriam's outburst is stopping my mind from working properly. Any prospect of assistance disappeared the moment I felt the atmosphere in this apartment. Nevertheless, I launch into the explanation I've rehearsed.

'The money laundering scheme at Associated Composites is a brilliant one. Cash from illegal sources is introduced to the motor racing business using people outside normal tax jurisdictions. That's the easy part. The clever bit is the way that Composites convert this into legitimate earnings. Their accounts say that they're paid enormous amounts on the pretext of supplying special components for racing cars. Whether these actually exist or are as good as they claim doesn't matter at all. Composites get tens of millions of pounds for supplying things that cost them almost nothing. That's the key to the whole business. Dirty money comes into the industry through tax havens and is converted into legitimate business profits here in the UK. Now that would be valuable enough for most money laundering schemes, even if UK tax had to be paid on profits. But Composites provide an even better return on the criminal investment by having the ability to re-export money that's clean and accounted for back to its source in the form of sponsorship. It really is the most efficient way of converting black money I've ever heard of.'

I pause for breath and to study the man's reaction. He looks disturbed and upset when he really should be interested and enlightened by what I am saying. The Composites scheme is so clever he should be giving me a round of applause for figuring it out. My own derivation, the caravan parks, is a pale imitation but one that's proving very effective as well. It's amazing what clarity of mind can be induced by the simple act of sitting quietly, without distractions.

'Are you accusing WOS of being an illegal organisation?' he demands. 'One of Britain's largest and most prestigious companies? A company famous all over the world for its quality and innovation?' His words peter out and I judge it appropriate to answer.

'Not at all, I believe WOS are entirely ignorant of what's going on at Composites. The acquisition must have been engineered by Composites to make it even less obvious what its primary purpose really is. As part of a huge conglomerate, it's much easier to hide individual transactions. No, I think WOS have been misled, that's what Martin discovered and that is why he was murdered.'

The faces on both father and daughter betray a growing antipathy to me and my explanation. Glances are exchanged, father nods some unspoken signal and she rises from her perched position.

'We have nothing more to say to you except that you are a liar. If you repeat these ridiculous allegations to anyone else we'll take legal action to protect our family name. Now get out.'

I fumble with my bag and extract the small item that Gary gave me under cover of a large tissue. Eyes are boring into me, she is standing above me in a threatening pose, arms on hips, jaw jutting out, like a chicken about to peck. If I wasn't busy trying to surreptitiously push the device between the cushions of the settee I might have time to appreciate the effort she was putting into the pose. Pushing my hands back onto the seat I stand up and turn to retrieve my handbag. The thing is nestled in place, camouflaged by its tiny blackness. No handshakes are offered, no goodbyes exchanged. My impression of these two is of intense dislike and I fully expect the relationship to deteriorate from this point onwards. These are cold-hearted, inhuman, self-serving people. Before I exhaust my stock of adjectives I am out of the flat and heading down the stairwell. A huge man waits for me on the next landing, smiling as he sees my approach.

55

Gary doesn't normally hang around work much after 4 p.m. except for football parking nights. Tonight his Range Rover is sitting askew, across the front entrance to the office, and he is sitting in it, eyes closed. Before I can walk over to tap gently on his window to rouse him, the peace is shattered by the roar from a large un-silenced motorcycle engine. As the three-wheeled beast pulls to a halt, it's revved up to its limit one more time before becoming still. The silence it creates is complete and welcome.

Michael Powell, or Big Mick as Gary calls him, eases himself out of an almost fully reclining position and staggers slightly as he disembarks from the trike. The predominantly bright orange machine consists of three big wheels, a large plush seat and a huge engine. It's not difficult to imagine that Mick built this thing himself.

Gary, fully awake now, winds down his window to hear our reports.

'You never told me you were sending Mick to keep an eye on me,' I complain half-heartedly.

'Not just Mick,' Gary smiles proudly. 'Ian and a few other lads volunteered to hang around the place, just in case. After all, you do their wages, they wouldn't want anything to happen to you.'

I shouldn't let this display of casual concern touch me but it does. It goes straight to my heart and melts me down into a puddle of need and vulnerability. Gary and the lads are looking out for me, that means a lot. I shouldn't be surprised, I shouldn't be moved, but I am.

'Thanks.' I turn to Mick who is so big he practically surrounds me. Now beyond his fiftieth year, most of his bulk is soft and flabby. He walks stiff-legged because his knees are bad and he complains about any job that keeps him on his feet. Looking at his bright-eyed smile, I see the magnificence of his youth shining through. At twenty, Big Mick must have been a colossus, a mountain of muscle and a man commanding instant respect.

'Didn't see nobody, boss.' Mick reports, double negative no doubt unintended. 'At least nobody lurking about, intending harm to our Jenny.'

'Did you think they were going to hurt me?' I can't help but feel alarmed by the thought. If I hadn't told Gary about my meeting I would have been completely unprotected. Gary seems to believe I was exposing myself to danger which is why he sent the lads. Come to think of it, the interview in the flat did feel quite threatening. Miriam and her father were unsympathetic, but would they cause me actual harm?

'You can't be too careful,' Gary answers. 'Anyway, did you manage to plant the bug? Did they notice it?'

'I put it down the side of the settee, I'm not sure it'll work there, won't it be muffled or something?'

'As long as they don't know it's there, that's the important thing.' Gary's eyes sparkle with excitement. 'We'll collect it tomorrow and see if there's anything on it.'

56

I can still hardly bear to look at the photograph. Even though it only shows the man's face, I know what the rest of him was doing when it was taken. It took a lot of bravery to carefully mask the bits of his body and mine, using a piece of card with an appropriate aperture. The photocopying was carried out in Carrie's absence and I now have fifty copies distributed.

If Miriam is not feeling helpful I have to pursue my own lines of enquiry. Gary has reluctantly passed them on to all the lads and told them to keep their eyes out. Short of pinning it up on every lamp post in Manchester with my phone number underneath, it's all I can do for now.

Since my meeting yesterday with Miriam and her father, Gary has been unusually attentive, popping in and out of the office with uncharacteristic regularity. The opportunity is too good to be missed and I force him to scan the pile of outstanding paperwork and make his childlike signature where appropriate.

Big Mick has been given my key to the apartment. It occurs to me that his massive bulk and dodgy knees don't make him an obvious candidate for a job requiring stealth. I think Gary is as anxious as I am to find out if the recording device overheard anything useful.

Carrie seems oblivious to the tension and is keen to elicit what information she can from me about the photograph.

'If I knew who he was, I wouldn't have had to distribute his picture, Carrie.'

'Yes, but is he a relative? Why do you want to find him?'

'He might have information about what we talked about, you know, the way I was imprisoned, what happened to me.'

'He looks funny with his face all screwed up like that,' she observes. 'What was he doing?'

'It's hard to say, Carrie.' I try to leave it at that, but she returns to the subject at every available opportunity, leaving me glad for once when she skips off home at the end of the working day.

The gloom is gathering outside and my stomach is crying out for its evening meal. I should have gone out for my run half an hour ago but I'm rooted to my chair, waiting for Gary, waiting for Mick, waiting for the device. To distract myself I look at the WOS website for the hundredth time. Already I can recite the long list of countries where they have offices or factories. I'm familiar with their products, their markets, their turnover, their profits and their shareholdings.

Almost idly, almost by chance, I flick to a graphic showing the Board of Directors, names and tiny photographs arranged in a nice circle. Some of the faces are familiar from my dealings at Landers Hoffman, but one of the others catches my eye. The photograph is very small and disassembles itself into a soggy blur when enlarged, but I'm convinced this is a picture of Miriam's father when he was younger and fatter.

The tag line reads: Lieutenant General Sir Algernon Tristan Wallace, KBE, Non-Executive Deputy Chairman.

My brain freezes, overwhelmed by the implications of this discovery.

57

The red light is flashing at my bedside. I am awake. The dull glow of the alarm shows 3:54 and someone is in the flat. There has been a break-in, exactly as Gary expected. It's as if I've never slept, as if I sat up all night waiting for the tell-tale shaft of red.

Sliding slowly and gently from beneath the duvet, I lie for a moment on the thin carpet, long enough to locate the smooth wooden nightstick. Grasping it firmly in my left hand, I slither to the bedroom door and listen. My breath seizes up, making me gasp suddenly as the oxygen deficit overwhelms my need for silence. Soft footsteps are approaching. Crouching behind the door, trembling with excitement, infusions of adrenalin fuelling my bloodstream, I pray for an intruder to come my way.

My bedroom door handle turns softly. Two men make a sudden entrance and glide over to my bed. They stand transfixed for an instant when they realise their quarry is not lying asleep and unaware. I take three steps, half crouched, fast, and transfer the energy into the point of my stick as it smashes into the nearest man where the base of the skull and the top of his neck meet. I scream my loudest kiai as I make contact. I channel every ounce of my being into the hit.

The second man dives across the bed to grapple with me but he becomes unbalanced as I step back to avoid his hands. As he overreaches, I hit his temple with my fist while I'm still clutching the heavy truncheon. He slumps forward and I rain blows onto his head and neck. These are the men who violated me, these are worse than animals, they deserve to suffer. I shout my pain at them as I make sure they stay down, that they don't leap up and harm me, even though they are lying still, even though my stick and hands and forearms are slick with blood, I keep on making sure.

Strong arms envelop me, calm words disturb my concentration.

'That's enough, Jenny, stop now, it's over, take it easy.' Big Mick is here, holding me. Lights flash on, my bed is scarlet. A man lies prone and bleeding onto my bedclothes, another is on the floor, this one leaking blood from his ear.

'Fucking hell.' I hear Ian's voice as he surveys the carnage. 'Are they dead? Did you kill them, Jenny?'

The words shock and freeze me to the spot. I discover that blood is dripping off the ends of my fingers onto the bedroom carpet. One of the intruders, the first one I hit, is moving in small spasms, legs and arms shaking in an uncoordinated way. The man lying face down across my bed is quite still.

Mick is already on the phone, reporting.

'Two guys, both in a very bad way. Might be critical. Head injuries. No not me, Jenny. Hit them both with a truncheon. Yes. Yes, Gary. No. Yes, I think we could. There's a right mess, carpet and bed clothes. Okay. Yes. Yes I will. Okay. See you later.' He rings off and looks up at me. 'Gary says to get them out of the flat.'

'What about the police?' I ask.

'Gary says we can't afford to involve the police, that they'll take a dim view.' Mick gestures towards the carnage.

'Okay.' I nod in the realisation that Gary is right, this doesn't look good at all. Two men broke into my home with the intent to harm me and I defended myself, that's the truth of it, but all the police care about is the dead or injured and arresting someone they can pin the blame on. And that's going to be me. I have a history of imprisonment and a record of violence, even though all of it is unwarranted and completely unfair. It's me they are going to arrest. Gary is right, I can't afford to have the police involved.

'What are we going to do?'

'Gary says to take them to Hope Hospital and leave them there. You need to tidy up a bit.' He looks down at my feet. 'There's a lot of blood on your carpet, might be hard to get out.'

My mind snaps into a vision of my mother sprinkling flour onto a red carpet stain, where my father's wine glass lies tipped on its side. While she kneels busy and distracted, he is giving me that look. Fear tightens my chest, stops my breathing. A sharp pain doubles me in two; I stagger off to the toilet.

58

My new office is really a caravan, a portable home modified to do the job. It sits in proud isolation at the entrance to the park, out of sync with the serried ranks and regimented rows that confine the other buildings. At least I don't have far to walk home, I can see my new accommodation from where I sit, an entirely unremarkable chalet, exactly like every other one on the site. Three from the end; one, two, three, I have to count in case I pick the wrong caravan and end up sleeping in someone else's bed. Not that they would mind, or in most cases even notice. My neighbours are generally quite elderly.

Gary insisted I vacate the Salford flat as soon as I'd packed and cleaned up the mess. Here in Fleetwood, I'm considered far enough away from marauding thugs and enquiring policemen. News of the intruders' condition is not encouraging. Both are still on the critical list, in intensive care. At least they're not dead and I ought to be grateful for that.

I'm more or less on my own up here, no Carrie for company, no Gary popping in and out. I do have a handyman, Gerard. What exactly he does to warrant that title I'm yet to discover. Gerard seems to be even older than the clientele he serves. When he potters off to oil a sticking door I half expect never to see him alive again.

Ian, or one of the other lads, arrives most mornings with the post and any other documents I need to see. My new location is fine in terms of getting my work done and being out of harm's way, but it feels like I'm in an old person's prison from which there's no escape.

Tim is still being an arse about Toby, still insisting I come to the house and only see him there. 'Under supervision,' he recites. 'Under supervision – that's what the court decided, can't go against the court.' He really is an even bigger arsehole now than he was when we were married. I can hear that woman's tinny shriek in everything he says to me. Notwithstanding, I'll be back down there again on Saturday and am looking forward to seeing Toby's little face, hearing his vocal cascade.

A man is standing in the reception area. Outside I can see a towing van hitched to the back of an aged Volvo.

'Do you have any overnight berths?' he asks. At first I hear the question wrongly and wonder why he's asking such a weird question. I have visions of babies newly born in the night.

'No, sorry, residential only, no touring vans,' I switch into caravan speak and resist admiring his dun coloured anorak as he slopes off.

It's not a bad idea, though, touring vans, overnight stays, cash payments. I make a note to gradually build up this additional source of income in the accounts. Things are looking good in the caravan business, this could make them better. A quick mental calculation involving ten berths and two hundred and fifty days' occupation at twenty pounds a night, that's fifty thousand a year, worth having, or rather worth pretending to have.

The wind must have shifted. I can detect the slightly sweet smell of decomposition wafting over from the immense landfill site that neighbours us to the east. A tram clatters purposefully along the track that divides us. In ten minutes it will reach the limit of its track and have to stop to avoid plunging into the Irish Sea. In ten more minutes it will make the return journey south to Blackpool and beyond.

After the hectic flight out of Salford, a couple of weeks of tranquillity and isolation have been a welcome relief. Now the novelty is wearing off. I need to make progress, stop hiding, become the hunter not the hunted. Now I know more about the WOS involvement in my situation I need to ask more questions. Miriam's father, Martin's father-in-law, is Lieutenant Colonel Algernon Wallace and this changes everything. The assumption I made that WOS were unwitting accomplices to the criminal goings on at Associated Composites no longer holds water. They are in it up to their necks.

211

After a distinguished military career, during which I feel sure he'll have been responsible for awarding large contracts to WOS, Wallace joined the company as the director responsible for negotiating sales overseas. His biography, conveniently published on the British Army website, confirms all of this and more. The Gulf States he saw service in are all major customers of WOS armaments. I can't be the first person to wonder about Wallace's connections, after all, the information is out there for anyone to find. Maybe this sort of issue would be dealt with during an Office of Fair Trading investigation. WOS successfully resisted such an enquiry during my time at Landers Hoffman.

As I sit in the cabin, engulfed in the sickly odour, watching the sun slowly set, more of my past surfaces for a new look. Now I'm aware of Martin's family connection with WOS, how does this modify my own view of events, beginning with Martin's death? Did Wallace have his son-in-law murdered to protect himself and his nefarious activities? Was Miriam a party to this? I find it hard to imagine anyone being so callous.

I think of Tim and Toby and the court and revise my opinion. If Tim had been having an affair, what would I have felt, what would I have been capable of doing? What am I capable of?

If Tim were dead then Toby would be all mine, it would be that simple. The thrill of this realisation is quickly followed by an admission that however convenient it might be, I would be sorry if Tim died and certainly not willing to actively contemplate murdering him, whatever the attraction.

Before I finish work for the day so that I can fit in a nice run before it gets too dark, I check my emails one last time. Among the usual promises of a better erection and a larger penis nestles a single item of note.

The device I left at the flat was successfully retrieved by Mick and taken to one of Gary's mates for downloading. 'If there's anything on the recording he'll find it' was the promise, but he seems to be taking his time getting round to it. Now I have an email with a voice file attached. My heart is beating faster at the prospect of eavesdropping on Miriam and her dad.

A long frustrating silence is all that I'm hearing, but I can see that there's over an hour of something on this recording. Five minutes in, I'm shocked to hear a voice, crystal clear and unmistakably Miriam Young's.

'This is my father,' she says and I'm instantly transported back to discomfort and awkwardness. When I speak there's an embarrassing period of coughing and throat clearing. My voice is tinny and cowering. I am making myself small in front of these people. By the time I'm finally invited to leave in no uncertain terms, the interview sits even more uncomfortably with me than it did at the time.

Had I known he would be there and who he was, I'd have been much more careful about what I said. As it is, I spill out everything I know and all that I conjecture. Why I should think I might have been among allies is a difficult one to answer now.

The fumbling with the device complete, I hear myself leave the flat. Now Miriam's voice begins to whine in complaint.

'That was horrible, seeing her like that. Was it really necessary, I feel humiliated.'

'You had to be here, darling,' his voice plummy and calm, 'she wouldn't have come otherwise.'

'Well, it was horrible, seeing her. I can't believe you made me do it. She must think I'm such a fool. I'll bet she's laughing at me right now, telling her friends about me.'

'Nonsense, my dear, she's a frightened little rabbit, you'll not be hearing from her again, you have my word.'

'What she said about Martin, is it true, was he killed?'

'Now, now, we've been through all that. Don't distress yourself just on account of that spiteful bitch. He died, it was his heart, nothing sinister about it, only sad, very sad. He was a special man, your Martin.'

'But he was having an affair, and with that woman, you told me. Why did you make me come here, why did I have to listen to all that?'

'It's important for the family. Look, I'll make sure she never bothers you again, I promise.'

Bright headlights, two pairs, swing off the road and head up the drive towards me. There is something disturbing about the aggressive way in which they are driving, not the stately progression I associate with returning residents in their Nissan Micras. These are big vehicles, vans.

As they come to an abrupt halt outside my window I duck out of sight under my desk. As a precaution I switch off the computer by pushing the button near my face. Loud voices, men shouting, make me curl up and cower in my precarious hide-out. Any worries I have about potential embarrassment are replaced by genuine concern and fear.

More voices. I hear my name being called. Boots clatter into the reception area beyond my open door. I hear Gerard, still pottering about aimlessly even at this time. He must be on his way to download the day's catalogue of minor defects onto my already over-loaded brain.

'She's not here, I'm looking for her myself.'

'Where then could she have gone?' The question is harsh and unpleasant, phrased awkwardly as if unused to speaking English.

'She'll be running,' Gerard offers proudly. 'She always goes running about now. Every day. Rain or shine.'

Footsteps recede, clumping outside, allowing me to breathe deeply.

'Oh!' I hear Gerard shout. 'She won't be long. That's her caravan over there, third one along. You can wait for her in the office. She'll be back very soon.' His overly helpful suggestions are making me cringe with exasperation. The footsteps return, as instructed. Gerard has his way. I am trapped here, cowering under my desk.

'I'll make sure she never bothers you again' runs around my mind. Not only the words, but the way he says them. There is certainty in the promise he makes. I'm sure he is the one responsible for the intruders at my flat and now these men are looking for me at my new home.

The footfalls are amplified by the suspended floor and rickety construction. The whole building vibrates to the comings and goings. I have visions of very large men with huge boots clumping around only a few feet away. Soon, surely, someone will take the trouble to come in here and look under my desk.

The rocking and shaking is stilled. I get the feeling that the boots have left the building. My knees are hurting. One of my feet has pins and needles, I need to move, this seems as good an opportunity as any.

Slowly I uncoil myself and peer over the parapet. A man is sitting on the reception table with his back to me. The tightness of his grey sweatshirt accentuates the saddle of thick muscle around his shoulders and neck. He is unaware of me, but I have to get past him to make my escape.

Looking around the office I can't see any useful implement with which to incapacitate him. Under the circumstances, a gun in my desk drawer would have been very useful but Gary's ban on firearms precludes that possibility. Stapler, computer keyboard, desk-tidy containing paper clips and drawing pins, small plant in a black pot of soil. Nothing useful like a baseball bat or pickaxe handle.

My desperate search is halted when I look up to see the man in the grey sweatshirt is looking straight at me. His face is square and handsome, his eyes gaze unconcernedly at me. No alarm, no shouting, no display of surprise, only a slow movement of his legs as he swings off the table and stands in the doorway. His arms and torso match the exaggerated musculature of his back and neck. If he's an obsessive body-builder, taking supplements and pills, concerned only with the look of his oiled body, I have a chance. Although he may look immensely strong and almost certainly is, I have sparred with his type before and found them slow to react, poor fighters, easily thrown off balance.

Speed and skill can beat pure strength. I hold this thought and pick up the stapler in one hand and my phone in the other. Heart thudding with tension, I try to match his apparent disregard and force a smile.

'Oh, hi!' I beam at him. Holding out my phone in my left hand I take a step towards him. He remains static, feet parallel, showing no sign of a defensive posture. As his eyes move to look at the phone I take another step, this time fast. As my hip swings into the stride I bring my right arm through and punch him in his temple with every ounce of strength and technique I can muster. The weight of the stapler adds to the force and momentum. My fist connects with immense power.

Instead of collapsing in a heap, instead of being knocked sideways and insensible, instead of flinching, this man stands upright as if nothing's happened. The pain in my fist is testament to the powerful blow I've just inflicted, but it has no apparent effect on him at all.

Before I can withdraw my arm and strike again, both of my wrists are grabbed by his strong hands. I'm standing helpless, arms aloft, locked in his unshakable grip. I try to deliver kicks but he manoeuvres away without any sign of effort. He calls out a few words, not in English, maybe Russian, another man appears, older and not at all handsome, but also dressed in a grey sweatshirt and jogging pants.

'Ah.' The older man grins to show crooked yellow teeth. 'Jenny Parker.' He fishes out a piece of paper from his back pocket, looks at it, then at me again. 'Yes, Jenny Parker, put her in the car.'

I'm shouting as loud as I can, things like 'Help, call the police, get off me, leave me alone,' until he steps forward and punches me hard in my stomach. Now I can't breathe, never mind shout. The pain overwhelms me, I sink to my knees, supported only by my grasped arms. My assailant loosens his grip on my wrists, allows me to fall, then picks me up by my waist and carries me under one arm. He deposits me in the luggage area of a white van, behind the rear seats. I'm still clutching my belly and trying to gasp in air when the vehicle drives away.

59

The relief at being taken out of the sweaty confinement of the van is short-lived. I'm grabbed again, carried inside a portacabin and lashed securely onto a table. My arms and legs are completely immobilised and I can barely move my head. All the resistance has been knocked out of me on the journey. I only had to move a little bit before a heavy fist swung into action. Every part of me aches.

The little I can see around the room fills me with dread. There are three video cameras on tripods in the corners, all pointing at me. The older, ugly man brandishes a bright knife in my face and grins his halitosis into my nostrils. The big man who caught me is by the door and I sense another presence out of my direct line of sight.

'Please!' I beg him. 'Don't hurt me, I'll pay you, I'll give you money, all the money I have, fifty thousand pounds, I'll give it all to you, please don't hurt me.' I am desperate, I have no other hope.

He makes no verbal answer, just pushes the cold blade under my shirt.

'Please...' My own voice sounds unfamiliar to me, distant.

The knife works its way upwards, slicing through the thin cloth, splitting my clothes in two. I am screaming for my life now, with the last vestiges of my strength.

A heavy blow to my abdomen stills my voice. The older man grimaces in disapproval, his face still looming above mine. 'Leave her, let her yell, he'll like it. He said to make her suffer.'

The tell-tale red lights show the cameras are filming, I am part of some perverted drama. The knife finishes with my top. He spreads the sundered clothing aside, baring my breasts. His face shows no sign of interest, no sign of emotion, no mercy or compassion, only cruel indifference in a cloud of bad breath.

He moves down to my feet, I feel him slicing each trouser leg in turn then my pants are torn away. I am naked, exposed, splayed out in front of these disgusting men. I wonder if this is another version of what happened to me when I was drugged. This time I'm fully conscious of what's happening to me but somehow I'm still able to detach myself. It's as if I've already abandoned my flesh to them and my spirit is preparing to vacate my body.

His smell is back, the point of his knife pressed against my throat.

'Anyone want to use her before I cut her up?' His words have no effect on me. I understand them but they mean nothing. A strange calmness has settled into me, my anxiety has been released. I know I'm lost and accept its inevitability.

'Me.' A new voice, younger, with an unmistakeable northern accent. The older man steps aside, I strain my head to see someone unzipping himself next to my head, taking out his penis, stroking it. A sudden jolt of recognition hits me. I know this man, it's Justin, Carrie's fiancé, the one who abuses her then gives her expensive jewellery.

'Justin?' I ask.

'Mrs Parker,' he replies. 'I'm going to do you a big favour. Give you one last bit of pleasure before he cuts you up.'

He leans over me so that I can see his face clearly, as he does so his hardening cock brushes my cheek and I grab it between my teeth. He shouts and tries to pull it away but I bite harder, fasten my teeth deep into his meat.

He starts to hit me and I twist my grip, trying to bite through his gristle, feeling his warm blood trickling down my chin. Before I can sever the end of his cock completely a savage blow to my stomach loosens my grip.

Justin pulls away, screaming with anguish. My mind can't help wondering how he'll explain to Carrie why he has my tooth marks in his penis.

I hear a familiar engine noise outside, the ear-splitting sound of Big Mick's motorised tricycle. Almost as soon as it stops, Mick appears in the doorway. I forget my pain and strain to look at him.

219

The strong man in the grey sweatshirt, the man who subdued me so easily, moves to block Mick's entrance. My heart sinks with the recent memory of his immense power and I fear for poor Mick. He attacks, but Mick absorbs his blows and grabs him around his neck. Remarkably, Mick manages to put this man in a headlock and continue his progress towards me.

The man with the knife flashes it towards Mick's chest, but Mick brings the head under his arm round to parry it.

Another vehicle arrives, men run into the room. Mick releases the bloody mess under his arm. Gary appears, pushes past him and fells the older man with a series of blows from a pickaxe handle. Strong arms pick me off the table and carry me gently to Gary's Range Rover. I can hear my own sobbing, but I can't do anything to stop it.

60

A man's face looks down on me as I open my eyes. It's a young face, cheerful and mottled, with untidy hair and an unthreatening smile. One corner of the poster has flapped free from the piece of Blu-Tack that should hold it tight to the ceiling. I remember I am in Sally's room, in Sally's bed, being stared at by one of Sally's Pop Idols. The place has a nice smell, fresh and clean, with a hint of wholesome cooking wafting through the door. I feel well enough to be hungry. There are a few twinges of pain as I sit up, the worst of these is in my stomach. I'm not sure if this is a result of the blows I received or a continuation of my fearfulness.

I swing my legs out of bed and find I'm wearing pink pyjamas with tiny white rabbits running around all over them. These must also be Sally's, she is a big girl for twelve and her things fit me quite well.

Downstairs, Gary and his family are already sitting around the kitchen table. Doreen, his wife, stands resplendent in her pinny and enormous quantity of red hair, doling out ladles full of steaming stew to the children. Sally, my room donor, is a be-freckled child with her mother's hair colour and her father's stocky build. She is the middle of three sisters; the eldest girl,

Siobhan, is fourteen, small, delicate and fair-haired. Sophie the ten-year-old is loud and boisterous, she pushes her dish to the front of the queue and complains vociferously as Sean, Gary's eight-year-old son, gets served first. It's either because he's the youngest or, as I fear, because he's a male, that he gets priority. I can't help thinking I'm sitting among a typical Irish family, three girls then a boy. It's as if poor Doreen was expected to produce offspring until a male popped out. This may be an unkind thought I am having and completely untrue, it's only that it looks that way to me. Nobody remarks on the fact that I'm sitting down to the evening meal in pink pyjamas, nor that I have occupied Sally's bed for two days solid now. The stew is delicious but I'm so hungry I could eat a tin of dog food.

My portion disappears almost instantly and I usurp the younger O'Donnells by being served second helpings out of turn. The chatter around the table is warm and good-humoured, the gentle banter among the children is full of fun.

'Aw Sean, don't you be slurping your food like that.' From Siobhan.

'Nah Sean, eat posh like this.' Sally places a tiny morsel of lamb on the back of her fork and takes a full minute, raising it slowly and elegantly to her mouth. There is a flash of steel as Sophie takes the opportunity to use her fork to purloin a choice morsel whilst Sally is otherwise engaged. Doreen and Gary sit proudly at either end of the table, smiling broad beams at each other. Carrie comes into the kitchen, takes the spare seat in silence and avoids acknowledging my presence with eye contact. She stares sullenly into her plate. All the pretend bickering stops and the atmosphere is suddenly flat.

'We need to talk.' I am addressing Gary but I could equally mean Carrie. Gary mops up the last of his gravy with a sizeable wedge of bread, then stands up.

'I'll go see to the horses.' He nods at me. 'If you like you can come and help.'

There are a row of green and grey coats hanging on hooks by the back door. Gary hands one to me and we walk outside to his car. The stables are barely fifty yards from his house, but he drives there and we sit quietly for a while.

Eventually I take a deep breath and ask, 'How come you managed to find me?' My voice falters towards the end of the question as I remember the teeth, the smell and the knife.

'We were lucky, so we were. They used the same van when they raided your flat. Ian put one of his trackers on it, just so we could see where it went. When Gerard called to say what had happened it was the only thing we could do, find their van.'

I breathe out heavily and gasp air back in as if my body doesn't believe I'll get another chance.

'Did you see it was Justin, Carrie's Justin, did you see what I did to him?'

'That little shit.' Gary screws his face in distaste. 'That's how they found you, it's how they knew where you were. Carrie told him, she was telling him everything. God help us you were brave. We took the cameras, I watched it through. Those are nasty bastards, especially that Yuri, the one with the knife.'

I feel surprised that Gary knows the names of these thugs.

'I suppose they're Popov's men, that's how you know them?'

Gary looks thoughtful.

'No. Popov told me who they are but they don't have anything to do with him.'

'I'm surprised, I thought Popov was the one that got me after the funeral. He says that wasn't him or any of his associates?'

'Popov had nothing to do with you being attacked.'

My heart sinks. Gary had been right to take Popov's advice and cast me out. A flash of fear for Gary's family, this place, his whole business makes me recoil with guilt. I am the cause of all this trouble, I'm bringing danger to his doorstep.

'They'll come here, they'll kill us all. I have to get away or you'll all be in danger.'

222

Gary says nothing. His tacit reply is confirmation of everything I say. He clicks open the car door, a smell of horse mixes with the scent of leather.

As he shovels straw, liberally laced with dung, into a wheelbarrow, I hover around him, hoping for some words of comfort. I need reassurance, I want him to say they are all dead, all gone away, never coming back. He shovels silently.

Cold feet bring me back from my desperate thoughts into the present. I am standing in a soggy stable wearing pink pyjamas under a waxed jacket. On my feet is a pair of fluffy pink slippers which are slowly absorbing the brown colouration of the liquid they are standing in.

A long muzzle sniffs inquisitively at my face. I clasp the horse's neck in both hands and lean my head against it. As I breathe, the aroma fills my lungs and the gentle kindness of the animal supports my spirit. I want to stay here, be with the horses, lie in the straw, share their oats, hide.

On the ridiculously short drive back to the house, I worry about the muddy imprints my soiled slippers make on the pristine grey carpet. Gary appears unconcerned about the state of his car's interior décor.

'Carrie looks upset, I think she's angry with me for biting her boyfriend's dick.' The words force a wry smile from Gary, even I can appreciate the dark humour in my words now they are said.

'No, not you, she's angry with me,' Gary replies. 'She knows nothing about what happened, only that Justin is no good; a thief and a killer of defenceless women, I told her. I said he'd betrayed you, led them to harm you. She knows he found out where you were from her, she's upset with me and with herself. She's scared of what you must think of her.'

My heart opens to the poor girl, no wonder she can't look me in the eye.

'You do know why I did that to Justin, don't you?'

'Oh yes, as I say we took the cameras, I watched the video, you showed real guts.'

A flush of blood suffuses my cheeks as I think of Gary being witness to my humiliation. But better Gary sees me than I am filmed being sliced to pieces. As I trail mud into the kitchen, I see Doreen clearing up and the children clustered around the TV. Carrie is among them, kneeling small and child-like. I sit beside her and hold her in my arms. She begins to sob her apology to me. There's no need for words, she can feel my love for her.

61

It's cold and wet; the smell from the landfill site is almost sick-making. I can't help but smile to myself at the thought that according to my accounts I have forty-two happy holiday-makers frolicking here. Understandably, none of them is in view as my quasi-presidential cavalcade comes to rest outside my chalet. Gary insists I go mob-handed to retrieve my belongings, although nothing untoward has happened since my abduction and rescue.

The more the merrier when it comes to moving house. I decide to keep watch while burly men labour over transferring everything I own into a big white van. Better this than the way they probably expect, me labouring and them watching over me. Gerard ambles across from the office, face densely creased with concern and a desperate need to find out what is going on.

'Mrs Parker,' he greets. 'Very glad to see you're all right. So, are you moving out, you leaving us?'

'It was only ever going to be temporary, Gerard. I need to be in Manchester, close to the office.'

'So,' he asks, 'what's your new address?'

Alarm bells go off inside my head at his intrusive questioning. My paranoia decides he's in league with my assassins and I feel myself begin to bristle.

'Hope it's as nice as here,' he continues without any trace of irony in his voice.

I look at this kind old gentleman and decide that he has only good, honest intentions, that I'm wrong to doubt him. My smile returns as I answer.

'How could anywhere be better than this?' I'm certain that my sarcasm would be transparent to most, but not to honest Gerard. He beams with satisfaction, God help him; he adores this rat-infested stink hole.

There are some mumblings of discontent when I announce that I'm walking over to the office.

'We should come with you,' they protest.

'Get on with the loading. Gerard will look after me, won't you, Gerard?' Gerard looks puzzled for a moment then nods vigorously.

Everything is where I left it, including the stapler and my old phone lying in the doorway. Whether Gerard left them there out of laziness or reluctance to disturb a crime scene I'm not interested enough to ask, preferring to be left alone to collect my files and papers. The computer churns into life, slowly and painfully performing all the arcane functions it deems necessary before it becomes responsive. I've found by bitter experience that clicking away too soon at it only makes things worse. If I bother it before it's ready, it recedes into a frozen sulk.

Of the eighty-four unopened emails displayed, I judge none of them to be of any relevance or interest. I see the one I was engaged with before my abduction and open the voice file again, scrolling through to where I left off.

'It's important for the family. Look, I'll make sure she never bothers you again, you have my word.' As I listen to the voice of that evil, wizened old bastard I remember the man with the knife telling me 'he' wanted to see me suffer. Well I have one or two ideas about whose turn it is to feel the pain. I've worked out a plan to expose Wallace and WOS as criminals without having to include myself in the proceedings. When I'm finished with them, they'll think that an OFT investigation is the least of their worries.

The van appears by the window. I'm being waved at to join the merry throng of men in the front. There's still ten minutes to go before the end of the recording, and I need to unplug the web of wires before I can extract the computer and take it with me. The cheeky beggars start beeping the horn to hurry me up. They do have a point, they have work to go to, paying work, not like the babysitting they're engaged in at present. I can get back to this later when I have peace and quiet. But I need to know...

They're calling me from the loaded van.

'Be out in a minute, need to make a call, won't be long.' I shout back. A door closes.

More honking outside. I wave them away, hold up five fingers, shake my head at them.

'Hello.' Miriam's father is speaking. 'Sorry to bother you so late, I'm a bit concerned about this Composites business.'

His voice has taken on a surprisingly hesitant quality.

'Yes, yes I know that. It's just that Miriam and I have been speaking to Jenny Parker...'

It goes quiet.

'I know, I understand, she met us here, spoke about a man called Casagrande, accused us of being in league with him, said he was a murderer, that he killed poor Martin.'

A long silence.

'No, don't get me wrong, I accept your reassurances, no, not a bit of it, I'll leave it with you. Speak to her yourself if you like, after all she is one of yours, even if she has gone off the rails. No, no, keep me posted. If you find out anything about this Casagrande, let me know.'

It's not Casagrande, then. I've been barking up the wrong tree, planning revenge on the wrong people. My anger begins to overwhelm me, anger at my blindness, my stupidity, but most of all my anger is directed towards whoever is trying to kill me. I might not know who that is, but at least now I know where I might find him.

62

Knotted with excitement and fear of discovery, I sit half crouched behind the reception desk at the Landers Hoffman offices. At this late hour the building is silent and empty. The alarms and cameras confirm that the only other occupants are Ian who is lurking by the entrance and Chris, the man next to me. Ian is the only legitimate inhabitant, Chris and I are both illicit interlopers, allowed in only through the laxity of the security firm paid to guard the place. Looking at the situation more positively, GOD Security is tripling its cover for no extra cost.

Chris is an older man than I expected from Gary's description. 'A high tech computer whiz kid,' Gary said. The languorous movements and receding hairline belie that epithet. At least he's wearing brown corduroy trousers so he ticks that box. He also has the scent of a man who lives alone, takes few showers and changes his clothes infrequently. He's no worse than most of the O'Donnell employees, though I'm desensitised enough by now to pull up a chair and sit close enough to view his computer screen as he works. My excitement is intense. Here I am at the heart of Landers Hoffman, hacking into their most closely guarded secrets, or at least that's what Chris is up to. I'm only sitting here watching his handiwork.

He assures me that he will extract the information I require whatever security measures might be in place. He also says that any mention of Casagrande will be picked up, whatever form it might take, and that another search is in progress looking for any mention of my name. Half an hour has passed like a flash, Chris is getting up to leave without offering me anything to look at.

'Where are you going?' I ask.

He turns his head reluctantly to answer.

'Home.'

'But we're not finished,' I complain.

'Obviously not. But I don't have to be here. Any results will come through to this.' He brandishes a small hand-held device. 'Could take several hours to get through everything. I've set it to be very thorough. You'll have everything you need by tomorrow. I suggest you go home and get some sleep.'

'Wait.' I feel flat, deflated. I want to see the evidence flashing onto the screen. I need to be here, to feel excited, busy, clandestine, surreptitious.

'What?' He looks irritated now.

'You can't be sure we'll search every computer, can you?'

'That's what we're doing,' he protests.

'What about the files on local hard drives, on laptops for example?'

'As long as they're connected to the network, we'll see them.'

'What if they're switched off?'

'Oh, I see, not then. Can't see them if they're off. Obviously not.'

'Then come on. Let's go and turn them all on, make sure.'

'Isn't that a bit risky? Someone might find out.' Chris looks around nervously.

'Let them, all I want is the evidence. Are you coming or do I have to do it on my own?'

He follows me to the lifts. I wave to Ian and he nods his acquiescence.

Most of the machines are on, but there are some that aren't. Chris finds a laptop in a bag and takes it out and turns it on. He grins at me, embarrassed that I was right all along. Some of the offices are locked, but I have Ian's full set of keys. Chris has no problem getting into any computer. When I switch one on, it immediately asks me for a password and I'm completely at a loss. Chris has a knack of quickly by-passing that procedure by jabbing a memory stick into it and pressing a few keys.

This is more like it. I'm enjoying the thrill of burglary and snooping around. While Chris works I have fun looking through desk drawers and peeping into filing cabinets.

'Bingo.'

The sudden shout shocks me and I quickly find Chris hunched over a laptop in the general office.

'Here's something with your name on it,' he announces. I watch over his smelly shoulder as he clicks away. A video flashes onto the screen. 'Oh shit, sorry...' Chris fumbles to close down the offending images. 'Sorry, it's porn.'

'Wait,' I instruct. 'Leave it on.' He does. I watch with disgust and horror. It's got my name on it because it's me. My video, the film of me being raped by grinning men. Numb, saddened and confused I sit and survey the office. My old seat is only a few feet away. I don't need the confirmation of the payslips in the desk drawer, I already know whose place this is. It belongs to Roger, that smelly creep who was always leering at me, the man who lectured me about money laundering and mauled me in the pub after Martin's funeral.

So it wasn't Wallace, nor anyone else. Roger, that's who spiked my drink and abused me. Now I know.

Chris announces his work is complete at 3 a.m. He projects an air of pride at a job well done and speedily carried out. My only disappointment is that there's no mention of Casagrande, at least none that he's picked up.

'That can't be right,' I protest. 'For a start I wrote a report that had his name in it.'

'Well, it's not there now,' Chris insists.

'I don't think your scan worked properly.'

He looks distressed.

'Well I'm sure it did. I know what I'm doing.'

'Then we'll try again tomorrow night, I need to know for sure.'

'Look Jenny, I've been thorough, honest I have.'

I have a hollow feeling. I didn't expect to discover what I have about Roger, but he's not the one I'm concerned with just now. I need to get to the man who is hell bent on having me tortured and killed and I doubt very much that Roger is that man.

'Before you go,' I turn to Chris, 'one more try.'

Ian hoves into view; long, pale and looking unwell, as always. The poor guy never sees the sun, I guess.

'Look,' Chris says, 'I've done all I can.'

'It's important,' I say, 'life-or-death-important. My life or my death.'

He frowns, not in annoyance; more like deep thought.

'How about calendars, diaries, appointments?' he asks. 'Anything like that of interest?'

'Yes.' My heart leaps and I grasp this second chance. 'Can you search in people's diaries?'

'Well yes, it's more difficult, the files are in a difficult format. But I can do it.' He begins to clatter away on the reception computer keyboard. Twenty minutes later he whoops and calls me away from a magazine I'm thumbing aimlessly through.

'Casagrande!' He is speaking with a hushed whisper. 'One entry, it's for the twenty-first of October a couple of years ago. It reads: Dinner with MY, MS and OR at Casagrande's house.'

'Who?' I ask. 'Whose diary is that?'

Chris fiddles about while I feel I'm falling through air without a parachute.

'Okay, got it. Does the name Eric Knowles ring a bell?'

Of course Eric, it has to be him and I should have known that all along. He's the one who set me up, sent me to prison; he's the one who gave me Martin's job so that I could take the blame for any problems with WOS. He's the one who killed Martin.

63

The annoying sound of a klaxon announces the arrival of a text. I regret letting Carrie fiddle with my phone yesterday. She thinks both the noise and my normal reaction to it hilarious. There's no point looking at it. It's 5.30 a.m. and I'm heading back to Gary's house with my head full of plans. At this time of night, I presume it must be my phone provider offering me some additional services. In any case my phone is buried in my bag and my bag is in the passenger footwell where I can't reach it without stopping the car.

The more I think about Eric Knowles the more I hate him. Everything he said, everything he did takes on a new meaning. How could I have been so vain as to think I merited Martin's job? Eric made me believe I was the star candidate when really he just needed me for cover. At the first sign of trouble he could make sure that everyone knew it was Jenny Parker who had the job of overseeing the WOS account, she's the one who takes bribes. In the event, he made sure I couldn't make my stand over the Associated Composites irregularities by having me arrested. A grim thought that I was too conscientious for my own good comes to mind. Maybe I should have buried my misgivings, signed off the accounts and started using Casagrande's money to buy my expensive knickers.

Those bastards had me where they wanted me right from the start. From the moment I let Paul drag me down to Northamptonshire I was heading for prison and ruin. First Eric took away my lover, then my child. Now he is hell bent on finishing me off, cutting me up and watching it on film.

Since Chris found the diary entry for Eric's dinner with Casagrande my mind has been churning with ideas for revenge. My problem is one of credibility. Mine versus his. I need to find some way to get to Eric, and I need to do it quickly, before he makes a successful attempt on my life.

There are lights on at Gary's house, but he's always been an early bird. Maybe Ian has already rung him and told him of our success. As I pull into the yard, I get a stab of disappointment when I realise his car is gone. I feel a little bit cheated that I won't have the immediate satisfaction of telling him what we found and how I'm going to nail the bastard that caused me all that grief.

The final details of what I need to do are still whirring around in my head. I need to discuss them with Gary, to enlist his help. I have to find a way to get the contract he has put out on my life cancelled so that we can all sleep easily in our beds.

As I bend down to retrieve my handbag from the passenger footwell, the car shudders slightly. A neat hole appears in the windscreen and tiny cracks begin to radiate out from it. Somewhere in the distance a door slams. Before I can sit back up to look out at what's going on, a second door closes with a loud thump. I can feel the vibration it makes. Another hole appears briefly then my poor windscreen decides it can take no more and rains shards of glass down onto my head.

As I rise, brushing the debris off as carefully as I can, two men come out of Gary's house and run towards me. The nearest one is Gary. He is waving wildly, shouting. The man behind him stops his chase, raises a handgun and fires. Gary stops waving, takes two more uncertain steps then pitches forward onto his face. The man calmly points his gun at me and fires again.

Ducking, I turn the ignition keys, fire up the engine and drive blindly forward. There's another gunshot and my Corsa strikes an obstruction, deflects off it, but keeps powering forward. The engine is screaming even louder than I am. I sit up and look where I'm heading only just in time to yank the wheel to the right so that I manage to career across Gary's lawn instead of diving into his ornamental pond.

I drive right around the house, onto the drive again and away. The wind buffets my face and hair, freeze-drying my tears even as they fall. There are headlights in my mirror now, they're following me…

At the motorway roundabout I have my doubts that I'll be able to drive fast enough for it to be a good choice but I take it anyway. The motorway is the only road likely to have other traffic for me to blend into.

Opening all the windows seems to help a little. That horrible booming noise is reduced. My hair is in rats' tails, whipping around my face, damaging me, hurting me. Apart from the odd lorry and occasional car there is nothing on the road. I have half a tank of fuel, can manage to keep up an eye-watering fifty-five miles per hour and now have several sets of headlights behind me.

As one draws close then pulls alongside, I glance fearfully to my right. One man, eyes forward, mobile phone to his ear, oblivious of me, of everything around him. I wonder who he's talking to at this hour and breathe again, waiting for the next candidate to whoosh alongside. This time with a leer and a weapon.

The services are one mile ahead. It's fully light now and I need to stop to pee, to get some respite from the hurricane blast. I have no idea if they're still following me. It's such a relief to stop, to get out of the freezing wind. I'm so cold I can hardly open the car door. My legs are shaking when I try to stand.

It's warm inside the building where a thin trickle of clientele shuffles wearily about, zombified by the early hour. The mirror in the toilets reveals a scared witch with a red face and streaming eyes. My efforts to repair the damage are feeble and ineffective. I leave the washroom almost as dishevelled as I entered it. I am cold, tired, hungry, scared for my life. When I think about Gary I'm filled with a desperate sadness that makes me feel like throwing up. The need to flee is uppermost in my mind. I know I have to keep moving, that they'll get me if I don't, but my body is incapable of complying with this imperative and curls up on a settee in the coffee shop and defiantly falls asleep.

Something touches my nose, first softly then harder. I open my eyes to see a plastic doll with unfeasibly large eyes in its tiny head. The little girl pushes it into my forehead. I sit up, brushing it aside with my hand. Seemingly satisfied with this, she bounces the doll's plastic feet across the table, lost in some fantasy where all this has meaning and life.

The place is horribly busy now. A long queue has formed for coffee and people vie for tables in the seating area. It's a wonder nobody has turfed me off my comfortable spot. The child's mother sits opposite, wrestling with a small baby, while her toddler runs amok with her intrusive doll. My heart leaps with hope when I fish out my phone and see a message from Gary.

'Stay away,' it reads. Timed at 5:07 a.m. It's now ten forty and I should have stopped the car and looked at it the moment it arrived. If I had, all this would have been prevented. Gary would be alive and I wouldn't be running for my life. It's all my fault, why do I have to be like this? Why do I cause so much pain?

My depression overwhelms me again. I feel like curling up into my protective ball and letting the world do its worst.

When I call the house it rings and rings, nobody answers, not Doreen, not Siobhan, not Sally, not Sophie, not Sean. No Gary. The tightness in my stomach is despair, the discomfort is unaffected even when I feed myself a welcome sandwich and drink a giant coffee-flavoured milky froth.

The little girl has stripped all the clothes from her doll, whose legs are twice the length of her trunk and which has no signs of sexuality apart from large nipple-less breasts that stand proud only just below shoulder height. There is something comforting in the way the girl is berating the doll, telling it off in no uncertain terms and poking it with her little finger. Serves her right for being a fraudulent impostor like me.

The urge to flee is overwhelming my stupor. Anxiety is building up on a monstrous scale. I expect rough hands to detain me at any moment. I scan the crowds filing into the place, wondering if any are looking for me. My car is a problem. I can't face another mile of wind-lashed agony. The little girl, bored with punishing her fake friend, starts rooting through her mother's handbag, a fat brown leather affair sitting plumply in the centre of the table surrounded by white crockery and small items of clothing.

The mother is occupied jamming a dribbling teat at the baby's mouth, trying to soothe its fretfulness. A bunch of keys appears and is discarded onto the table, followed by a small pack of tissues and a fat purse bulging with cash. A black tube of lipstick is clutched triumphantly, its top wrestled loose and the bright pink stick revealed. The little girl starts smearing it on her face, a large stripe from nose to ear. Her mother looks up from gazing into the baby's eyes and jolts the infant into crying mode again as she reaches out to restrain the little girl. The table rocks, the handbag slides towards me, pushing the keys in front of it. As the mother wipes away at the child's face, I pick up the keys and walk away.

Outside the day is ridiculously bright, but not warm enough for a seventy mile an hour wind to be refreshing. My car is no longer sat in isolation. Cars are parked everywhere around it. A lone policeman stands peering into it as if curious to learn more. The mother's key fob is in my pocket. I press the button as I walk, watching for a reaction. The red Audi A4 has a child seat in the back, a baby seat in the front and is strewn with tissues, wipes, drink cartons, crisp packets, blankets, coats, toys and plastic bags. It has a windscreen without any bullet holes. It is warm and comfortable. My guilt level reduces steadily as I speed southwards. There are more inhospitable places to be marooned than a motorway services. She and her children will be fed, watered and toileted in reasonable comfort until rescue. I would gladly swap places with her, exchange her plight for mine.

64

Finally Mick answers his mobile. 'Jenny, are you okay?'

'I'm alive, if that's what you mean by okay. Gary was shot. I ran away. Is he dead?'

'No, but he's in a bad way. The hospital aren't saying much, but we're all worried for him.'

'What about Doreen, the kids, are they all right?'

'Yes, all okay. Obviously shaken up and scared and such but uninjured.'

'Are the police looking for me?'

There is a pause before Mick answers.

'No, why should they?'

'Well, it was me they were trying to kill, it was me caused it all, got Gary shot.'

'The police are treating it as burglary, they assume they were after Gary's money. Nobody's mentioned you as far as I know.'

'I stole a car.'

'You should be used to driving stolen cars by now...' Mick laughs.

'No, I'm serious. I took it off a woman at Stafford services. Will the police be watching out for me everywhere?'

'I doubt that, not unless you shot the woman dead when you stole it.'

'What about cameras?'

'They do you for speeding. If you drive too fast they'll send three points and a fine to the poor woman – add insult to injury.' He is laughing now. I feel amazed that anyone can find humour in this desperate situation. My spirits are lifting slightly, even though the humour is directed at me.

'It's all right for you to laugh,' I say, 'you're not the one being hunted by armed thugs.'

'We'll protect you, come back up north, we'll get it sorted out.'

'Soon. There are things I need to do down here. Keep me posted, Mick. Give my love to Doreen and the kids, tell her I'm praying for Gary.'

When Mick hangs up an empty hole opens inside me and I am swamped by grief. I need to stop this self-pity, this collapsing into what ifs and what might have beens. Of feeling that I don't deserve this pain. I do deserve it and more. Everything bad that happens is a direct result of my own inadequacy. Admit it, move on – that's what I need to do.

The hotel receptionist looks at my crumpled state, contrasts this with the shiny new suitcase. If he looked inside it he would find everything still had a price tag attached and become even more suspicious. After clucking and staring at his computer for a long time, he finally announces that I can have a room for the night. It's as if he is granting me a big personal favour. His name tag says Jean Phillipe and I hope he has a bad day.

'Only one night, we're fully booked after tonight. It's the motor racing at Silverstone, we're very busy. Only one night, is that agreeable?'

'Yes,' I say, 'that's all I need. Do you have internet access and a computer I can use?'

'Oh yes,' he says, 'over there in the lobby, compliments of the house, free of charge.'

'Printing?'

'Certainly, madam, but we make a small charge of five pence per page – to cover costs, you understand.'

*

I am amazed at what Chris has done with the information we gathered. It's all there, up on the cloud, so he assures me. All I have to do is log in to the dropbox he created. The lobby is completely empty, even the reception desk is unmanned. Four in the morning is a good time to work undisturbed, even in a public place. Twelve hours' sleep is what dictated my schedule.

Two hours' work, twenty pounds to the night porter for letting me use the printer and I'm done. What I have is a fat envelope containing everything Giuseppe Casagrande does not want to see. All I have to do now is make sure he sees it.

The Audi is parked in a field with several thousand other cars to keep it company. I have no intention of returning to it, and have no regrets about leaving it where it is. Once the motor racing is finished and everyone has gone home, a solitary red car will remain. There should be a quick return to its rightful owner. I consider putting it through a car wash and filling it up with petrol as some small compensation for the trouble I've caused, but I need it to look like it was stolen by joyriders and dumped at the motor race. A really bright policeman might even conclude that the same vagabonds who trashed my Corsa were probably the ones who stole the A4. As long as I don't have to meet the owner again things should be fine. According to Mick, car crime is so commonplace as to be almost ignored by the authorities. He reckons little or no investigation will be carried out.

It's one of those rare British summer days, twenty-five degrees, sunshine, clear blue skies, gentle breeze occasionally wafting the heat away. The world, his wife and all their progeny are descending on Silverstone. I am joining this throng but feel none of the fun and excitement that animates them. The smells of unwashed bodies, cheap perfume and burgers frying in old fat fill my nostrils. As I stand in line to buy an entry ticket I marvel at the amazing variety of paraphernalia being worn and carried by the heaving masses around me. There are even flags with cars' names on them so that people can wave them as they pass, I presume.

I ask the family behind me if they have heard of Crugnolla Racing. The father has a huge T-shirt with Aston Martin emblazoned on the chest. I'm amazed they make them this big. His wife and children are mere moons orbiting around his vast planet.

'Oh yes, they're leading the championship. We aren't far behind though. When we win this weekend, we'll be in with a chance ourselves.'

'Where will I find them? I have to speak to their owner, you see.'

'Get a paddock pass. They'll be in there. Look out for the blue and black Lamborghinis. That's what they run.'

Sure enough, there they are, in a massive tent. Proudly unattended, protected only by a thin tape stretched across the front of the awning. Beside the racing cars, which look smaller than I expected, is a big grey motorhome. Unlike the rest of the rubberneckers, I don't feel constrained by the flimsy protective device and push myself into the tent, walk past the cars and bang on the motorhome door.

The young man with a slightly irritated expression on his baby face is peering down at me from his elevated position inside the huge pantechnicon.

'Casagrande!' I demand. 'Giuseppe Casagrande, I'm here to see him.'

He's wearing an all-in-one suit peeled down to his middle with the arms tied around his waist. Underneath, he has a white vest with long sleeves and roll neck. Hardly suitable attire for a hot day like this, no wonder he looks flustered. He throws anxious looks at the crowd which has swelled in number and become much more animated at his appearance. A few of them are shouting 'Pedro, Pedro,' and waving autograph books.

'He's not here.'

He has to be here, it's my big chance, maybe my only chance.

'He said to meet him here,' I insist.

'You're in the wrong place, he's at the hospitality tent.' Pedro waves his arms as he gives me directions. 'Did he give you a pass?' I shake my head and he disappears inside for a moment and then comes back with a bright orange plastic strip. 'Put this on your wrist, he should have sent you one, you can't get in without it.'

The hospitality tent is the size of a large mansion and has aluminium decking at the front of it that accommodates four gleaming sports cars, one yellow, one red, one black and one

240

white. I presume these are road-going versions of the tiny racing cars. When the smiling girl sees my wrist band she gives me a sheaf of paperwork, including a race programme and photos of the cars and drivers.

Pedro's face looks much more relaxed as it smiles back at me from one of the cards. Inside the vast tent there is a ballroom-sized area with dozens of tables occupied by eaters and drinkers bedecked in a variety of brightly coloured race wear complete with sponsors' logos. Along one wall a sumptuous buffet is laid out. A long queue is filing past it, filling plates. Behind the bar, pretty girls in white pinafore dresses squirt lager into stemmed glasses and scrape off the froth with a plastic spatula.

I scan every table for Casagrande, but in vain. I stare at everyone in turn again in case I missed him the first time, but still have no success. My elation at getting this far is waning, my doubts are returning to slow me down to a pathetic crawl. There are two areas cordoned off at the far side, one marked Press, the adjacent one VIP. Casagrande emerges from a doorway at the rear of the VIP area. My breath catches in my chest, refusing to be expelled until I force it out, then I have to consciously breathe in and out, in and out, as I walk towards him.

'I'm Jenny Parker, you must remember me,' I say.

He nods but shows no emotion or sign of interest at first, then his face transforms gradually, his uncertainty changes into recognition and his mask of bonhomie reappears.

'Ah yes, of course, how charming it is to see you again, and after so long.' The smile is full and beaming, the voice bright and animated, but his eyes tell me exactly how little he is enjoying my sudden appearance.

'We need to talk,' I say. 'This whole thing is about to collapse around your head.' He looks up at the tent fabric gently flexing and moving in the wind. It's as if he's taking me literally for a moment.

Two men in full Lamborghini livery come up beside me and begin to speak volubly in Italian, arms waving wildly, as if they're ready for a fight. Casagrande stills them with a raised hand and turns and motions me to follow him through the door, down a corridor and into a large office with polished desk, boardroom table and enormous television on the end wall. He invites me to sit down in one of twelve black leather chairs, cool to my touch even in the heat. I realise the room is air conditioned and am grateful for it. I need to regain my own cool and this is certainly helping.

'I am surprised to see you here,' Casagrande says.

I don't detect any malice in his voice, but get a sudden shock of fear. Perhaps I'm wrong, perhaps this is the man trying to kill me. Perhaps they all are.

'I've had a few difficulties along the way, been through some hard times since we last met,' I say. 'Now I need your help, Signor Casagrande.'

'Ah, young lady, how can I possibly be of assistance to you?'

I push the envelope towards him, now covered with sweaty fingerprints from clutching it tightly for so long on a hot day. He smiles, as if remembering it's he who usually delivers the brown envelopes to me.

'What is this?' He puts a hand on the documents but makes no move to examine them.

'Those are a record of the money laundering transactions carried out by Associated Composites, names, sources, amounts, dates, everything.'

He smiles. 'Are you expecting me to pay you for this, give you some money? Are you trying to blackmail me?'

'No. These aren't my documents and they are not for blackmail. They've been prepared for submission to the EU Commission. The investigation that follows will destroy everything you've built.'

'And you are threatening me, therefore?' he says without a trace of anxiety or concern.

'No, as I said, these are not my documents. I have access to Landers Hoffman, illegal access I might add, and these have been secretly prepared by Eric Knowles himself. He's decided to protect his own interests by alerting the authorities. He thinks he's had all he's likely to get from your business and he's about to blow the whistle on your activities. The authorities will give him immunity from prosecution if he does, and this way he keeps everything and you lose everything.'

Now Casagrande's face betrays his serious concern. I'm getting through, hitting him in a weak spot at last. I press home my attack.

'There's still time to stop him, I can make sure the computer records are wiped, that none of this ever gets out.'

'Why should you help me? What is it that you want in return?' he asks.

'My life, to be left alone. Listen...' I lean forward and fix his gaze. 'I'm in the same business as you now, small fry in comparison, but the same. Eric Knowles has put a contract out on me, they've tried to deliver three times, but I have my own resources...' I pause to try to gauge the effect of my words; his face gives me little feedback and no certainty that I'm on the right track.

'Get Eric off my back. All I want is to be left in peace. We have a common objective, you and I – stop Eric Knowles.'

Casagrande smiles at me but I detect no warmth or humour.

'Wait here, please.'

Before I can say anything more he leaves, taking my documents with him. Despite the cooling atmosphere, I am beginning to swelter in my own anxiety. Did I really expect Casagrande to take me at face value and deal with Eric? The chilling realisation that I'm acting in ignorance overwhelms me. Panic begins to take hold. I have to get out of here, away from the racing circuit, back to the relative safety of Manchester.

The two men who meet me by the door are obviously under instructions to detain me.

'This way, please,' sounds polite enough, but loses its gentle invitation when the double grip under each shoulder is added. I am half guided, half propelled out of the hospitality area and through the crowd of race-goers. When we reach a silver Mercedes people carrier they thrust me inside and it begins to push its way slowly through the human tide.

It's possible that I'm being taken to comfort and safety but my escorts are unwilling to discuss this in any detail.

'Signor Casagrande asks that you kindly come with us. It's for the best. Signor Casagrande, he a very busy man. Will join us very soon.'

This is all the information I can elicit. Asking 'Where are we going?' meets only with shrugs.

It's also possible that these two men are taking me somewhere quiet where they will kill me. A man in Casagrande's position would certainly give serious consideration to this option, if only to be on the safe side.

Then there's Eric. What if Casagrande actually works for Eric rather than the other way round? I haven't given this possibility any thought until now. I hope this isn't a fatal error. If it's true, I'm in deep trouble.

I wonder if the van doors are locked. If I grab the handle and try to escape it will give a bad impression. Gaining Casagrande's trust is my only real hope. If I attempt to escape, even if I succeed, any chance of that may be lost completely. It's me who has taken all this trouble to see him, not the other way round. Toby has made me aware of the effectiveness of child locks in vehicles. The driver will have deployed them if he wants to make sure I don't escape. If this is an innocent journey, he may have left the doors unlocked, in which case escaping is the last thing I need to do.

By the time I make up my mind to stay put, the van has cleared the crowd and is moving too quickly for me to get out even if I wanted to.

Our destination is so unsurprising I feel almost disappointed. We turn into the industrial estate and park in front of the Associated Composites offices. They take me to a large room on the ground floor and leave me with the promise: 'He says he won't be long. Please stay here.' I hear the lock turn as the man closes the door. Perhaps he's worried that someone might steal all these plastic chairs and formica tables.

I'm in the canteen. There's a serving hatch that opens to a small kitchen where I find a kettle, tea and a fridge full of milk and other edible perishables. After a nice cup of tea and a toasted cheese sandwich, I feel stronger but no less anxious. Once again, I examine the possibilities in my mind.

Casagrande believes me, has sent a hit squad after Eric and is keeping me safe until any danger has passed. I like this version, I only wish I believed it.

Casagrande doesn't believe me, doesn't trust me, has sent for Eric and is waiting for his arrival. This one chills me to the core and has me trying window locks to see if anyone has been lax enough to leave one undone and put the entire contents of the canteen at risk. They haven't.

Casagrande doesn't know what to make of what I've told him, is checking through the documentation, is seeking corroborative evidence, is communicating with his superiors. Most likely it's this one. But this one leaves me in no man's land, neither dead nor alive, neither damned nor saved.

All I can do is wait.

65

I take some consolation from the fact they've left me with my phone. Some of the gloss is taken away by the discovery that I can't get a signal. Letting Mick know where I am would have been a big comfort. I doubt I could have prevented him from turning up mob-handed, I'm not sure I would have even tried.

Plastic chairs are bad enough to sit on long enough to eat lunch. Now that night has fallen I'm faced with the prospect of trying to sleep on them. I line up three and try to lie across them, but either they're too narrow or I'm too wide. When I put another row opposite, the width problem is solved but when I lie down they move apart and I drop down the hole in the middle. A table is harder, less flexible but much more stable. I use my handbag as a lumpen pillow and try to sleep.

Headlights and voices rouse me. I clamber stiffly off the table and move over to the door.

'Leave her to me, I'll take care of her.'

Eric Knowles's voice leaves me quivering with alarm.

'What are you proposing, Eric?' It's Casagrande. 'You are going to beat her to death with a chair or maybe stab her to death with a kitchen knife? What do you mean you'll take care of her?'

'She's caused me a lot of trouble, believe me. A lot of trouble. All I want is her out of the way. Permanently. If you'll help, then fine, help.'

'Maybe we shouldn't be so hasty, Eric. First we should speak to her. Then we should consider carefully our next course of action.'

The door opens, I step back quickly. The two men who brought me here walk in, followed closely by Casagrande and Eric.

'Sit down, please.' Casagrande looks sternly at Eric. I sit down at my sleeping table, they sit opposite.

Eric looks at me as if I were a piece of excrement stuck to his expensive shoe. He doesn't look at all happy. He does look angry but he doesn't look confident. Maybe he isn't in control here. I decide that accusing him of my rape might shake him, it will at least be an unwelcome surprise.

'You bastard.' I turn to Casagrande. 'He had me raped and photographed. He sent pictures to my husband.'

Eric laughs. 'Why would I bother?'

'Why? So that you could control me, that's why. So you could blackmail me, make me do what you wanted, approve the WOS audit, turn a blind eye to all the criminal goings on.'

'Absurd,' Eric turns to Casagrande. 'She's making all this up. We already had her exactly where we wanted.'

I feel myself colouring up, I am losing my belligerence. Of course he had me where he wanted me. He was my boss, he paid me well to do everything he told me. He knew I had accepted a substantial bribe. It's the wrong thing to accuse him of, an error that might prove fatal.

'You had me drugged, raped and filmed,' I insist, 'because you're a sick bastard and you like to see women suffering degrading abuse. It was the same when he had me kidnapped. They were hired to make me suffer horribly and film it all for him.' I stab a finger at Eric.

'She's deluded,' Eric says. I haven't actually convinced myself but the look on Casagrande's face indicates he isn't altogether sure about Eric now.

I try to use what little advantage I may have earned. 'No, it's not me that's deluded. It's all on your personal computer at Landers Hoffman, I had the hard drive ghosted, I've got everything, even the stuff you thought you'd deleted. How do you think I got all the information I came here with? How many other poor women have you been preying on, Eric? What kind of sick demented psychopath are you?'

Eric's gaze is like steel. Either he's innocent of everything I'm accusing him of or he is completely devoid of remorse. Either way, he's not helping my cause one bit. Casagrande shifts slightly in his plastic seat. Perhaps I've touched something in him. Not enough to save me but a small crack in Eric's armour that I can work on. If Eric's predilection for cruelty is insufficient concern for Casagrande then I have to find something that is.

'You're not the only ones he's laundering money for,' I address Casagrande. 'He's got bigger fish to fry than you. If he drops you in it he stands to make more money than you could ever pay.'

Casagrande looks puzzled for a moment, as if confused by my clumsy English idiom.

'Tell him, Eric,' I continue, 'tell him all about your Chinese friends.'

Eric slaps his hands on the table and stands up. His chair makes a girlish squeal as it slides backwards.

'Enough!' Eric shouts, 'enough is enough. There's no point to this. Either you sort her out or I will. Just get on with it. I've got better things to do than listen to this lying bitch.'

Casagrande remains seated, hands together in front of him as if in prayer. 'Enough of what?' He asks quietly. 'Tell me, Eric, about your Chinese dealings. I am interested.' He motions to the empty seat but Eric stands his ground.

'It's all nonsense, she's making it all up. She's a poisonous scheming little bitch and she's costing us time and money.'

'You could start with the boy in the Hilton,' I prompt. 'The Chinese student living in a suite at Manchester's most expensive hotel.'

'I have no idea what you're talking about.' Eric's face tells me he does. The bluster has gone, he looks tense as if bracing himself for what I'll reveal next. Truth is, I can only guess but it's got me this far and I have to go for it.

'If you won't tell Signor Casagrande about your Chinese dealings, then I'll have to,' I taunt him, hoping for some reaction. I'm rewarded by a spike of alarm in his eyes. I hope that Casagrande caught it.

'There's no such thing,' Eric says. 'Landers Hoffman have a couple of Chinese restaurants in Manchester as clients. Other than that, nothing. She's making it all up.'

'Chengdu Industries,' I say, 'you put the owner's son in the Hilton. You covered it with your footballer accounts. Chengdu are your real paymasters. It was them who told you to pull the plug on Signor Casagrande and World Ordnance Systems. Chengdu are ten times the size of WOS, they're the big payers now.'

I take a breath, swallow. Is this the right direction? It has to be.

'Associated Composites showed you how it all worked, you took that knowledge to Chengdu where you can make much more money. Now you're getting rid of your old friends, concentrating on your new ones.'

Eric leans across and slaps me hard across my head, I flinch with the blow and this puts me off balance. Eric is on me before I can rise from my seat, dragging me to the floor. His hands circle my neck, I manage a weak punch to his nose but he pins me down and is throttling the life out of me. I manage to slide a hand down the front of his trousers, underneath his shorts, grope among the disgusting warm hairiness until I reach his scrotum. I squeeze a testicle between thumb and forefingers as hard as I can. This gets his attention, slackens his hands, makes him try to pull away. The gap between us becomes sufficient to allow my legs to move, I knee him between his legs and bring my arms up to break his grip. Twisting, I slide my body out from underneath his moaning bulk, get to my feet and begin kicking him around his unprotected head. Before I can inflict any serious damage, strong arms restrain me and pull me away.

Eric is pulled roughly to his feet by the biggest of the two bodyguards. Casagrande nods towards me and I am released.

'Come on, Eric,' Casagrande's voice is calm. 'I see what you mean. Accusations mean nothing. Don't worry, Luigi here will drive you home.'

'No, that's not necessary, I have my own car here.' Eric looks terrified, tries to shake himself free.

Luigi reaches inside his jacket and brings out a large revolver which he points at Eric's head.

'What about her?' Eric's face oozes blood and hatred as he is manhandled through the door.

I am alone with Casagrande who rises gracefully and offers me a white handkerchief.

'What about me?' I ask.

Those eyes bore into me and for a moment I'm very afraid. When I see that faint smile, I breathe out my relief and I know that we have an understanding.

66

It is a bright August afternoon. The cars are queuing up to pay their money and be shown where to park. As they spill their beer-filled cargoes clad in red shirts with misleading names on the back, I walk about chivvying the lads, getting them to move more quickly, to form two lanes, to get the money in quicker. Some of the punters are new, it's the first match of the season and they baulk at the ten pound charge. If they do I am summoned over to deal with them.

'You can get cheaper, mate,' I smile, 'but you'll be blocked in. If you want to wait half an hour to get out after the match, be my guest.'

Most of them stump up. In any case, the place will be full in less than half an hour and then we can go, taking the supervised parking signs with us. In this weather I can see why Gary used to be so keen on the job. Two hundred and fifty cars, money worth having for a couple of hours' work.

I promised Doreen a visit after I've finished here in Trafford Park. It's been hectic recently and I've been neglecting her. She's in the stables, standing between two horses, her arms resting gently on one of them. Even when I stand quietly beside her, feeling the manure sticking to the bottom of my shoes and smelling the earthiness of still-sweating horses, she remains transfixed, staring into space.

I'm close enough to see the tears welling in her eyes and to understand that here is the only place her grief can be allowed to manifest. The knife in my stomach reminds me that it's my fault she's grieving. Gary died trying to protect me, when he should be alive to look after his wife and children. And me.

Eventually she speaks.

'Gary loved his horses.' My own tears join hers, dripping softly onto the hay-strewn floor.

'I am sorry,' is all I can manage.

She turns to look at me and reaches out to pull me into a warm hug.

'It's not your doing, don't feel so responsible. It was those men with guns who killed him, not you. I only want you to know how much I appreciate you looking after the business, God knows what I'd do without you. Me and the kids are so grateful, Jenny.'

I can't hold back. All the pent up feelings pour out of me and onto this good woman's shoulder. It's a long time since someone held me like this.

Back in the house, brave cheerfulness reinstated for the children's benefit, we sit, Doreen and me, nursing cups of tea and listening to the subdued chatter amidst the televisual babble.

'I never understood why those men were trying to kill you, Jenny. Gary never told me anything about work, well hardly anything.'

'They were hired by a man called Eric Knowles, he used to be my boss at Landers Hoffman. He made an arrangement with some very serious criminals who needed to launder huge amounts of illegal cash. You know, legitimise it, make it look like it came from a normal business.'

'Like a caravan park?' Doreen's eyes twinkle as she asks.

'Exactly like a caravan park, but much, much bigger,' I continue, smiling. 'Eric arranged for WOS, a large multinational company, to buy the small business they were using to take the proceeds of crime and trickle them into UK bank accounts. As part of WOS they could increase the volume of their activity and stand less chance of being caught. The clever part was arranging for Landers Hoffman to be appointed auditors for WOS, that way Eric could make certain the illegal payments remained hidden.'

'But what did all this have to do with you?'

'Eric made me responsible for the auditing. He thought I'd be too weak and inexperienced to see anything untoward. And anyway he knew I'd taken a bribe and he thought he had complete control over me. When he found out I was prepared to stand my ground he told the police about the money I took and had me arrested.'

'But why does he want you dead?'

'I started to make waves with WOS, the big company involved. He must have felt I was getting too close to finding out about him.'

'So it was this Eric Knowles who killed Gary then?' Her lips are thin and clamped tightly. 'What do we do about him?'

'Nothing,' I say, smiling wider, 'nothing at all. His business partners found out he was about to betray them. There was an unfortunate road accident. Eric's car was found burnt out in a ditch with him inside.'

67

O'Brian is sitting on the corner of my desk, exactly as Gary used to do. He is detailing all the ways in which business is bad. I am half listening and less than half concerned.

'We've got machines standing in the yard,' he continues, 'nobody needs to hire them any more. There's fuck-all happening out there, the construction industry is on its arse. As for sales, I bought a dozen small excavators six months ago at what I thought was a good price. I've sold one. One! The rest are standing idle, going nowhere, the manufacturer is giving such a big discount now there's no prospect of offloading them except at a massive loss.'

Mick blocks up the doorway and allows me to interrupt.

'Excuse me,' I say to O'Brian. 'What is it, Mick?'

Mick looks towards O'Brian and then back to me.

'Please would you wait a moment?'

I walk out of the office and see that Mick's face is even redder than usual.

'It's all going to kick off this evening,' he says.

'What? Riots? Here in Manchester?'

'Yes, for definite. The police are sure of it. They've cancelled all leave and rest days, they're issuing riot gear to everyone, even my mate who does pub licensing is expecting to be out there with a baton and shield. All he's done for the past five years is fill out forms and talk to landlords. He's not a happy bunny, I'll tell you.'

'Don't you think the police will cope?'

'You saw what's been happening in London. Complete anarchy, fires, looting, mobs with firebombs. It's spreading. All hell is breaking loose. Anyway, half our bobbies are down in London helping them out.'

'It'll be the city centre, then? Is that where they'll be?'

'Could be anywhere, but that's a safe bet. All the high value shops. Deansgate, King Street, the Arndale. That's where.'

'So do you think the stores we guard might get hit?' I'm getting caught up in Mick's obvious concern.

'In London they've been wrecking everything, shops, offices, the lot. Torching them as well.'

'OK.' My mind is beginning to race. 'Get everyone in. Everyone. And if they can bring any friends, the more the better. Tell them it's double time and an extra wedge for anyone they bring.'

I return to O'Brian, who is literally kicking his heels on my desk. Before he can continue his soliloquy of doom, I tell him about the impending riots.

'Bastards, someone should teach them a lesson.'

'Anyway,' I say, 'I need to make some arrangements to safeguard our customers. Was there anything else?'

O'Brian gives me that long stare of his and I look straight back into his eyes and wait. I remember when one look from him made me unsteady, but compared to Casagrande, this man is as gentle as a baby.

'Well,' he begins slowly. 'There's the matter of the business now that Gary's gone. As I've put so much money into it, I have to protect myself. Control my assets, so to speak. You understand, I'm sure you do.' He pulls out a sheaf of papers from his jacket pocket with the air of a magician. 'You and Mrs O'Donnell need to sign these to transfer your shares into this holding company I've formed.'

The consternation I feel must be obvious because his tone becomes a little more placatory.

'Don't worry, I'll still need you to run the business and I'll pay you a good wage. Maybe even a bit of a bonus from time to time.' He winks.

As I pretend to look through the paperwork, I use the time to breathe, steady my body and slow down my mind. The urge to slap his preposterous face recedes slightly but there is enough residual anger to keep the possibility alive.

'Leave it with me,' I sigh.

He stands up and turns to leave.

'Wait.'

He turns, still smiling smugly.

I tear the papers in half and drop them into my waste bin.

'I've had a think about your suggestion, Peter, and I've decided to reject it. This is Gary's business. Whatever personal arrangement you two had is no longer valid. He might have promised to sign over the company to you for all I know but it belongs to his widow now, and to me. As her representative, I can tell you that we're intending to carry on as we are. You'll get the same service, the same treatment and the same return on your investment. Business as usual.'

He flushes, whether in embarrassment or anger I can't decide, then he leaves without another word.

I have no time to worry about O'Brian. I settle down to make some serious phone calls.

At 4 p.m. I inspect Mick's recruits in the car park. He's issued them all with high visibility bibs but they don't look convincing to me. The idea that they might deter an angry mob seems a little farfetched. They're more likely to be taken as miscreants than guardians. At least there's a good turn-out, thirty or so regulars swelled to twice that by casual volunteers. It's just as well; I have twelve new customers to cover. Ten independent shops and two national chain stores, all in or around Deansgate and St. Ann's Square. News is already coming in that Salford precinct is in uproar and that several fires have been started.

*

The two guys in my shop are casuals, neither has done this kind of work before. At least we have that in common. Both are big lads, heavy rather than muscled, and I'm glad they're here with me. The atmosphere in town is eerie, distant shouting, the smell of smoke, constant police sirens and the jangle of numerous intruder alarms. It got dark a while ago, there have been several bunches of hoodlums walking past shouting but no attempt to get in here until now.

The steel shutters are being rattled, I can see three men pulling at them. I hold up my hand to stop the lads making themselves known.

'Wait,' I instruct. 'See if they give up and move on.'

The rattling increases its intensity then gets replaced by banging. They're using a steel barrier from the road repairs outside to smash the shop front. The barrier was placed there to protect people from risk of injuring themselves by falling down the shallow hole someone has dug to reveal a blue pipe. Now that safety item is being used to destroy.

The window caves in with a crash, showering glass over the display of cameras and lenses. Only now do I realise that we should have taken everything out and hid it in the back. I quickly forgive myself for this lapse, it's my first riot after all.

'Right,' I shout above the banging. 'One either side of the doorway. Hit anyone who comes through, hit them hard but try not to hit them on the head. Anywhere else, not the head. I can't afford fatalities, even in this situation. The police will take a dim view if we cause any deaths. Even looters have more rights than shopkeepers these days.'

The shutter is forced half open and the door is now taking terrible punishment. I wade through the broken glass and yank it open. Three men in hoods and masks pause in their destructive process and stare at me in disbelief.

'Go away,' I yell at them. My knees are weak but my voice is strong. 'Find somewhere else to loot.'

'We like this shop.'

The nearest lout steps towards me and I kick him hard in his groin. The kick is swift and powerfully assisted by the steel-toed safety boots I'm wearing. He doubles up, holds onto his genitals and moans softly. The other two discard their battering ram and walk away. The injured man looks at me with disbelief then hobbles after them.

Two more groups show casual interest but move on when they see us. A slow-moving cordon of riot police arrives to shepherd miscreants towards waiting vans. Mick radios to report a minor skirmish on the other side of the square. One of our lads was attacked when he left his post to deal with a fire in the shop opposite. Mick says he has a few bruises and is in much better shape than his assailants.

I arrange for broken windows to be boarded up when it all seems quiet and am home in bed by 3.30 a.m.

*

O'Brian again. Sitting on my desk again, kicking his heels again. He doesn't make an appointment, doesn't ask if I'm busy. He materialises in my office, a wild-haired, sharp-eyed manifestation. After last night, I could have done with a lie-in, but today is a day for grasping opportunities, not resting. The phones are ringing constantly and I'm busier than I've ever been. The last thing I need is O'Brian and his avuncular menace.

'Lot of damage in Manchester.' He is speaking softly, I can hardly make him out above the sound of the phone. 'Shops looted, fires started, people attacked. Dreadful state of affairs. The police need more powers, we can't let those nasty toe-rags get away with trashing our city.'

'Excuse me.' I pick up the phone, it's an order from one of our new customers. They now want us to provide comprehensive security at all their locations nationwide. I arrange to meet them in London next week.

O'Brian continues to loom over me. 'I heard about your exploits last night. Word is that your lot protected all your customers and that all the other security firms were either absent or ineffective.'

'Maybe they were doing the rioting.'

My poor attempt at humour tickles him more than it should. He throws back his head and barks with laughter. I notice tufts of black hairs in his nostrils that contrast starkly with the universal whiteness elsewhere.

'Have you heard about the Irishman who looted Argos?' His laughter subsides but his eyes retain an amused twinkle.

258

'No,' I answer dutifully.

'Well, he's got five hundred catalogues if you want one.' O'Brian's laughter returns and he gives his own joke full appreciation.

The phone rings again. He stops laughing abruptly and places his hand over it.

'Before you answer that, I want you to know that I'm impressed with the way you've coped without Gary. Last night was a spectacular illustration of your smartness and your courage.'

He plonks the fat holdall on the desk.

'Here. More investment. Consider it a vote of confidence. Use it wisely.'

I certainly will. I certainly will. With O'Brian behind me, I've got a chance. One I shan't be letting go.

The End